Tim Renton was a Member of Parliament for 25 years and a Government Minister for nine. As Minister for the Arts, he was an architect of the National Lottery. He was made a Life Peer in 1997.

He lives on the Sussex Downs with his wife, Alice Renton, also a writer. *Hostage to Fortune* is his second novel.

Also by the same author

THE DANGEROUS EDGE

HOSTAGE TO FORTUNE

Tim Renton

ARROW

Published in the United Kingdom in 1998 by Arrow Books

1 3 5 7 9 10 8 6 4 2

Copyright © Tim Renton, 1997

The right of Tim Renton to be identified as the author
of this work has been asserted by him in accordance
with the Copyright, Designs and Patents Act, 1988

First published in the United Kingdom in 1997 by Hutchinson

Arrow Books Limited
Random House UK Limited
20 Vauxhall Bridge Road, London SW1V 2SA

Random House Australia (Pty) Limited
20 Alfred Street, Milsons Point, Sydney, New South Wales 2061, Australia

Random House New Zealand Limited
18 Poland Road, Glenfield, Auckland 10, New Zealand

Random House South Africa (Pty) Limited
Endulini, 5a Jubilee Road, Parktown 2193, South Africa

Random House UK Limited Reg. No. 954009

A CIP catalogue record for this book is available from the British Library

Papers used by Random House UK Limited
are natural, recyclable products made from wood grown in
sustainable forests. The manufacturing processes conform to
the environmental regulations of the country of origin

Typeset by Deltatype Ltd, Birkenhead, Merseyside
Printed and bound in Great Britain by
Cox & Wyman Ltd, Reading, Berkshire

ISBN 0 09 946831 X

*He that hath wife and children hath given
hostages to fortune; for they are impediments
to great enterprises, either of virtue or mischief.*

Francis Bacon,
Essays, 'Of Marriage
and the Single Life'

*Britain had not been conquered or invaded:
she felt no need to exorcise history.*

Jean Monnet,
a founding father of the
European Community

To Ann Harvey
with thanks for many years of friendship
and forbearance

I am particularly grateful to Jonathan de Ferranti for his creative help in working out the arithmetic in the lottery part of the plot. I also want to thank for their advice on very different matters: Mr Bill Young, Head Keeper on the Firle estate; Mr Reg Homard of Lewes Gun Room; Christopher and Primrose Arnander; Bertrand Coste; Marianne and Dominique Frachon; Sir Peter Petrie; Christian Gudgeon; Polly Renton and Dr Paul Elkington.

CHAPTER ONE

There was a nasty atmosphere in the hall. The Prime Minister felt it from the moment he entered, four security guards close to him, his wife a few yards behind. As he walked up the centre aisle, consciously smiling and waving to the few faces he half-recognised, a smell of hostility rose from the crowded benches in the middle and at the back of the meeting. He noticed the Union Jacks printed on T-shirts wrapped round beer bellies, the slogan BRITAIN FOR THE BRITS stamped in red, white and blue letters on backs that turned away as he went by.

Jim Bishop was an old pro. He had fought his first election when he was twenty-five in a hard steel town where unemployment was high and politicians of all parties were despised. He had been in the Commons twenty years, a Minister for eight, Prime Minister for the last three, but he still felt the sweat starting to dampen his hands. The hatred came at him in waves as tangible evil, waiting to gather momentum.

He looked ahead and realised immediately that the lights above the platform were far too bright. He would not be able to see the audience through them, and that would make it even harder to put his message over. He silently cursed the organisers of the meeting, regretting the impulse to help out Angus Fyffe that had made him accept the engagement. He saw Angus coming to the edge of the platform to greet him and turned to give a reassuring smile to his wife, but he could not catch her eye. Something in the toecap of her shoe was

1

captivating her and all he could see was her head of deep brown hair, glistening from the glare of the television lamps.

He felt himself pushing back his shoulders like a young recruit in the army. Then, with both arms stretched out in front of him, he half-ran up the steps to the platform and seized hold of the chairman's hand. 'Angus,' he said, 'Margaret and I are delighted to be here. Thank you so much for asking us.'

Smiling broadly, they turned together, paused for the television cameras and then Lord Fyffe moved forward to kiss Margaret Bishop lightly on the cheek. 'Welcome to you both,' he said.

Fifteen minutes later, the first missile was thrown. The Prime Minister was well into his stride, explaining the economic difficulties for Britain if France, Germany and their Continental neighbours were all in a single currency but she failed to join. He prophesied that new investment from Japan and the United States would bypass Britain, that rival manufacturing companies on the Continent would have lower costs as, tied into the Euro, they would not have to cover exchange risks, that in the third millennium there would only be four international trading currencies: the Chinese yuan, the Japanese yen, the American dollar, and the Euro. He had been through all the arguments countless times at public meetings in the last year.

'If we don't hang together with our European partners, we'll certainly hang separately. We *must* . . .' He never finished his sentence.

A thickset man rose from the middle of a row halfway down the hall, holding a plastic bag in his hand. 'Hang your bloody self,' he shouted and threw an egg with a cricketer's expert flick of the wrist.

The egg landed an inch below the knot in the Prime Minister's tie and exploded. Egg yolk ran in an expanding stream down his House of Commons tie, over his white shirt-front and towards his trouser belt. Another egg soared through the air, missed Angus Fyffe by inches and fell on to the platform where it spattered yellow, sticky fluid over the varnished planks. In quick succession, a third broke on the pleated front of Margaret's shirt and the yolk spread rapidly, blending with the silk material.

'This is wrong! Stop it at once! You must stop!' yelled Lord Fyffe, a touch of panic already in his voice. But the throwing of the first egg had acted as a signal to the benches around. Twenty T-shirts were now on their feet, all with plastic bags in their hands. Out came an assortment of apples, tomatoes and eggs that hurtled towards the platform.

'Traitor!'

'You bloody Hun!'

'You're selling us to the Germans!'

'Get out of Downing Street!'

'Long live the Queen!'

'Bleeding arsehole!'

The T-shirts moved in a solid scrum up the aisle towards the platform, shouting and throwing as they went. The front rows, comfortably dressed in jackets and cord trousers, turned round and gaped fearfully.

Angus Fyffe tried again. 'Stand back! Go back! You can't threaten the Prime Minister like this.'

A barrage hit him in the chest and he put up his hands to protect himself. 'Shut up, you stupid cunt! It's him we want, not you,' shouted a bearded six-footer. 'He's the one who's selling us out to the Krauts.'

The television cameras swung away from the platform and focused on the mob moving up towards Jim and Margaret Bishop. To five million viewers, they looked as if they might disappear in a few seconds in a welter of flailing arms and bad eggs and rotten apples. But then came the sound of commands being shouted, and police moved in from the ends of the aisles, pulling out their truncheons. Curses poured into the sound booms and the cameras zoomed in on hand-to-hand fighting just in front of the platform. A loud crack was

3

heard all over Britain as a truncheon landed on the shaven head of a man who had neatly kicked a policeman in the groin.

'It's time to go,' the senior security guard said quietly, hooking his arm firmly through Jim Bishop's.

'I don't want to go.' The Prime Minister sounded angry. 'It'd be running away. I can calm them down.'

'I don't think you can, sir. There are professionals out there. We didn't do any body searches, and some of them might have knives. I must ask you to leave.'

Another security guard latched on to Bishop's other arm, and as he glanced round he could see that Margaret and Fyffe were already being led to the back of the platform.

'Damn! This is the last thing I wanted to happen.' As he walked away, he felt a thud at his back and then a metal dart fell at his feet, its three-inch spike shining in the arc lights.

In the small room at the back of the hall, Jim Bishop finished washing the egg off his shirt and tie and turned to the Assistant Chief Constable. The police officer fiddled nervously with the peaked cap in his hands.

'Why didn't your men get into it more quickly?' Bishop asked.

'Our instructions from the Chief Constable were to wait till the last possible moment. We were told that's what you wanted.' The officer sounded defensive. A critical report to the Home Secretary could put his whole career at risk.

The Prime Minister drew in his breath sharply, then relaxed and said, 'No, of course you were right. It's just that I hate being seen scuttling off the stage. I'd much rather slug it out.' He turned to Angus Fyffe, who was hovering behind the police officer.

'Well, Angus, I suppose there's no point in our hanging around. I'm sorry, we haven't done the cause of European Union much good tonight. Those bastards – they'll have known it would all be on television, so it'll be in the European

papers, too. Another British mob fighting to preserve the past
– I can see the headlines in Paris and Berlin.'

'Don't blame yourself,' Fyffe said. 'Not even your powers
of persuasion could turn an organised band of Little Eng-
landers into enthusiastic friends of France and Germany.
Wisdom and sincerity are not going to make any difference to
a gang like that.' He turned to greet Margaret as she
reappeared from the washroom, the pleats in her shirt wet
from where she had dabbed them with soap and water.

'Are you all right?' he asked anxiously. 'Is your shirt
ruined?'

'Jim will have to buy me another if it is, and it'll cost him
three hundred pounds. It's Armani.' There was a mixture of
fear and resentment in her voice. Bishop slipped his arm
through hers and piloted her protectively towards the door,
followed by Fyffe and the security guards.

'You shouldn't go yet, sir,' said one of the policemen.
'Better wait for a few minutes, there's still a nasty crowd
outside.'

'But I need to get back to London,' Margaret protested. 'I
can't stand waiting here any longer. I really want to get out.'

At that moment, a policewoman brought in cups of tea and
Margaret reluctantly sat down. Bishop accepted a cup of tea
and turned to Angus Fyffe. 'I gather you've let Strudwells to
Sheikh Matab, the Medevan ambassador. I saw him the other
day and he invited me to shoot there with him. I've said I'll
go, but it won't be the same as shooting with you, Angus. I so
enjoyed those holidays at Strudwells with you. They were
some of the best times of my life.'

'Me too,' Angus said. 'Matab's only renting the place till
Christmas. D'you know him well?'

'Yes, quite well, he's a good friend of this country. His half-
brother, the Emir, keeps most of his money in sterling and
buys a lot of equipment from us. He's one of our best
customers in the Gulf.' Bishop smiled. 'You're safe with
Matab, Angus. But why have you let Strudwells to him?'

'Money,' said Angus with a rueful smile. 'Nothing more complicated than that.'

The Assistant Chief Constable returned from a consultation with his colleagues outside and told them it was now safe to leave. Seconds later, they were standing on the pavement. A hundred lights flashed, cameras clicked and reporters shouted, asking whether the Prime Minister was hurt. He assured them that he and his wife were fine and waved vigorously to prove his point. He muttered to Margaret that she should do the same, but she appeared not to hear and slipped quickly into the back seat of the Jaguar.

As they sped back to London along the motorway, a police car in front and two others following, with detective, private secretary and security guards on board, Bishop reflected on his commitment to European Union. It would be so much easier if he could get it out of his blood . . . But he could not abandon it. With every day that passed he found it harder to see an independent future for Britain in the new millennium.

He appreciated the genuine anguish suffered by many of his colleagues and friends about the issue. It would be much less effort if he joined them in revelling in the strikes in France or the collapse of yet another government in Italy but, as the arguments became angrier, he kept on thinking of his father's words to him when he'd first entered Parliament: 'Remember, son, it's for politicians to make the big leaps forward; it's for technicians to work out the details.'

A simplistic approach, perhaps, but it increasingly reflected the way he thought himself.

He glanced out of the window at the town lights that flashed past. Swindon. How that had grown. A very successful example of devolution, of manufacturers moving their headquarters out from Central London. He might use it in a speech. He wondered who was the MP – was it one of theirs? He couldn't remember and his thoughts turned back to his father, Karl Bischoff, a fifteen-year-old refugee from Hitler's

Germany in 1935, whose parents had changed his name to
Charles Bishop. Isle of Man internment camp in summer,
1940; from there to the army; fought in Africa and Italy;
ended the war a captain in Intelligence with a Military Cross
and no right leg, blown off by a German mine. Never
complained but always in pain, died seventeen, no, eighteen
years ago. Jim wished he had talked to him more about the
war but it had never been easy to draw him out on the subject.
He would say it was a long time ago and there would never be
a war like that one again.

Jim looked across the back seat and saw that Margaret had
woken up. She was staring straight ahead of her as if there
was something of great interest on the windscreen. Jim
noticed with pride the clear, straight line of her jaw. There
were no traces of a double chin or of wrinkles in her neck. He
leant over and stroked her cheek gently with the back of his
fingers.

'You've got a fantastic profile,' he said quietly.

Margaret did not reply for a moment. Then she said, 'The
car's going far too fast. We must be going well over eighty.'

'No one's going to stop us and we'll get back to Downing
Street that much quicker,' Jim protested.

'Please, Jim, you know how I hate it.'

'All right.' He leant forward and muttered in the ear of the
driver, who immediately slowed down and switched to the
middle lane. 'Thank you, that's better,' Jim said.

They sat in silence for a few minutes and then Jim said, 'It's
easy to forget about the car crash. It's quite a few years ago
now.'

'Not for me,' said Margaret. 'I can never forget. Never,
ever.' She turned away slightly, and went on, addressing
herself to the car window. 'Practically every night I dream I'm
standing in that little lane and in front of me is Sally's little
white car, the one we had just given her for her birthday,
upside down in the hedge, and there are her legs hanging out

7

from the side.' She paused and then said in a low voice, 'I don't see how you can forget. I can't understand it.'

Jim reached out to take her hand but she pulled it away from him and sat, fingers laced between each other, looking straight in front of her.

As they passed Reading, Margaret unclasped her hands and turned to him. 'Jim, do you have always to make speeches about Europe? It makes people hate you so much. That audience tonight, I've never seen so much hatred in people's faces. Actual hatred. Some of them looked as if they'd kill you.'

'It's the biggest issue of our lifetime, Margaret. It's all about the future of this country and of Europe. That's why people get so passionate. I don't blame them for that.'

An aeroplane, lights all along its fuselage, looking like a giant moth in the night sky, flew slowly past them, wheels down, ready to land at Heathrow. Another minute passed and then Margaret said, 'I'm not coming with you again. Not to a meeting like that. I loathed every minute of it.'

'I didn't much enjoy it myself. But, darling, I so like having you there. It gives me . . .' Jim sought for the right word '. . . comfort,' he finally said. 'Do come sometimes.'

Margaret shook her head. 'I'd rather be playing backgammon with Angus Fyffe and my friends. That's more amusing, more fun.' She paused as she thought about their different likes and dislikes. 'You know,' she said, 'I suppose a bit of gambling gives me the same sort of kick as speechifying to enemies gives you. A strange sort of thrill. You never know what's going to happen next.' She paused again and then added, 'But I'll come sometimes, perhaps.'

The heavy, bomb-proofed Jaguar swept along the Hammersmith flyover and down into Cromwell Road. The driver looked at the clock on the dashboard and switched on the radio. The chimes of Big Ben filled the car, immediately followed by the voice of the BBC announcer. 'The Prime

Minister and his wife were mobbed by an angry crowd at a public meeting in Wiltshire this evening. They had to . . .'

'Turn it off, please, Joe,' said Bishop. 'I don't think we want to be reminded.'

'Come on, Zeppelin, come through here.' Colin Old pulled open the sagging barbed wire and urged his black Labrador through the gap. Then he followed, bending low under the top strand. The stile, a yard or two away, had been broken at the end of the last shooting season, and it was still broken. Either he would have to mend it himself or he would have to have yet another row with the farm manager.

Colin sighed as he set off down the path between the ashes and sycamores, all stripped of their leaves and quietly waiting for winter. It was his job to look after his pheasants from the moment of their hatching till he sold them, dead and tied in pairs with a scrap of binder twine, to the local game merchant. It was the farm manager's to see the fences were repaired, to drill the game crops rather than just scattering the seed, and, every year, to have the honeysuckle and bramble cut right back.

He thought about the Strudwells estate as he walked along the moss-covered path, so well known to him that he bent instinctively into its curve round the side of the hill. It seemed to him that just as the owner of the woods and the land around had gone up in the world, so the estate itself had gone downhill. First, it had been Mister Angus, then Sir Angus, and now it was Lord Fyffe.

Colin Old missed Mister Angus. He missed his interest, his laughter when the birds flew the wrong way or guns jammed in the middle of drives. Now the shooting was all let. Commercial days, they called them. It paid for the wheat and the new hatchery and the beaters – and his wages, the farm manager said. All Colin knew was that it was city types who came, and they knew precious little about shooting. They said they only wanted to shoot high pheasants, and then, when he

9

showed them high pheasants, they couldn't hit them and complained to the agent about the size of the bag. Still, give him a southwesterly wind and an old drive like this one off the hill, and he would show them higher birds than anywhere else in Sussex. And that, the agent said, was why they could go on letting days at such good prices. It was the new drives he worried about, the ones lower down round the game crops. Last year, some of the birds there just hadn't wanted to fly at all, not even in a good wind in January.

Colin turned to his right and walked towards an old metal bin with a rusty lid of corrugated iron. As he struggled to lift the lid, a rat slid out of a hole in the bin's side and ran past Zeppelin's nose towards the nearest honeysuckle bush. Zeppelin had hardly to move. Four bounds, and a heavy paw smacked down on the rat, breaking its back and pinning it to the ground. Zeppelin picked the rat up in his mouth and, tail waving furiously, carried it back to Colin, who banged its head hard against the side of the bin and threw it into the bush.

'Clever boy, Zepp,' he said as he filled the blue canvas bag hanging down from his neck with wheat out of the bin. And then, whistling a quiet, even birdsong through his teeth, he set off again down the path, dipping his hand into the bag and rhythmically scattering the wheat, two yards to the left, two yards to the right, three yards into the open patch of ground on the left, four yards to the space between the bramble, everywhere where the birds could find it easily.

Jauntily and idly, the cock pheasants appeared from the undergrowth, heads held high, tail feathers sweeping over the ground, and started to pick up the grain. Immediately behind them came the light brown hens, dowdy by comparison, and nervous. Within a few minutes Colin could see several hundred pheasants moving around him and he threw heavier handfuls into the open spaces on the ground.

Zeppelin suddenly moved forward, pushed his muzzle hard into the bottom of a bush and brought out a hen pheasant.

Colin took it out of his mouth and saw that a wing was broken. Holding the pheasant by the legs, he put his fingers on either side of its neck just below its head and pushed downwards until he felt the neck bones slide apart. The wings flapped for some seconds and then went quiet, and Colin slipped the bird into his pocket. Zeppelin, sitting down, watched him quietly, while, all around him, pheasants went on pecking elegantly at the wheat on the ground.

Colin had been on the Fyffe estate for more than thirty years. Other keepers just let their birds feed from hoppers, but Colin walked through the drives in the woods every day in order to know what had been happening in the last twenty-four hours. If birds had been shot with a rifle during the night, or if badgers or brown owls were taking the eggs, he knew it immediately. He protected his pheasants until the day of the shoot, and then he took pride in putting them over the guns as high as possible and seeing them well killed. Months of painstaking work gone in a second, but that was the nature of the job.

Whistling the same birdsong – any other whistle would not be right – he climbed through the wood to the point where the drive would start. There he put his hand into his second bag and scattered handfuls of what he had always told Angus Fyffe was his magic mix.

He looked at it in his large, hard palm for a moment and scratched between the grains. Linseed, peanuts, sunflower seed, buckwheat, cut maize; they were all there – it was a treat for any pheasant – but it was the millet they went for. That would keep them hanging around for days. It was like a drug to them. And that's what he needed. Birds that were driven from this point in the wood were like dots in the sky by the time they went over the line of guns below. The agent had told him that the big days till Christmas had all been taken by a rich Arab who had booked the house for the weekends as well. 'Stinking rich,' the agent said. He had shot here last year with Lord Fyffe and enjoyed it. He was paying a top price –

£20 a bird – and a bonus if they shot more than three hundred birds in the day, so it had better be good.

His second bag empty and Zeppelin at his heel, Colin walked to the fence. There he noticed a cock pheasant standing on one leg, not moving, watching him. He checked himself with the thought that they always looked as if they were watching him. But there was something strangely familiar about this pheasant. Then he saw the patch of blue feathers on its back, and he remembered another one just like this, blue feathers between the wings and a very black head, who had often stood close to him last winter when he'd been feeding. Melanistic and Michigan blueback, he thought to himself. Very unusual. The Michigans are strayers; they fly well but they never hang around. That's the trouble with them, but this one must like Strudwells. The hope filtered through his mind that the bird might survive this new season as well, and then he shook his head in self-reproach. He never allowed himself to get sentimental about the pheasants. The more that were killed, the better. That's what the farm manager said, and on that point Colin agreed with him.

CHAPTER TWO

Jim Bishop picked up the oatmeal-coloured mug in front of him. It had the words TREATY OF MAASTRICHT on one side and, on the other, the signatures of the politicians of all parties who had led the debates on the Treaty. He took a gulp of black coffee, now quite cold, and started to reread the pile of faxes from British ambassadors. They were an unpleasant start to the day.

Germany was always on the top of the pile.

BERLIN   7 NOVEMBER   2015   NO 1734

UNHAPPY MEETING THIS AFTERNOON WITH FOREIGN MINISTER. BUNDESTAG WILL AGAIN DEBATE EURO SINGLE CURRENCY NEXT WEEK. PROPOSED INCREASE IN RESERVES OF EUROPEAN CENTRAL BANK UNDER THREAT. FREE DEMOCRAT AND SOCIAL DEMOCRAT PARTIES AIM TO DEFEAT THIS. IF THEY SINK TRADITIONAL DIF-FERENCES AND VOTE TOGETHER THIS WILL DESTROY CHRISTIAN DEMOCRAT MAJORITY AND LEAD TO CONSTI-TUTIONAL CRISIS. FOREIGN MINISTER AND CHANCEL-LOR URGE FAVOURABLE BRITISH DECISION ON EURO URGENTLY.

HILLYARD

Next was Sir Roderick Carmichael KBE KCVO from France.

PARIS   7 NOVEMBER   1715   NO 3498

AT LENGTHY LUNCH AT QUAI DORSAY ALBERY
EMPHASISED FRENCH DECISION ON REMAINING IN EURO
NOW IN BALANCE. PRESIDENT AND PRIME MINISTER
STILL IN FAVOUR BUT SUPPORT AMONG GAULLISTES
WANING DUE TO CONTINUING RISE IN UNEMPLOYMENT.
BOURSE VERY WEAK AS A RESULT. THIS MUST LEAD TO
HIGHER INTEREST RATES WHICH WILL BE SELF-
DEFEATING AND WILL FUEL MORE STRIKES. SUGGEST
PRIME MINISTER USES FORTHCOMING VISIT TO ASSEM-
BLEE NATIONALE TO MAKE BRITISH POSITION KNOWN.
AWAIT INSTRUCTIONS.

CARMICHAEL

Before Bishop could read the faxes from Rome and Madrid,
the telephone on his desk rang and his private secretary told
him that the Chancellor of the Exchequer was on his way to
the second-floor flat at Number 10.

Bishop did not offer the Chancellor a Maastricht mug.
Instead, he poured coffee into a white and blue Minton cup
and then pointed the Chancellor to a deep chair in one corner
of the study. He sat in a chair at the other end and the thought
crossed his mind that, sitting there, they were like two boxers
waiting for the bell to ring so that they could start the first
round. One in the blue corner, one in the red corner. He
wondered who was in which. The European issue crossed all
normal political divides.

Bishop waited while Graham Blackie took his first mouth-
ful of coffee. Despite all their work together, the man was a
mystery to him. Blackie was twenty years younger, so there
was a generation gap, but even so Bishop could not
understand how someone, who loved life and was a brilliant
economist, could be such a primitive nationalist. He thought
all that would have been knocked out of Blackie at the LSE,

14

but evidently no such thing had happened. And the summit meetings of European finance ministers Blackie attended every fortnight only made him more insular, more critical, more determined that the civilised world began, continued and ended at the White Cliffs of Dover.

Bishop remembered him campaigning years ago against the Channel Tunnel – outrageous meetings up and down the country in which Blackie claimed that any physical linking of Britain to the Continent was unnatural and would lead to disaster. But then Blackie had fallen, heavily and surprisingly, for a French girl and that had made him, at least, see the advantages of Eurostar.

Bishop sighed and decided he had to start the conversation. 'Thanks for coming at such short notice,' he said. 'I didn't want any private secretaries present to take minutes.' He paused. 'I thought you and I had better have an entirely frank and private talk together.' He paused again but Blackie said nothing. Bishop gestured at the pile of faxes on his desk.

'You've seen these, the faxes from our European Union ambassadors after they had confidential talks with all the Foreign Ministers?'

'Yes, I glanced through them. Typical whingeing lot, I thought. Obviously, the Germans are wondering whether they did the right thing in sinking the Deutschmark into the Euro, just as I told them they would, though God knows how they get out of it now. And the French are, to put it in the language of one of my less elegant LSE professors, pissing in their *pantalons* about the death of the franc. *Noyau dur.* Hard core. What a joke. *Noyau faible*, rather. Or rotten core, that's what I call it at the Treasury. And bound to get faibler yet.'

Bishop picked up his Maastricht mug and rolled it gently between the palms of his hands. 'You know, Graham, our predecessors signed this Treaty,' he said reflectively, 'and spent months and months discussing it first.'

'I know it all too well, and a bloody disgrace, I call it.'

Both men fell silent, as if waiting for a storm to break.

'By the way, Jim, I'm sorry you had such a bad time at that meeting the other night,' said Blackie, throwing words into the painfully quiet void between them. 'It must have been horrid for Margaret.'

'Yes, it was. I'm afraid she got quite frightened.'

Silence again filled the room until Bishop took an audible deep breath and straightened his shoulders against the back of his chair. 'I'm afraid, Graham, this can't go on,' he said. 'We have our Community obligations. We are meeting all the economic criteria for joining the single currency. I don't want to see the Euro break up; I think it would be disastrous for Europe if that was to happen.' He saw Blackie getting ready to interrupt, but he ploughed on. 'Graham, I know what you think, but my father and grandfather went through the thirties and the last war. European Union is only a generation old. If we start to go backwards, it will mean a break-up of our free trade area, more protectionism, like the thirties, and all the new jobs will be in China and Latin America. Perhaps we'll end up with war.'

'No, Jim, you really can't say that. You're talking just like the Germans,' Blackie broke in angrily. 'That's an emotional argument that has no base in fact.'

'But you can't say that either,' said Bishop. 'The fact, the simple fact, is that neither of us knows for certain. And I think to let the Euro go under now is much too great a risk. Getting ready for it has been a discipline for so many countries – Belgium, Italy, Spain. If we abandon it now, we'll end up competing with each other for lower exchange rates and then we'll fight each other for jobs and investment, and Germany's so much the strongest, she's bound to win. Who knows where it will end? I don't, you don't.'

Prime Minister and Chancellor looked at each other across the room, and both knew this was their personal crisis. They had worked together for three years in Cabinet, fought two elections, shared ten years in the party. Neither wanted to part company with the other. Each knew that it was inevitable.

Graham Blackie got slowly to his feet. 'Prime Minister,' he said formally. 'What do you propose to do?'

'At the next Cabinet, I shall announce that I am going to use my visit to Paris the following week to say that Britain intends to join the Euro.'

'You can't say "Britain". Britain doesn't want to join. *You* want to join, most of us don't, and it'll be the death of our party.' Blackie could not keep the fury out of his voice.

'It's all a question of leadership, Graham,' said Bishop. 'If you and I, and Roger Beacon for the Opposition, were to go round the country preaching that the single currency was best for Britain, we'd have a majority for it in no time. There'd be no problem. Just like the referendum in 1975. People don't understand. They get told so much garbage about their pensions being threatened and their jobs being at risk – poor devils, they don't know what to think. But you and I,' he spoke sadly and thoughtfully, 'we could do it together, even without Beacon.'

Blackie shook his head and started to walk towards the door. 'Not a chance. It would be total hypocrisy for me,' he said. 'And disaster for Britain.'

He had had weekly meetings in this room for the last three years. Bishop and he had plotted Budgets and economic strategy and interest rates. They had steered Britain out of recession into prosperity, but they would no longer be working together. From now onwards, it would be insults and shouting personal abuse at each other. Graham Blackie remembered his last quarrel with Marie Claude and shuddered.

'I'm going to be against you, Jim, all the way. I'll fight you as hard as I can because, simply, I don't believe in what you're doing. And I'm a mean fighter. I'll use every weapon I can lay my hands on.'

'I know that,' said Bishop, 'but I still wanted you to hear my decision from me, not just round the Cabinet table.'

'Thanks for that.' Blackie paused at the door and added, 'And I think perhaps, out of courtesy, too, I should let you know that Marie Claude has left me. For good. She has found,' he tried to sound light-hearted, 'another lover in Paris, or so helpful friends lead me to believe. You were always very kind to her, Jim, at all the pompous parties. You turned a blind eye to some of our indiscretions. She was very fond of you, but you won't be seeing any more of her.'

'I'm very, very sorry. I thought she had gone just temporarily, to visit her parents, perhaps.' But Bishop was speaking to an empty space. He listened to Blackie's steps receding down the corridor, then picked up a bundle of papers from the floor and moved back to his desk, where he started pencilling a shortlist of replacements for the Chancellor's job – until the thought occurred to him that the parliamentary party might decide to get rid of him rather than Blackie. He put down his pencil. He needed to think that one out.

Like all the most exclusive clubs in London, the Montclare looked discreet from outside and splendidly shabby inside. The marble floor in the hall usually seemed in need of a wash, the green baize on the notice board had been torn for many years and the leather on the fender round the open fire in the ground-floor bar had faded to a gentle shade of black. But the food was excellent, the cellar contained some of the best first growths in London and there was a five-year waiting list for membership. One blackball, quietly registered in a confidential note to the club secretary, and the individual concerned would be excluded for life.

The Montclare had three unusual features. Women had been admitted to full membership since the 1970s, thanks to an energetic chairman who enjoyed bedding a wide variety of the opposite sex in the club's two spare rooms. Ambassadors and foreign visitors were regularly given temporary membership. And, on the second floor, there were four discreet little rooms which were reserved for private gambling parties. The club charged a large reservation fee and asked no questions. The practice had started in the 1890s, when the Prince of Wales of the time, who was devoted to cards and dice, had been a member. It had thrived ever since. The more puritanical members consoled themselves with the thought that it all helped to keep down their annual subscription.

Sheikh Matab Rashid bin-Omanyi Hassan was a member of the club, besides being half-brother of the Emir of Medevan and that country's ambassador to the Court of St James for the last fifteen years. He was also their ambassador to Ireland, Sweden, Norway and Denmark, but he kept his visits to those countries to the irreducible minimum. He liked London and, in turn, many enjoyed his Pol Roger and caviare parties. One guest had commented to a London paper that the ambassador had bigger sturgeon's eggs than anyone else in town, and his name had promptly disappeared from the invitation list. Matab and his half-brother liked discretion in public, whatever debauching took place in private.

Over the years Matab had built up an exclusive group of gambling friends whose company he enjoyed and who could be relied on to keep their mouths shut. They regularly met at the Montclare to play poker or bridge for high stakes. Tonight it was progressive backgammon. The opening stake in each game was the final stake in the previous game. As the opening stake could be doubled up to six times in any game and all the players were committed to playing a minimum of two games, the tension was high and the sums of money large. Starting with a £5 bet, it was so easy to win £160 on the first game and then lose £10,000 on the next.

Margaret Bishop finished her first game against Harold Plank with a modest win of £80. They had both already come several times to Sheikh Matab's Evenings of Chance, as he always described them on his thick, engraved cards, but they

19

had never played against each other before and had scarcely talked.

'Call me Harry,' he had said as Matab matched them with each other and directed them towards a baize-covered table, and he introduced himself as an American businessman with interests in casinos and fruit machines in Britain and the United States.

Plank suggested an initial stake of £5 and Margaret felt an inner sigh of relief as she accepted and put the doubling-die on the central ridge of the board between them. She knew that, in coming to these gambling sessions, she played well beyond her purse but the excitement gnawed at her. She spent the whole day beforehand imagining the dice tumbling across the table, or the crisp feel of new cards in her hand, and as she opened fêtes and spoke at tea parties, her mind wandered to challenges and bets and huge sums of money lost and won.

The first game passed easily. Margaret and Harry Plank each doubled twice when the game swung in their favour but, at crucial moments, Margaret threw double threes and then, two turns later, double fives. Harry made an obvious mistake in his back-game, leaving an uncovered piece which Margaret immediately took up, and she won comfortably with Harry still having seven men on the board.

'Eighty pounds to you. You certainly gave me the run-around then,' he said as he started to reset the board. 'Do you play often?'

'Whenever I can get away,' Margaret replied. 'I love it.'

Each threw a single die to start. Margaret threw a six, Harry a one. 'I'll take that,' she said and moved two pieces to block the last point before her home. She suddenly felt extraordinarily confident, as if she knew she was bound to win. This was to be the evening when she would sweep the pool and pay off all her overdraft.

As soon as Harry had played, she said, 'I'll double you,' and turned the doubling-die round until the figure two was visible and pointing upwards.

'Christ,' said Harry softly, 'so you'd like a fight.' He put the two dice in the shaker, jostled it in his hand for a few seconds and then threw the dice on to the board. Double fives. He grunted with pleasure and moved two pieces to start building up in his own home. Margaret felt a tautness in his play, an avid watching of her moves that had not been there before.

After the next few moves, Harry had doubled once. There was little to choose between their boards until Margaret threw a five and a six. Again an overwhelming sense of confidence possessed her. 'Lover's leap,' she said, smiling. 'My favourite throw.'

After Harry's next throw, she asked if he would accept another double. He nodded his head without speaking and turned the doubling-die to eight.

Both players steadily moved their pieces towards their homes until Harry rubbed the dice for some time between his fingers and threw them out of the back of his hand. Double fives again. This gave him the chance to build up outside his home and to take up one of Margaret's uncovered counters.

'Damn!' Margaret bit her lip. She threw a five and a two, got her man down but could not move it out of Harry's home.

'I've gotta double you, honey,' said Harry, American accent starting to break through the careful British overlay.

Margaret looked at the board. Harry clearly had the advantage, but not an enormous one. Eight times eighty, £640. She really didn't want to kiss goodbye to that, and there was some way to go with the game. She said she would accept, and Harry turned the doubling-die to sixteen.

Two turns later, Margaret threw a double six. Harry threw a three and a four which left one of his men exposed as a blot. Right, thought Margaret, I can get him now if I throw four. She rattled the dice for a long time and then threw. Three and one. Good. She took up Harry's piece and put him momentarily out of play. To her surprise, Harry smiled broadly, took a cigar out of his pocket, licked one end and then started quietly to munch. 'Great,' he said, 'this is getting exciting.'

Margaret felt herself getting angry. For some reason, she thought the large man sitting opposite was laughing at her. Her own board was now covered, in her home, on the six-point, the five- and the three-point. Harry had to throw a four, two or one to get his man back into play. He threw the dice quickly, got double threes and shook his head with a faint grimace. Serve you right, Margaret thought. The game must be turning in her favour.

'D'you wanna a cigar?' Plank asked. 'I've got some small ones.'

'Of course not!' Margaret spoke crossly. 'And, if I had one, it would be large, very large.' She knew she was being patronised and for a moment she lost her concentration. She stared at his tie, brightly patterned with fishing flies. She felt as if a metronome was moving inside her skull, tick-tock, tick-tock, going from one side of her head to the other with a noisy, distracting rhythm. On an impulse, she asked the American to accept another double.

'Sure,' he said without hesitation, 'if that's the way you wanna play it.'

Margaret had no sooner spoken than she regretted her suggestion, but there was no way out of it. She turned the doubling-die to thirty-two. That made, she calculated quickly, £2,560. Too much, much too much for just one game of backgammon.

A turn later, the game went in Harry's favour when Margaret threw a three and a two and had no choice but to leave one of her men exposed. She found herself quietly praying, Please God, *please* God, don't let him take me up. But God wasn't listening. With a sense of inevitability she watched Plank also throw a three and a two and remove her man from the board and up on to the central ridge. She threw double threes but the three-point was now blocked in Harry's home and she could not get her man down.

'Luck's not being a lady for you,' said Harry smugly, with complacency, and again Margaret felt angry. She found his sympathy bogus. 'I'm going to double you for the last time, but I guess you're not going to accept.' He pretended to count on his fingers. 'If you don't, I shall be two thousand five hundred and sixty pounds the richer. Four thousand dollars, not a helluva lot, but just enough for my bill at the Savoy tonight.'

Margaret's cheeks flushed. She was damned if she'd let this brash businessman get the better of her. She knew she should not accept the double but there was still a chance that the dice would go her way. 'Of course I'll accept,' she said, keeping her voice light. 'You're not much ahead of me.' She turned the doubling-die to sixty-four and felt the sweat gathering in the palms of her hands.

She threw and the dice rolled over the table, taking an age before they settled. Five and a one. Damn. She couldn't come down.

Harry left the shaker on the table and, with the same curious movement as before, rolled the dice between his fingers and then jerked them out of the back of his hand. Double fives. He moved the last two of his men in to his home and blocked off the last of his open points.

'Fortune smiles on the bold,' he said with a wide smile, 'and I sure guess I'm one of those.'

For the next two throws Margaret could only watch as Harry removed pieces off his board without allowing her to come on. On his third throw, he removed the last of his fours from the board but every other point was still blocked. Margaret shut her eyes as she abandoned the shaker and rolled the dice around in her damp palms before throwing them. Please God, she prayed and then looked up. The first that came to a stop was a four. Thank God. The second hit one of Harry's pieces, bounced back and settled with a two facing upwards. She came down on to the board but was blocked from moving out of Harry's home. She needed at least a three for that.

She started to panic. However cool and sophisticated she wanted to appear, she knew that her cheeks were turning red as the sweat gathered on her forehead. If she didn't get at least one of her men off the board before Harry finished, she'd be gammoned and the stake would double yet again. God, she couldn't think how she had let herself get into such a stupid position.

'You all right?' queried Harry.

'Of course,' she tried to keep the defensive edge out of her voice, 'I was just ill-wishing you.'

Harry smiled. 'You've got guts,' he said and threw the dice again.

Three turns later, Harry had only two men left on his board and he needed just a two and a three to take them off and win the game. Mary still had two pieces just outside her own home. If only she could throw a double, almost any double, she could get them into her home, get one of them off and stop the gammon.

This time, she put the dice into the hard leather cup, rolled it back and forwards in her hands and smiled across the table at Harry. She had regained her cool, determined not to let him see her rattled.

A six appeared. The second took a very long time to settle and then she saw that it was a five. At last, the high numbers she needed, but it was too late. She did not have another move with which to take a man off and prevent the gammon game. Unless Harry threw only a one or a two.

Harry looked across the table and saw two beads of sweat running down Margaret's neck and into the collar of her dark red blouse. It all seemed to be turning out as he wanted. He picked up the dice in his fingers, rolled them and tossed them back on to the table. A five and a three. He took his last two men up from the board and said, 'Thanks. That was great.

Maximum on the doubling-die and then gammon. That's pretty rare.' He paused and picked up his wet cigar from the ashtray. 'Do you want a return game? A chance to win it all back?'

Margaret breathed in and clenched her hands together under the table. She would not, she just would not let her emotions show. She forced herself to laugh. 'Not tonight, another night perhaps. I'll give you a cheque for –' she paused '– eighty times a hundred and twenty-eight.' Her face wrinkled.

'Ten thousand two hundred and forty pounds,' said Harry. 'Call it ten thousand, and I'll get us some champagne.' He rang a bell and a waiter came scurrying.

'Tell me about you,' he said a few minutes later, glass of champagne in one hand, chewed and wet cigar in the other. 'Matab told me you're married to the Prime Minister. How come you're here?'

It was a question Margaret often asked herself. She knew it was dangerous. Although Matab continually assured her that his circle of friends kept their mouths shut, a leak to any gossipy journalist and then a mention in *Londoner's Diary* would be enough to cause Jim a great deal of distress.

But she needed the danger; it was an essential distraction. She had to put the memories of Sally out of her mind during the day – nursing Sally at her breast, brushing her long dark hair, dressing her in pretty clothes for birthday parties, her young brown legs running undamaged at school, long, long telephone calls from University about boyfriends and holidays. Her daughter had been such a friend, such an escape from all the duty work and entertaining she did for Jim. And then, three years ago, the car crash had happened and Jim, a new Prime Minister, had just been too busy to pay much attention. Of course he'd been sad, very sad, but not broken the way she'd been. They should have gone away together for a long journey, looking for the sun, looking for new adventure. But there just wasn't time.

Margaret forced a smile as she looked over her glass at the American. 'My husband thinks I'm playing bridge with a group of close and respectable friends,' she said. 'I do it quite often.'

Harry Plank poured more champagne into her glass. 'And he wouldn't mind your losing money like this?'

'He'd be horrified.' Immediately Margaret regretted this admission. Politics had taught her that too much openness was always a mistake and she hardly knew the man opposite her. But Plank did not react. He stared at the wine in his glass, twiddling the stem and looking at the bubbles fizzing to the top.

After a long pause he said, 'I guess you're a friend of Angus Fyffe, aren't you? Matab knows him, too. I thought he might turn up here tonight but he won't show now. It's too late.'

'Yes,' said Margaret. 'He's an old friend of mine. I got to know him through politics and now we share,' she paused and searched for the right words, 'a bit of a passion for gambling, bridge, horses, and things like that.'

'I'd like to meet him. We might be able to do some good business together. He's big in your lottery here, isn't he? I know a lot about lotteries; I've made a helluva lot of money on them in the States. Yours is just about the largest in the world now. Stakes of over a hundred million pounds, prizes of twenty-five million when there's a rollover – that's the sort of game I like to play. But I need some . . .' He looked across the table and suddenly smiled at Margaret, a wide, surprisingly attractive smile. 'What's the word? Associates, I guess. Or partners.'

Margaret said nothing but found herself, almost against her will, smiling back.

'I guess there's no hurry for you to pay me the ten thousand pounds,' Harry said, refilling her glass. 'Hell, if we can work things out, it could be, like, your first dividend from my lottery project. An advance, I'd call it, of future prizes and profits.'

Margaret twiddled her glass. There was a cheek about this man, but she found it a relief after all the careful politeness of her ordinary day. 'And what's your price?' she said eventually. 'As the saying goes, there's no such thing as a free bet.'

'You're a clever woman and . . .'

Margaret interrupted him in mid-sentence. 'No,' she said, 'I'm not particularly clever, but I've been in politics a long time.'

'Okay,' said Plank, 'I'll be straight with you. The deal is this. You bring Fyffe here as soon as you can, soften him up a bit about me, and then I'll tell you about my plans for your lottery. If Fyffe's the right man, I'll need his assistance, and I guess you may be able to help me persuade him.'

Margaret realised she was being bribed. In a careful, discreet way she was being offered what she thought the courts might call an inducement. She started to bite her lower lip as she thought about it. Her instinct told her that this was the moment to turn back, to say goodbye to Harry Plank and leave the club, but there really didn't seem any obvious harm in what he was suggesting and she didn't want to write him a cheque.

'Is Matab in on this?' she asked.

'Of course. He'll be much the biggest investor if we can pull it off.'

That decided Margaret. She liked and trusted Matab. After all, he was the longest-serving ambassador in London and an old friend of Jim's. It was only because of Matab that she came to the Montclare in the first place.

The room had become stuffy and the air, which seemed now to be hazy-blue with cigarette smoke and brandy fumes, felt to Margaret as if it had gone in and out of too many lungs without recharging. She saw Matab get up from one of the further tables and start to walk towards her, and she felt a sense of relief.

'Here comes Matab,' she said quickly, anxious not to dwell on Plank's proposition. 'He's going to drive me home. All right, I'll try to get Angus Fyffe here soon. He's a party-going bachelor, and he and I often pair up when Jim is just too busy with red boxes and visiting Prime Ministers.' She leant down and picked her handbag up off the floor. 'Thank you for the game, Harry, and,' she paused, 'for the grace period for my losses.'

'Grace period? What the hell's that?' Plank raised his eyebrows and his forehead filled with wrinkles.

'Oh, I mean, giving me a little time before I pay the ten thousand. But I'll pay you soon, of course.'

'Of course,' said Plank and formally accepted her hand and shook it.

Sheikh Matab's car was a stretched grey limousine, specially built for him by Rolls-Royce. It seemed to Margaret to have become even more stretched while they had been playing backgammon. There was an ocean of space between the deep, tilted back seat where she sat with Matab and the sliding glass windows that separated them from the white-robed driver and which were tightly shut.

Matab sat close to her, his hand resting gently on her knee. She tried to identify his subtle perfume. It reminded her of the warm south wind in the Mediterranean, and there was something else behind it, something spicy. Cloves? Or was it musk, she pondered as they drove smoothly along Piccadilly and past the lights of Fortnums.

'Come closer, come closer, my darling, come closer.' Matab murmured the words of the old song as he put an arm round her shoulders and pressed her towards him.

She laughed and pushed him gently away. 'Dear Matab, you are impossible. You don't feel content unless you seduce,' she corrected herself, 'unless you try to seduce every woman you meet.'

'That is not correct. I only seduce the very beautiful ones, and you are beautiful. I looked at you playing with Harry and I saw how beautiful you were.'

Margaret did not reply and the car turned into Trafalgar Square. 'Tell me,' said Matab, 'how did you get on with Harry?'

Margaret wondered whether to tell him how much she had lost and decided not to. Instead, she told him of Harry's wish to meet Angus Fyffe. Matab thought it a good idea. Plank would interest Angus.

'What's Harry Plank like, really?' Margaret asked. 'He seems quite a . . .' she searched for the right word '. . . powerful person.'

Matab purred. 'You found him attractive?'

'No, that's not what I meant . . .' Margaret began.

Matab interrupted her, his voice full of cream and honey. 'I wish, dear Margaret, you would come on my yacht for a holiday. It's in the Caribbean. In February perhaps, after the shooting season. It's very beautiful; you would love it.'

Margaret smiled. 'Beautiful seems to be the only word in your vocabulary tonight, dear ambassador, and cruises on yachts are very old-fashioned.' She removed his arm from round her shoulder as the car passed the Banqueting Hall and slowed down for the turn into Downing Street.

Margaret found a note waiting for her on the small walnut table opposite the lift door in their flat. It was handwritten in pencil: 'It's past one, boxes are finished, darling, and I'm off to bed. I'll sleep in the dressing room as I have to be up at six for a flight to Brussels. Rather a panic there, I'm afraid. Hope you had a good time with Angus and company, and didn't lose too much money! Missed you at supper. Jim.' After his signature was the familiar hieroglyph of an anchor going through a heart which they had both used to sign off letters to each other for the last thirty years. Looking at it, Margaret felt an odd pang of nostalgia. The anchor seemed like a symbol of their past closeness, painful to contemplate now. Switching off the hall light, she walked quietly to her bedroom, careful not to disturb Jim.

CHAPTER THREE

Brussels was a disaster. Belgium held the presidency of the European Union, to run until the end of the year. The Flemish Prime Minister was under pressure from the Walloon opposition, who were demanding a referendum on Belgium's move into the single currency, and unemployment in the industrial area round Liège had soared after two steel mills were bankrupted by competition from Poland and the Czech Republic, both future members of the European Union.

The Belgian Prime Minister, a veteran of many European crises, had decided to call an emergency Summit. Fourteen heads of state or government groaned with frustration, cleared other engagements from their diaries, cancelled foreign visits, and flew to Brussels in their official jets – except the President of France, who came in his own high-speed train. They were not in the best of tempers when they arrived, and nineteen hours of talking and eating in the Palais de Berlaymont did nothing to calm fraying nerves.

The President of the Commission explained that the present membership of the European Central Bank, and the reserves that had been transferred to it, were simply not big enough. There were signs of a speculative run against the Euro that brought to mind the mad weeks before sterling was brought down in autumn, 1992. The name of George Soros was frequently quoted.

The German Chancellor, Franz Kepler, spoke for two hours without a note but drank three litre-bottles of mineral water during his speech. He complained that Germany, France, the Benelux countries and Austria, so far the only countries that had converted to the Euro, could not carry the burden alone. Other countries had to join quickly, and, as he spoke, he pointed his chubby index finger first at Jim Bishop and then at the thin figure of Antonio Malavinti, the Italian President. If the Euro were to collapse, if Germany were forced out of this most powerful development of European Union for which his country had prepared for so long and subsidised everyone else, then *es geht um alles*. Everything would be at stake. No more single market; German commissioners would be withdrawn from Brussels; no more subsidies from the German taxpayer for Spain and Greece and Ireland and Portugal.

But if only Britain and Italy were, finally, to make up their minds, then . . . *Kennst du das Land, wo die Zitronen bluhn?*

The quotation from Goethe's poem took the interpreters by surprise, and there was a distinct pause before the other heads of government heard the words 'Do you know the land where the lemon trees bloom?' crackle through their headsets.

'Bloody silly, ending his speech with a fanciful quote from German poetry,' said Graham Blackie on the way back to Northolt in the HS-120.

'I thought it was rather marvellous,' said Bishop reflectively. 'And surprising. But, of course, the Germans are desperate romantics at heart. That's why they like music so much.' And he quoted from a few lines later in the same poem: '*Dahin, Dahin! Mocht ich mit dir, o mein Geliebter, ziehn!*'

Blackie interrupted him before he could translate. 'Christ, you're cultured, Jim. That's your trouble. You don't understand the ordinary man, the man who goes to watch Arsenal every home game, who listens to Kiss FM and then goes to the pub for a few beers. And that makes you out of touch.'

'You're wrong. I do those things, too, whenever I have time, except Chelsea's my team. And I listen to Test Matches on the car radio, although it makes Margaret very cross. I admit I love shooting – but so do you, so it can't be all that exclusive.' He began to laugh at Graham, and then his mood changed as he remembered the split that lay inevitably ahead of them.

Graham guessed his thoughts and turned away to stare out of the little oval window at the clouds. Eventually he broke the silence. 'Jim, I didn't believe a word about the Germans pulling out of the market if we don't join the single currency. That really is bullshit, you know – we're far too important a customer for them. There's a visible trade surplus in their favour of six billion a year. They'll never give that up.'

Jim shook his head. 'That's where we disagree, Graham. I think Kepler meant every word he said – there's no bluffing on this issue. But let's not argue about it now. Plenty of time for that in Cabinet tomorrow. What Kepler said will be at the core of our discussions.'

Blackie pursed his lips, torn between frustration and anger, and pulled out a thick folder of papers from the black, crested briefcase by his side. 'It's all going to go very wrong,' he said, just loudly enough for Jim to hear. 'And it's Britain that'll suffer.'

Angus Fyffe pushed aside the silver coffeepot and milk jug and spread out his morning mail in between the marmalade jar and the butter dish. He wondered which letter to open first. A thick white envelope with the stamp of the Royal Academy on it? That could wait – it would be an invitation to the opening of their Christmas show; they had to ask him in view of the lottery money he had given them. Four dismal-looking circulars? They could wait, too. They would either be asking for money for a charity or offering a softback copy of a book he didn't want to read. And he was in no hurry to open the window envelope with the words British Gas printed in blue in the left-hand corner. That left a plain envelope marked STRICTLY PERSONAL. He turned it over and saw the bird standing on one leg embossed on the back. A personal letter from his bank – this was worrying. He slid a thumb under the seal and ripped the envelope open. 'Bloody hell!'

Crane's had been established in 1832, the year of the first Reform Bill, as the letterhead proudly announced. The contents, though, were thoroughly up to date.

Dear Lord Fyffe,

It has come to my notice that you have again exceeded your agreed overdraft limit of £600,000 despite your commitment, when you came to my office in July, that this limit would be strictly adhered to. The overdrawn amount on your account is, at today's date, £717,247.36.

Furthermore, I have been advised by your members' agents at Lloyds, whom you authorised to communicate directly with me, that you have not yet paid calls that were made on you by various syndicates at the end of July in the amount of £217,000. Your agents further advise me that there are likely to be more cash calls on you from Lloyds in the very near future.

As you will know, your underwriting at Lloyds is secured by a bank guarantee from Crane's, which in turn is secured by the first mortgage that we hold on the house, land and cottages at Strudwells.

My directors have asked me to advise you that, unless positive steps have been taken by the end of the year that will enable Lloyds' calls to be paid and your overdraft reduced, the bank will have no option but to instruct our estate agents to put Strudwells on the market. As we have been bankers to your family for six generations, I can assure you that we will only take this step with deep regret.

If you wish to come to my office to discuss this, I will, of course, be pleased to see you, but I have been advised by my board to tell you that their decision is imutable.

Yours sincerely,

Bernard Fareweather

Christ, thought Fyffe, the man's a prick; he can't even spell immutable. He poured himself another cup of coffee and had

33

just started to read the letter again when the telephone rang. He picked it up with relief.

'Angus, good morning. I'm glad I caught you at home. It's me, Margaret.'

'Dear, lovely Margaret, thank goodness you rang. I was just about to leave when the postman brought me the nastiest possible letter from my bank. I need to win the pools to keep them happy.'

'Oh . . .' Fyffe sensed the slight reluctance in Margaret's voice and wondered what was coming. He opened the invitation from the Academy as she went on. 'Angus, I met an American businessman at Matab's backgammon party last night. I liked him a lot.' She paused. 'He's very keen to meet you. He seems to have won a lot of money on lotteries in the States and . . .' She paused again and then said quietly, 'Angus, we're both in terrible trouble moneywise. I think this American's got some sort of scheme which might help us.'

'What's he called?'

'Harry Plank.'

'What a ridiculous name.' Angus laughed. 'Did you check up on him with Matab?'

'No. I was too busy fending off Matab's crawling hand as we drove home, but Plank suggested you come and meet him at the Montclare one evening. Why not ring Matab yourself and find out all about Plank?'

Fyffe thought for a minute before he replied. 'Margaret, politics has made you a good judge of people. Do you really think he can help us?'

Margaret recalled the hawkish, angular face in which the bones seemed set at odd angles to each other. She remembered the intense look that had come into his eyes when she doubled at the beginning of the second game, and the strange way in which he had sometimes flicked the dice out of the back of his hand, always throwing doubles. A ruthless man.

'Yes, I think he might. He's got some scheme in his mind. I

don't know that I'd trust him but he could make us a lot of money.'

Fyffe glanced across to the letter from Crane's sitting on the breakfast table. If they foreclosed on Strudwells, it would become public knowledge and everyone would know he'd gone bust. Jim Bishop would make him give up the job that had been created for him at the lottery, obviously – the politicians and the press just wouldn't let him stay there – and that would reduce his income to zero.

'Are you still there? Have you gone back to bed?' asked Margaret anxiously.

'No, no. I was thinking about what you've just said.' Angus paused and then said slowly, 'I really don't think I've any option.' Margaret sensed him smiling down the telephone. 'And in any case it may be exciting, and I'm all for that. I'll come to the Montclare tomorrow night. Will you tell Plank and I'll ask Matab about him? You'll be there, won't you, so we can keep each other company?'

Margaret looked at the diary on her desk and saw that she already had an engagement: the annual dinner for retired political agents, to be held at the Berkeley. A formal, black tie, pompous, boring affair. It had been in her diary for months and Jim would not forgive her if she did not go with him. 'Damn! There's a ghastly thing I've got to go to. I can't get out of it, but whatever it is that Plank's plotting I'll join in. I think he's a winner. Ring me afterwards and tell me about it.'

She put down the telephone and stared out of the window at the rooftops of Whitehall. It was raining and the slates glistened in different shades of grey and deep blue, merging into black. Thursday Jim would have a Cabinet meeting starting soon. No point in asking him to do anything with her. She looked at the typed list of engagements for the day lying on her desk. Except for the two hours allowed for Cabinet, Jim had something happening, someone coming to see him, every half hour. She didn't have anything till the evening. Lucky old Jim.

35

She picked up the paper and, with a conscious effort of concentration, started to read the front page. There was a large picture of a hundred-year-old veteran selling poppies. Of course, it was Remembrance Sunday in three days' time. November the eleventh. Just thirty-five months and two weeks since Sally slid on black ice, hit two other cars, turned over and killed herself. If only she had told her the weather forecast that morning. If only she had not asked her to go and pick up her brother, Giles, from the choir school in Coventry. She turned quickly to the last page and started to scan the list of runners at the Doncaster race meeting.

There were moments when it looked as if the Chancellor of the Exchequer would hit the Prime Minister. 'Don't you see,' he bellowed across the Cabinet table, 'you're giving up British sovereignty? We won't be able to decide our own interest rates; they'll be decided for us in Frankfurt. We won't control our own growth or jobs; that'll all be decided by European Central Bank Governors. We'll be no better than Alaska,' he paused but couldn't think of any better analogy, 'or any other small state in the USA,' he added lamely.

Several voices mumbled their approval on both sides of the Cabinet table. Bishop knew that he would never get the support of all his Ministers, but he was not going to weaken now. 'Look, we all feel passionate on this issue. I realise that we're split, the country is split, the party is split. But at the end of the day I have to do what I believe is right.' A few groans came from the far end of the long table. 'So far some one hundred and forty million Europeans have given up some of their sovereignty in abandoning their old national currency, but' – he emphasised his words by slapping his hand on the table as he spoke – 'they have acquired a share in a new sovereignty by joining up to the single currency.

'That's a hugely significant event for Europe, and I'm determined, absolutely determined, that, this time, Britain should be part of the event from early on, not lagging behind as we've always done before.' There was silence all along the Cabinet table.

The Prime Minister continued: 'And I'm sure that being part of the single currency is the only way for Britain to compete in the twenty-first century. The United States is becoming much more protectionist; wage costs in China are only a fraction of ours. We simply cannot expect to survive as a high-technology economy unless we are an integral part of the European Union.'

He paused and looked up and down the long table at his colleagues. Then he spoke with slow emphasis, again thumping his fist on the table in front of him. 'This is the moment when Germany and France need us. They have taken the lead on the Euro and they're right. We must support them. I want us to join as soon as possible.'

Bishop could feel the calculations going on in the brains around him, a weighing of personal fortunes, a balancing of odds, an assessment of outcomes. On top of that, there was a deep hostility from some of them towards himself. He sensed that at least half the Ministers were waiting for Graham Blackie to give them a steer. He might be twenty years younger but he was the clear leader of the Nationalists. They had started openly to give themselves that label and were planning rallies up and down the country with speakers from all the political parties.

Blackie duly obliged. 'I can't believe my ears, Prime Minister. You said it was time for us to support the Germans. Why? They're our greatest rivals; they run the Commission and the Central Bank. They're not part of the problem; they *are* the problem. That's why we've fought two world wars against them. They want to rule Europe.' He hesitated, then added, 'Prime Minister, it's hard for you to get away from the German blood in you.'

Silence fell like an invisible curtain on the Cabinet table. Everyone was anxious not to catch the Prime Minister's eye, and Ministers fell to straightening their papers into neat piles.

The carafes of water that stood in the middle of the table were suddenly in great demand and were passed backwards and forwards. Someone started to cough and was immediately clapped on the back and offered a drink by all around him.

Jim Bishop rocked gently back in his chair, clasping and unclasping his hands. Finally he said, 'Graham, that was unworthy. I'm sure you'll regret it.' He paused and then added in a reflective tone, 'But perhaps you're partly right. It's the German blood in me that makes me so determined there mustn't be any reason for the Germans to start another war.' He continued sadly, 'Most of you have been listening to me making these points for years. I'm not going to take a vote today but we're going to have to split and go our own ways.'

'What do you mean?' asked Blackie.

'I'm going to talk to Roger Beacon. He thinks much the same as I do. As Leader of the Opposition, he'll bring a lot of his party with him. We will both give a lead round the country, like they did for the Referendum in seventy-five.'

Blackie grimaced. 'You'll tear our party to bits. They'll never forgive you.'

'I've thought of that, but there are worse fates.' A wistful smile spread over Bishop's face as he spoke. 'And there comes a time when you have to do what you think is right, and damn the consequences for the party.'

'Christ!' Blackie sounded incredulous. 'I never expected to hear you talking in such high moral tones. You've lost your judgement.'

'No, I haven't. Perhaps I've got it back after a long absence. And about time, too.' Bishop paused and then added firmly, 'Beacon will see things the way I do.'

There was no formal ending to the Cabinet. There just suddenly seemed nothing more to say. Ministers shuffled their papers together, then stood up and walked towards the double doors, silent, not talking to each other, knowing they were staring over the edge of a cliff and uncertain where and how far they would fall.

As Ministers, they all had certain problems in common: their lives were far too busy; their pay was inadequate; their hair went prematurely grey; their stomachs thickened. But at least their voices were listened to, their speeches delivered, their smallest thoughts turned into tabloid headlines. BISHOP SEES RECOVERY ROUND CORNER. BLACKIE EXPECTS TAX CUTS. They had got used to being treated like Moses carrying a new tablet of stone down the mountainside. And now all that was at risk. The cliff was crumbling at their feet. The red boxes would disappear and with them the deference, the drivers, and all the other perks that went with the job.

'What the hell's got into Jim?' an angry voice asked Blackie as he got into his black Rover. 'How come he's suddenly got morality?'

'This has been brewing up for a long time,' Blackie said. 'I'll have to do something about it.'

Harry Plank had been born in a small village on the edge of Chesapeake Bay, the vast stretch of water that divides Delaware from Virginia and Maryland. His father owned a tumbledown clapboard house and a skipjack, a wooden sailing boat from which he lifted several hundred crab-pots during the summer and autumn. Whether there was money to buy food and heating oil depended on the number of crabs in the pots and the price for them in the market.

Harry was first taken crabbing when he was four, and he still remembered the interminable hours spent pulling in pots, sorting the jimmies from the female sooks and spotting the ones that were about to shed their shells. When he got it wrong, his father cuffed him on the head. The only fun was betting on the number of crabs they would get out of each pot, but even then his father won nine times out of ten.

Winters were long. The westerly winds poured through the cracks in the house and, by February, the money for heating oil had always run out. Harry's father spent hours bent over his boat, repairing and caulking it, painting it when he could afford the paint – anything to get out of the house where his wife cooked, sewed, patched and complained that she never knew from one year to the next whether they would have enough money to last till the spring.

Harry decided to move out before his father died and left him with the responsibility of looking after his mother. He was fifteen when he crept out of bed at five one morning, walked three miles along the dirt road to Oyster and caught the Greyhound bus to Baltimore. He was tall for his age, thin and tough.

He prospered in Baltimore. He knew much more about soft-shelled crabs than the wholesaler who gave him his first job. In the market he was able to tell at a glance which were the barrels to bid for and what price they were worth, and in two years he was running the business. The following year he bought it. The owner had a heart attack and offered it to Harry at a low price. Harry massaged the profit figures, got a loan from a small Maryland Trust and Savings bank and found himself the proprietor of a battered shed, a conveyor belt and some freezing equipment. A week later, he was visited by the local Mafia representative who demanded the usual thousand dollars. He refused and was beaten up on his way home that night. His nose and left cheekbone were broken and he was promised more of the same treatment as a three-inch knife was drawn suggestively across his neck. The next day, after another difficult visit to the bank, he paid.

Two years later, Harry's business was growing rapidly and he received an invitation to join a Mafia-owned club in Scarlett's Ridge, on the edge of suburban Baltimore. There, on the golf course and in the poolroom, he learnt about the state lotteries of Maryland and neighbouring Virginia and Delaware, and the changes in New Jersey law that were turning Atlantic City into the Las Vegas of the East Coast. A regular golfing partner told him that there was much more money in fruit machines than in fish. At first, Harry thought the remark was just insulting, but he considered it carefully, as was his habit, and concluded that his golfing partner was correct.

Harry looked across the bar at the mirror behind the row of brandy bottles and straightened his black bow tie. He thought it strange that he should have to put on a dinner jacket to come and gamble at the Montclare. On the Boardwalk, in Atlantic City, you didn't have to wear a jacket, let alone a tie, but there it was. If that was what Matab wanted, that's what Matab would have.

The door opened and Matab ushered Angus Fyffe into the room. After he'd made the introductions, Matab gave both men balloon glasses half-full of pale brandy. 'I hope you like it,' he said. 'It's Napoleon.' He pointed to the elegant brown-green bottle with a gold N above the label, topped by a crown. 'Gagneur et Compagnie, 1811.'

'It's extraordinary,' said Fyffe, swilling the brandy gently round the glass and sniffing appreciatively. 'It has the most amazing bouquet, but it really can't be 1811, and I've never heard of Gagneur.'

'Well, you are learning, my friend. I bought it at an auction of bin-ends in Oxford. It came from one of the Colleges. It was brought there by a White Russian in 1917, together with some cases of excellent claret, all presumably from the family cellars in St Petersburg. He didn't pay his bills, so they confiscated his wine. Seventy years later, he still hadn't paid so they sold his stock, and I bought. A speculation, of course. Some of the claret is a little weary – it's gone a long way and it's over the top – but I agree with you, the brandy is excellent. And, I think, unique.'

'Please, can we talk business? I have a very early start in the morning.' Plank had started to jingle the coins in his pocket impatiently. 'Is it just the three of us or is anyone else coming?'

'It's just us three. I thought that . . .' Sheikh Matab paused and searched for the right word '. . . would make it easier.

And Margaret Bishop had to go to some important dinner with the Prime Minister, but she sent you her best wishes, Harry. You seem to have made quite a hit there.' Matab sat down at a card table, put his glass down on the green baize and gestured to the other two to join him.

'Now, you have each asked me about the other and I can vouch for you both,' he said. 'Harry, I have known Angus all the years I have been in Britain. He is a respected and influential figure here. Angus, I have known Harry for less long – two years while he has been building up his casino business here – but he came with recommendations from good friends in the States. I have watched him here at the Montclare. He is an excellent gambler, very good with figures, and he can keep a secret. You can, can't you, Harry?'

Harry smiled. 'I've been keeping secrets all my life. I'm here, Lord Fyffe, because I want to make a proposition to you, on Matab's suggestion.'

Angus regretted the crunch moment was coming so soon but he was determined to be businesslike. 'I'd like to hear it. That's what I came for, not' – he smiled – 'the brandy, delicious as it is.'

'Well, it's like this,' said Harry. 'For the last fifteen years, I've been building up a business in soft gambling on the Eastern seaboard. Fruit machines, Keno, Instant scratch cards, operating casinos – I and associates have done them all and made money. And, as a sideline, I organised a syndicate that set out to win lotteries.'

'Scams,' said Angus.

'I wouldn't call it that,' Plank said calmly. 'We won a lot of money in Virginia, for example, and that was all legal.'

'How did you do it?' Angus asked.

'There were two roll-overs and that was the key. The jackpot went up from one and a half million dollars at the end of January to nearly twelve million dollars a week later, and twenty-seven million dollars the week after that. I had organised a syndicate with seven million dollars just waiting for that to happen. There were seven million possible combinations and the syndicate set out to cover them all in three days, between the thirteenth and fifteenth of February.'

Harry laughed. 'It was crazy. We had couriers carrying ten thousand dollar bank cheques all over the state. They worked from three small offices in Norfolk, and they just managed to cover about five million combinations in the time.

'But we won. We won with a ticket bought in a Farm Fresh grocery store on St Valentine's Day. Can you beat that?' He looked at Sheikh Matab and Fyffe and was pleased to see that they were now both hanging on his words. The showman in him started to come out.

'It was the greatest day in my life. First waiting to make sure we had the winning combination and then finding that we were the only winner. We went wild. We had a helluva party.'

Angus Fyffe leant forward and asked, 'How much did you make, Harry?'

Plank swilled the brandy round in his glass, prolonging their suspense. 'We cleared just on twenty-two million dollars on a five million dollar investment.' He laughed. 'And then the taxman in the great old US of A tried to get thirty per cent of the prize, but we screwed him. We had organised it offshore through an Australian investment company, and he couldn't touch us. I still remember the numbers to this day: 8, 11, 13, 15, 19, 20. Every one was a low number. That was important.'

Angus repeated the numbers as if they were a mantra. 'You were very, very lucky to be the only winner.'

'I know, and that's why I want to try something kinda different in England.'

'What's that?'

Plank looked across the bar at Fyffe and saw a grey-haired Englishman in a midnight-blue silk dinner jacket with an immaculate velvet bow tie. He noticed the worry lines that cross-hatched the forehead. The mouth hung slightly open and, despite the smoothness of the clothes and the double gold chain that wove through the buttonhole, Plank sensed an air of anxiety, almost desperation, coming off Sheikh Matab's guest.

'D'ya really want to know?' he asked.

'There's no harm in telling me,' Fyffe said, a slight slur in his voice. 'I'm the special adviser to our lottery, you know. Maybe I can help. If I can't, I won't tell anyone. I'll keep your secret to myself. Absolutely to myself.'

'That's fair,' said Harry. He turned back to the bar, asked Matab if he could have some more brandy and watched as his and Fyffe's glasses were refilled. 'It's like this,' he said. 'I need to see the combination frequency data from your lottery. I guess you keep them?'

Fyffe looked puzzled. 'You mean which combinations are most frequently backed?'

'Specifically, which ones are least frequently backed. That's what I want.'

Fyffe thought for a long time before replying. 'Strangely, we do keep them. I'm never quite certain why, but it's something to do with establishing the random nature of our computers that do the draws, in case that was ever queried. Also, our statisticians absolutely love them. They're crazy about numbers. The science of numbers they call it. It seems more like chaos to me. Whenever they have a chance, they love to point out how daft people are, always backing the same numbers and the same series of numbers. Silly sods. You know . . .' The glass in his hand trembled slightly. He put it down, missed the edge of the bar, and it fell on to the carpet. 'So sorry, Matab. Hasn't broken, though. Carpet too thick.

'As I was saying, the ninth week of the first lottery, before the Government took control and I became the special adviser, there was a roll-over. The jackpot went up to sixteen million pounds, and seventy million tickets were sold. Odds were fourteen million to one, then as now, so there should have been five winners. Five.' Matab had given him another glass and he jerked it towards Harry, emphasising his point. 'But there weren't five. Guess how many there were.' He gazed at Harry, who said nothing, waiting for him to make his point. 'There were a hundred and thirty-three winning tickets. Think of that, Mr Plank. Twenty-seven times the proper number on a random basis. Why?'

Fyffe peered at Matab and Plank, but both kept silent. 'You don't know, I don't know,' he said aggressively. 'There was nothing particularly funny about the draw numbers. I remember them: 7, 17, 23, 32, 38, 42 and bonus 48. But it meant that the winners got just a hundred and twenty thousand pounds each instead of three million. Think of that. They were part of a herd, all drawn by some instinct in the same direction.'

Plank moved over and put a hand on Fyffe's shoulder. 'Angus, you're right on the ball, you're making my point for me. We must go into business together'. He paused for a few seconds, then asked, 'Can you get me a list of those combinations that are backed in your lottery by just one punter in fifty million or less?'

There was an awkward silence while Angus put on a consciously wise, almost offended look. 'That's a strange suggestion,' he said. 'I don't know. I'd need to know more. I've an official position, of course, I'd never put that at risk.' He stared at Matab and Plank, both of whom looked sympathetic and said nothing.

'If I may ask, what's in it for me?' The second glass of brandy helped Angus to ask the question with what he thought was the right combination of firmness and insouciance.

Harry Plank walked over to his briefcase, took out a bulky envelope and gave it to Angus. 'Read that in the morning,' he said. 'My syndicate's proposal's inside. If you get me the low frequency combinations, the first time we win the jackpot, you'll get five per cent of our winnings.'

Fyffe picked up the envelope in his hand and appeared to be weighing it. 'And how long will that take?' He could not quite keep the anxious tremble out of his voice.

'On a mathematical average, anything from eight weeks to fifty-six. It's all in there. And you're welcome to come in as an investor yourself. The return is very attractive. I can provide business and bank references if necessary.'

The telephone on the bar rang, and the doorman told Angus that his car had arrived. He muttered his thanks to Matab for a stimulating evening, told Harry Plank that he would read his proposal and wove his way through the chairs to the door. His foot slipped on a loose Turkish carpet but he grabbed at the door handle and steadied himself without falling.

After he had gone, Sheikh Matab looked at Plank and a small, restrained smile crept across his lips. 'Your fish is nibbling at the fly,' he said quietly.

'I guess so,' said Plank. 'Now that the Government here have announced they're halving the lottery tax after bringing in the Health Service drugs bill as one of the good causes, the return on our scheme looks great. Fyffe needs money like a duck needs water for sex. He'll lick his lips when he reads the papers I've given him. By the way,' he added, 'I always give our schemes a code-name.'

'I remember,' said Matab. 'You called the Virginian "Blue Crab". I could never think why.'

'A common delicacy in my part of the States, ambassador.' Plank smiled. 'This one will be "Magic Flute".'

Matab looked puzzled. 'Why?'

'Don't you know? You'll reckon it's out of character but I'm a Mozart freak. Mozart wrote *The Magic Flute* for the freemasons of Vienna. That's why Sarastro is there in the plot, the High Priest. The *Flute* is full of odd references to numbers which were important to freemasons. Papagena's age is linked to the Saros cycle from which Sarastro takes his name. They're both just over eighteen years. All very obscure.

And it's obscure, unlikely combinations of numbers that we want to win this British lottery.'

'Yes, yes, very clever,' said Matab. You have surprised me, but I still wonder whether you will convince Lord Fyffe.'

'I'll bet you. A thousand pounds?'

'No,' Matab replied. 'I have just too much faith in you and not quite enough in Lord Fyffe.'

CHAPTER FOUR

They met in Room J, the small conference room in the basement below the Transport office, beyond a door marked 'Members of Parliament only'. The room was windowless, lit by harsh neon lights, and the only furniture it contained was a plain wooden table and some hard chairs. Blackie knew that many good plots had been hatched here, about Maastricht and leadership elections, rebellions and the removal of whips. When David Armitage, his parliamentary private secretary, asked where they should meet after the ten o'clock vote, he automatically replied 'Room J'.

There were three back-benchers in the room when he entered, all talking at once to Armitage. He knew them well. The donnish-looking figure with heavy glasses and balding forehead was Doug Mesurier, one of the best brains in the new intake. Then there was Spencer Gray, wearing his trademark, a violently striped tie. Gray's speciality was to find the weaknesses in Opposition speakers and bait them accordingly. The fat man standing next to Gray had a deceptively amiable appearance. In fact, Wally Wallace was brilliant at leaking to the press stories about his enemies that contained enough grains of truth to get wide coverage and front page headlines. He had recently lost a libel suit which would have bankrupted him if the whips had not persuaded a rich supporter of the party to bail him out.

Blackie told them briefly about the Cabinet meeting. They listened, grimacing and shaking their heads, until Blackie got to Bishop's plan to run a joint campaign for the single currency with the Opposition leader.

'Treachery!' exclaimed Gray. 'Guy Fawkes was hanged for less!'

Blackie laughed. 'You're right,' he said, 'and we'll draw and quarter Bishop before we're finished. I plan a run on the pound, usually loyal MPs demanding the PM's resignation, an ugly demo in Trafalgar Square with an angry mob marching on Downing Street, and so on.'

'And does he resign at the end?' Mesurier asked quietly.

'Wait and see,' said Blackie. 'Let's get through the first act before we write the script for the finale.' He started to issue instructions. Mesurier was to make his worries about sterling known, hinting that, if Britain joined the Euro, it would have to be at a much lower exchange rate. Sterling would fall. When that process started, Wallace was to tell his friends in the lobby that the Chancellor wanted to put up interest rates but was being prevented from doing so by the Prime Minister. It could be a resignation issue for the Chancellor. That should bring down sterling even more, Blackie was respected as a tough-on-inflation man, and the stock market would then tumble as well.

'Black Monday,' said Wallace with a grin.

'More like Black bloody Week if we play our cards right. We'll get all the tabloids on our side. Imagine the headlines: SON OF HUN DITCHES BRITAIN.'

'That's a bit over the top, isn't it?' Armitage protested. 'Sort of racism, really. Unfair on Bishop.'

Blackie shook his head impatiently. 'We can't afford to be held back by niceties. This goes beyond hurting people's feelings. I've never felt so strongly about any political issue since I left school. This is life and death for Britain and all its institutions. Monarchy, Parliament, the armed forces. They're all under threat. I feel like Martin Luther starting his moral crusade. "Where there is no vision, the people perish." That's what it's all about. There's no doubt in my mind that the Germans want a European army, as in Hapsburg days, an army with many different countries in it but blurring their national identities. A common defence policy, a single currency, a European army – they're all facets of the same coin, a merging of individual nations' history and inheritance into a European dimension in which the Germans will be much the largest partner and therefore the dominant one.

'They're doing again what Bismarck did in 1871, when Prussia took over the Hanovers and Saxonies and Bavarias and merged them all into one Germany. That's why Kohl took back East Germany and unified it with the Federal Republic. He wanted a Germany ninety million strong ready, like a giant octopus, to take over the rest of Europe.'

Sweat was beginning to pour off Blackie's forehead and he stopped and pulled out a handkerchief.

Armitage took advantage of the pause to object, 'This is all a bit far-fetched, isn't it? The truth is that West Germany took over the East to save it from economic collapse after the Berlin Wall came down, and Frankfurt and Munich stepped in to help Leipzig and Dresden. They're all the same family.'

'No,' said Gray and Mesurier in the same breath, and then Mesurier went on, 'Graham is absolutely right, but too many of our colleagues don't see it. We've got to educate them. They've got to have the guts to fight for Britain.'

'That's it,' said Blackie, 'and there's very little time before Bishop sells us irrevocably down the river and into the Euro. David, do you remember the Jesuits' tag, *Exitus acta probat*?'

'Of course,' said Armitage. 'The end justifies the means.'

Blackie nodded approvingly. 'The Jesuits got it right,' he said, and swept on before Armitage could offer any more objections. 'Now, David, I'd like you to arrange for as many friends as possible to be in the House when the Prime Minister makes his statement about joining the single currency.'

Wallace interrupted him, 'I've got the first question to the Prime Minister next week. That'll be a chance to get this all started.'

Blackie agreed. 'We need as many friends in the House as possible, from all parties. Plenty of attacks on the PM, sensible attacks that will read well in the papers. In the end we've got to force a vote before a final decision is taken.'

Wallace, Gray and Mesurier nodded their heads enthusiastically and were beginning to list people they should approach when the division bell rang. They all looked up at the annunciator on the wall, saw it flashing DIVISION in bold capitals, and started to move towards the door.

'Gentlemen, before you go,' said Blackie, 'may I remind you of the need for the strictest secrecy? The battle ahead is the most important in our lives.'

They all nodded wisely and Gray said, pompously, in Armitage's view, 'And may I say, Chancellor, that I am very proud to be part of your team.'

The National Lottery Board had had a bad few weeks. It all started with the public boycotting the lottery after the Prime Minister and the Chancellor agreed that too much money from the lottery was going to Arts and Heritage. They decided that the two should be combined together, receiving the same sum between them as Sports.

The hunt was then on for a new good cause. Every government department put in a bid. Transport thought they should get it for a fourth London airport and Environment put forward the case for replacing the rock and stones on south coast beaches with clean white shell sand from the Hebrides. Both suggestions were touted as good for employment and the British tourist industry, and both were rejected by the Prime Minister as either old hat or impractical or both.

Then a small British pharmaceutical company, Polypaul plc, announced that they had invented a drug which prevented the onset of AIDS. They were near the end of successful clinical trials and planned to launch it in the next few months. In medical journals, it was heralded as a triumph for British research, potentially as important as Fleming's discovery of penicillin. It would save thousands of lives. It was also prohibitively expensive, and there was no new money in the Health Service drugs budget.

The chairman of Polypaul put an advertisement in the national press, asking all those who wanted the drug to be available, free, on the NHS to write to their MPs. Within days, 422 MPs, overwhelmed with correspondence, signed a motion requiring the Government to increase the drugs budget to accommodate the Polypaul discovery.

Jim Bishop, realising the pressure was becoming irresistible, urgently summoned the chairman to a private lunch at 10, Downing Street. The only other guest was the Chancellor. Over coffee, they did some back-of-an-envelope calculations.

'The cost of the treatment,' Polypaul's chairman said, 'is an average eight thousand pounds per patient, covering a course of twenty-five injections and then eight weeks of heavy dosage of pills.

'The number of those recognised as HIV positive is twenty thousand, but there's no way of knowing how many more will come forward once it's announced that a drug's available that would prevent the onset of full-blown AIDS.'

Bishop suggested that they work to a total of sixty thousand, to be, in his words, on the safe side. They did the calculations and reached a total cost of £480 million.

Blackie refused outright to consider an increase in the drugs budget of that size: 'There are many other miracle cures round the corner just waiting to be discovered, and their patent holders will all demand the same treatment. We cannot set a precedent.'

But Bishop persisted. 'Government's got a duty, Graham, to make Polypaul's drug available. If it was free on the NHS, anyone who was scared because they had swollen glands, or a rash, or something they didn't understand, would come and get tested. If they were HIV positive, they'd take the Polypaul injections and they wouldn't pass on their virus. That would save the State millions in the long run. Apart from saving lives.'

Polypaul's chairman agreed enthusiastically, but Blackie pointed out sourly that, in the long run, they were all dead anyway.

Over a second cup of coffee, a compromise was reached. The new good cause for the lottery would be the AIDS drug, once it had passed all its tests and won the approval of the Committee on Safety in Medicines. In return, Polypaul would reduce their price by 20 per cent, with a further 10 per cent off after the first 30,000 patients.

Afterwards the Chancellor was congratulated by his civil servants. They had not had to find any money for the AIDS drug and the principle had been established of the lottery paying instead. This could surely be extended to some other expensive discoveries in the pharmaceutical pipeline.

But that was precisely where the rub lay.

The tabloids led the uproar. GOVERNMENT CHEATS, they cried. Lottery money was *our* money. It must not be used to pay for the NHS. That was the Government's duty, which they had promised to fulfil in their election manifesto. BOYCOTT THE LOTTERY, one scribbler suggested, pressed by his news editor for a fresh idea two hours before the paper went to press. And the idea was picked up by television and radio.

Lord Fyffe became a frequent visitor to Downing Street, reporting a huge fall in sales of lottery tickets. For two successive weeks, ticket sales fell to under ten million and the jackpot to well below £1 million. Panic was spreading among the arts promoters, heritage consultants and sports advisers who had come to rely on the lottery as the goose that would for ever lay rich golden eggs.

Another motion appeared on the Commons Order Paper demanding that Lord Fyffe be sacked immediately.

Blackie's civil servants pointed out that, at this rate, the tax paid by the lottery to the Treasury would fall dramatically. It had been £700 million a year; it could now go down to £100 million or even less. And, they added with gloomy satisfaction, once people gave up the habit of buying lottery tickets, who could tell when they would start buying again? If ever. Cursing the day that Polypaul discovered their AIDS drug, Blackie asked Fyffe what would help the lottery recover most quickly.

The answer was simple. The only way to restore sales was to increase the jackpot.

And so Blackie came to the dispatch box in the Commons and announced that the tax taken by the Treasury would be reduced immediately from 12 to 6 per cent. Based on the average ticket sales of the past two years, this would give the lottery another £6 million a week, and all of that would be added to the Saturday jackpot. The mid-week lottery was cancelled: it had never caught on, and sales had been disappointing.

The Opposition hooted with laughter, the pools companies protested to their MPs, bishops protested to the House of Lords. But it worked. GIANT JACKPOT, the headlines screamed. Like alcoholics at the end of Lent, the buyers flocked back to the lottery terminals with doubled enthusiasm. And Harry Plank called Sheikh Matab and said it would be to their mutual advantage to meet Angus Fyffe.

Lord Fyffe looked with pleasure at the daily sales sheets that were laid out for him in one corner of his large office blotter. Twenty million so far this week, and Friday and Saturday still to come. They should hit sixty million at least, perhaps seventy. That was back to the old form. He had worried about his job but the fuss in the House had died down, thank God.

He opened the envelope he had been given by Harry Plank the night before and pulled out several sheets of paper. He switched his private telephone line over to his secretary next door and settled down to read. Each page was headed STRICTLY PRIVATE AND CONFIDENTIAL.

Inside was a covering note from Harry Plank.

Dear Angus.

I attach the detailed calculations of my lottery scheme, which I have christened 'the Magic Flute'.

Its success depends on our betting, every time there's a roll-over, on two million number-combinations that are very infrequently backed, say by one punter in 50 million, rather than the average one in 14 million.

If we can do that, I reckon I can guarantee you and my other investors a return of at least 70 per cent, I repeat, *70 per cent*, on the money you put in. Better than your return on the shooting at Strudwells!

Of course, we'll be paying tax at 6 per cent like everyone else. So, every time we play the lottery and put in our £2 million, we'll be contributing *one hundred and twenty thousand pounds* to your treasury. Sounds like we're some damn charity!!

Matab is very keen.

Give me a call when you've read the papers.

All the best,
    Harry Plank

Angus pulled open the bottom drawer in his desk where he hid his cigarettes, fumbled for a match and drew the smoke into his lungs. His hand shook as he turned to the pages of calculations.

THE MAGIC FLUTE

SUMMARY OF THE INPUT ASSUMPTIONS:

1. The syndicate operate only in roll-over weeks. There is only one lottery draw a week.
2. Roll-over weeks occur, on average, at least once every eight weeks.
3. The syndicate buy two million 'low frequency' coupons, which are backed by, on average, one in 50 million tickets bought by other punters.

4. Other than to the syndicate, 60 million tickets are sold in non roll-over weeks, 80 million in roll-over weeks.
5. There has been a lottery tax reduction from 12% to 6%. The 6% extra has been used exclusively to increase the jackpot.
6. There is a significant correlation among frequencies that give the best jackpot prizes and those that give the best match 4, match 5 and match 5 + bonus prizes.

In a non roll-over week, with 60 million tickets being sold:

	£Million
Prize fund (45% of sales)	27.00
£10 prize money paid out (£10×60M × 1/57)	10.53
Pools fund left	16.47
First jackpot fund (52% of pools fund)	8.57
Additional jackpot fund (6% of sales)	3.60
Total jackpot rolled over	12.17

The following week, 82 million tickets are sold, including 2 million to the syndicate.

Prize fund (45% of sales)	36.90
£10 prize money paid out (£10×82M × 1/57)	14.39 (note 1)
£10 prize money paid to syndicate (£10×2M × 1/57)	£ 351,000 (note 2)
Pools fund left	22.51
Pools fund paid to 4/5/5+ winners (48%)	10.80 (note 2)

Pools fund paid to 4/5/5+ syndicate winners		£ 527,000 (note 3)
First jackpot fund (52% of pools fund)	11.71	
Additional jackpot fund (6% of sales)	4.92	
Roll-over (see above)	12.17	
Total jackpot rolled over	28.80	
Jackpot fund paid to syndicate		£1,585,000 (note 4)
Net return on £2 million of tickets		£2,463,000

Christ, this was complicated. Angus stubbed out his cigarette in the engraved glass ashtray presented to him by his constituents and immediately flipped open the pack for another one. The match broke as he struck it and he swore out loud. His secretary put her head round the door. 'Is there anything I can do to help, Lord Fyffe?' She had a sixth sense of knowing, even through the partition wall, when the special adviser was getting upset.

'No, thank you, Angela. I'm just embroiled in some rather complicated work. Thanks.'

Angela looked at the ashtray from a distance and said, archness creeping into her voice, 'You really shouldn't smoke so much, Lord Fyffe.'

Fyffe did not reply. This time he struck boldly and successfully on the match folder and the door shut. He turned the page and read on.

NOTES TO CALCULATIONS

(1) The number of £10 prizes paid out in a roll-over in which the syndicate win the jackpot may be slightly lower, because their low frequency combinations may see fewer punters

getting three correct. The correlation is, however, weak and difficult to quantify.

(2) The syndicate can expect a fairly steady £10 prize fund return of £351,000 on their 2M tickets.

(3) The syndicate can expect to get the same proportion of 4/5/ 5+ winning tickets as the other punters. Therefore it might be argued that they can expect 2M/82M of the 4/5/5+ pools fund. The syndicate would then win £10.8M × 2M/82M = £263,500.

In fact, assuming input assumption 6 is correct, this will not be so. There is hard evidence from the figures that low frequency combinations, when they win 4/5/5+, are, like the jackpot, shared with fewer other winners than other frequencies. This is logical. Therefore, although the syndicate will win about the same ratio of such prizes as everyone else that week, they can expect the prizes they do win to be significantly higher.

The factor is very hard to quantify. We have assumed they win double, i.e. £527,000. It could well be more. The amount would vary from roll-over week to roll-over week, in accordance with prize amounts, but would be generally reliable over several months.

(4) The syndicate have a 1 in 6.99 chance of winning a share in the jackpot. If they do, they can expect to share their jackpot with one other ticket for every 50M other tickets. If there are 80 million other punters, they can expect to share with an average of 1.6 other jackpot tickets. Including the syndicate, there are therefore likely to be 2.6 jackpot winners. The syndicate can therefore expect to win an £11.07 million jackpot once every 56 weeks, or, on average, £1,585M of jackpot every roll-over week.

Added to their lesser prizes, the syndicate can expect, in the long run, £2,463,000 back for every £2M of tickets they buy in each roll-over week.

HOW QUICKLY CAN THE SYNDICATE DOUBLE THEIR MONEY?

The time taken to double one year's outlay is 4.32 years without reinvestment of profit. The figures are:

Average annual outlay: $52.14/8 \times £2 \times 10^6 = £13.04 \times 10^6$

Average annual profit: $52.14/8 \times £463{,}000 = £3.02 \times 10^6$

Profit as % of outlay: $3.02/13.04 \times 100 = 23.16\%$

Time to double one year's outlay: $100/23.16 = 4.32$ years.

If there is reinvestment of the running profit at normal interest rates, this falls to approx. 3.7 years.

RATE OF RETURN:

Each roll-over week, the syndicate must invest £2M. Of this, £878,000 will be returned to them, near enough steadily, in lesser prizes. Each roll-over week they fail to win the jackpot will therefore likely cost them £1.12 million. They must expect to wait 56 weeks, after which they will have invested £7.85 million over an average of 28 weeks. They can then expect their £11.07 million jackpot, giving them a net profit of £3.22 million over 56 weeks.

Their mean annual capital outlay will therefore be £7.85M × 28/52 = £4.23 million.

Their net annual profit will be £3.22M × 52/56 = £2.99 million, i.e. 70.7%.

SOUNDS LIKE THE GREAT DEAL OF ALL TIME!!!

Fyffe read the papers twice. He had never been brilliant at arithmetic although he found it easy enough to play around on his Apple Mac. Why should it take four years to double a year's outlay when there was a net annual profit of seventy

per cent? Still, either way it was a damn good return. And
much better, infinitely better than the rent from Strudwells.
The trouble was, there were so many wages to pay at
Strudwells: Old, the keeper, the farm manager, the beaters . . .

What was it that Plank had promised the night before? 5
per cent of their winnings. Did that mean 5 per cent on the
gross, £11 million once every 56 weeks, or on the net, £3.2
million? Either would be useful, very useful indeed. A pity he
couldn't tell his bank manager about this new income – it
might make him more relaxed. But he'd risk it, run up his
overdraft a bit more and invest £20,000, no, £30,000 in the
syndicate himself. It sounded far too good a chance to miss.

He needed a drink. He walked over to the mahogany wine-
cooler at the far end of the room, pulled out a bottle of dry
vermouth and one of Stolichnaya vodka and poured a
generous measure from each into a short tumbler. He
dropped a handful of chunky ice cubes on top.

Then there was the question of the frequency combination
data. He knew the lottery had them all on computer, as he
had sat in on a meeting just the other day when the chief
statistician had given the Board a demonstration of the series
of numbers which were either very popular or very unpopular. He had made the point that people's likes and dislikes in
numbers simply never changed. It was rooted in their
subconscious. No matter how many times seven was a
winning number, it went on being backed more than anything
else, although in logic it should be avoided like the plague.

The statistician had told them that chaos played an
important role in the lottery draw; their business was the
knowledge and organisation of that chaos. Fyffe rather liked
this analysis, and he wondered briefly how he could explain it
to the Chancellor of the Exchequer. The trouble with Blackie
was that he was too clever – LSE trained and all that. Still, he
was a surprisingly good shot.

The telephone rang on his desk.

'Sorry to disturb you, Lord Fyffe.'

'Yes, Angela.'

'It's the Parliamentary clerk. He says a question has been put down by an MP, asking for your salary to be reduced by a thousand pounds. He wants to know what the answer should be.'

'What bloody impertinence!' Fyffe checked himself. 'I'm sorry, Angela, but these MPs simply haven't a clue. They have no idea of the responsibility involved. Anyway, I'm much too busy to worry about it just now.'

'Of course. I'll tell the clerk. He'll draft a standard answer, I'm sure.' Angela shook her head as she put the phone down. Poor Lord Fyffe. He had so many things on his mind.

Angus realised he was putting off making a decision about Plank's proposal. Should he give him the data he needed to make his Magic Flute work? It was a damned silly name for a business venture.

Strictly speaking, what he was being asked to do was against the rules, he supposed. On the other hand, he couldn't see there was actually any harm in it. After all, Plank's syndicate would simply buy an extra two million tickets and that would mean roughly half a million pounds going to good causes, apart from the tax. And it would produce some more money for the AIDS drug, which was what the Government wanted.

He walked across to the window and stood looking down on the stream of buses and taxis circling Trafalgar Square in endless pursuit of each other. Even if he were to agree to give Plank the information he needed, he wasn't sure how he would actually get his hands on the combination frequency data. Would he be able to access it from his own modem, or would he have to ask for guidance? Fortunately, he had always insisted on having the highest classification of password, in case he wished to do a spot check on any aspect of the system. Fyffe prided himself on his computer literacy.

He poured himself another drink. This time he put the ice

cubes in first, before tipping in equal measures of vodka and vermouth.

There was also Bishop to consider. Jim certainly wouldn't like him leaking data to Plank. But equally it would be very embarrassing for Bishop if he went bust – 'Creditors take Lottery Peer to Court', and all that sort of thing – particularly as they were known to be very good friends. And it would definitely be bad for the party.

Plank's scheme really did represent a marvellous escape route – not just for him, but for Margaret too. He would insist that she be allowed to invest in the scheme as well, and in that way he could help her win back some of her gambling losses. She would bless him for that, and so would Jim, although of course he would never know of it. A good deed unseen.

He took another, long sip of vodka martini, then turned round and unlocked the safe in the wall behind his desk. He took out the thick computer manual, marked in heavy red letters COPY NUMBER ONE, and turned to the index. Finding the reference to combination frequency data, he began flicking through the pages.

He had just found the series of instructions which gave access to the data when the telephone rang again. He snatched it up. 'Yes?'

'I'm sorry to disturb you, when I know how busy you are . . .'

'For goodness' sake, Angela, get on with it. Do the MPs want to sack me again?'

Angela laughed nervously. 'No, no, of course, it's nothing like that, Lord Fyffe. You remember the opening of the new all-weather sports track in Coventry, funded by the lottery? Your driver thinks you should leave now if you're to get there by five.'

'Oh, I'd forgotten all about it. I'm afraid it'll be impossible for me to go, Angela. Something has come up that I must work on. Please ring and give them my apologies. Tell them . . .' Fyffe thought for a moment '. . . tell them we're working on a campaign to help promote the new AIDS drug. It's urgent work, but ask them to keep that strictly confidential. All right?'

'Yes, of course, Lord Fyffe. I'm sure they'll understand.' She hesitated. 'Would you like a sandwich?'

'Yes, please, that's very thoughtful of you. Brown bread, not white, please. Smoked salmon or crab would do.'

Fyffe turned back to the computer screen and clicked his mouse to call up the frequency data.

There they all were, arranged in descending series, starting with one in a hundred million down to one in two million. Angus flushed with excitement. It all seemed so extraordinarily easy. He could move his mouse and call up whichever series he wanted and print them out.

He slipped a blank disk into the machine and started to copy on to the disk, then reached for the telephone.

'Harry,' he said as soon as Plank answered, 'it's Angus Fyffe. I've read your papers.' There was no comment from the other end. 'I'm . . .' He paused. 'It's very difficult for me. Very difficult indeed.'

'That's great.'

Angus was nonplussed. 'What do you mean, "great"? I said it was very difficult for me.'

'That means you're interested. If you weren't, you'd just tell me to get lost.' Plank's voice sounded sharper.

Angus felt he had to move the conversation on. 'I take it that my five per cent would be on the syndicate's gross winnings, the eleven-million-pound share of the jackpot when we win it.'

'Hell, no. It's on the net, whatever that turns out to be. And after expenses.'

Fyffe mentally gritted his teeth. 'I must have ten per cent then,' he said in the strongest tone he could muster. 'Five's not enough.'

There was a long pause and then Plank replied, 'Let's not horse around, Angus. I'll agree to six per cent but not a cent

more. Hell, that way, you're going to make a hundred and
eighty grand every year for doing nothing, once you've got us
the frequency data. Of course, we'll need to keep that
updated. How soon can you get us the material?'

Fyffe realised Plank was taking his acceptance for granted.
Bloody man, he thought. But he needed the money so badly.
'I'll need to think about it, of course,' he said, trying to make it
sound as if he was doing Plank a favour, 'but I'll want to come
in on the syndicate myself, and I want Margaret Bishop to be
in on it as well.'

'Margaret Bishop?' Plank sounded surprised. 'Fine, if you
think it's a good idea. You know her much better than I do.
How much d'you wanna come in for? Fifty grand is the
minimum. I don't need a bunch of small investors.'

Fyffe gulped. He heard his voice saying, 'I'm sure we'll
both come in for fifty.' He must try to sound more
businesslike. 'If you can handle IBM compatible disks, I can
copy the information out for you. It will take some hours. I
could give it to you at the Montclare once it's ready, and then
we can talk more about terms, and security.'

'As soon as you've done your side of things, I'll send a guy
round from my office, Tom Bobbins. I know I can trust him.
After we've looked at your data, we'll meet at the club on
Saturday or Sunday, whenever Matab can manage.' Plank
paused, then said, 'I'm glad you're on the team, Angus. I'm
sure we can work together.' The phone clicked and was silent.

Fyffe thought back over their conversation. He found
Plank's words disturbing. He hadn't considered himself as
working with Plank, rather as a straightforward investor – on
favoured terms, of course, because of the information he was
providing. Still, he felt certain he could make a lot of money,
and that was the key point. Plank certainly sounded very
confident. There was a gentle knock on the door, and Angela
came in with two sandwiches on a tray.

'Here's your lunch, Lord Fyffe, I'm sure you must need it.

And a glass of apple juice. I'm afraid the canteen didn't have any smoked salmon or crab.'

'Thank you, Angela. Looking after me as always.' He peered at the inside of the sandwiches. 'Egg salad and prawn mayonnaise. Splendid.' He paused. 'Angela, I'm going to be very busy for the next few hours. Can you see that I'm not disturbed? And bring me a lot of paper and some more blank disks. I'm working on a new idea for the lottery which ties in with the campaign for the AIDS drug. It probably won't come to anything but I want to try one or two theories.'

'Of course. It's lucky we cancelled going to Coventry. That will give you some time.'

Angela shook her head in wonder as she went back to her desk. Lord Fyffe was amazing. He did so much for the lottery and he was so creative. No wonder they employed him as a special adviser.

There had been little wind so far in November and there were still plenty of leaves on the trees – too many, from Colin Old's point of view. Some of the guns would have difficulty in seeing the birds clearly enough in the drives in the woods, which would mean they'd have to be very quick to get on to the bird in time. If they missed too many, they would certainly complain to him at the end of the day.

Still, that was next week's problem. That was when his Arab boss was having his first big day, bringing all sorts of grand people, the agent had told him, politicians and ambassadors. They would shoot the main woods round the release pens, and some of them would stay the weekend at the big house. It would be more like the old days before Mister Angus spent so much time in London.

Tomorrow there was to be a small shoot round the woods on the boundaries and driving the game crops under the Downs. The agent had asked a few local guns he knew well and he wanted to give them a reasonable day. Colin planned to entice some more pheasants towards the fields of fodder radish and linseed. It was their first year, and he wasn't certain how well they would hold the birds, whatever the farm manager told him. There was a covey or two of partridges down there as well.

He filled the two green bags slung round his neck with groundfeed mixture, whistled to Zeppelin who had his nose down a rabbit burrow, and set off out of the main wood. A dozen cock pheasants were outside the wood, pecking idly at the grass in the sunshine, and they scuttled towards the nearest cover, leaving a solitary dark cock looking at him. You again, thought Colin, always hanging around. He walked towards the bird and was within a few feet of it before it turned and started to move with a dignified strut back to the wood. Zeppelin watched from his heel and slowly wagged his tail.

Colin walked along the hedgerow, scattering grain on either side of him with a rhythmic flick of the wrist. The pheasants would follow him soon enough, and then he would throw some millet seed down where he wanted to hold the birds until the next day. Ahead of him, across two fields of grass, he could see the first game crop, a broad strip of maize. He kept on telling the farm manager it was no good just planting maize by itself in straight lines. You had to mix it up with another crop, otherwise the birds just ran down one line in front of the beaters, turned at the end and ran back down another line. If a dog caught them, they never got up, but just died of a heart attack. He often wondered about pheasants. They seemed awfully stupid to the average gun who didn't know much about them, but they were like humans really – a mixture of fear and greed. You had to lure them to get them to do what you wanted.

Colin looked around and saw that Zeppelin was busy investigating a small heap of dried cow dung. He whistled and the dog instantly bounded back to him. If there had been an expression on his face, Colin would have described it as one of injured innocence.

CHAPTER FIVE

'I'm going to need your help, Roger. Without it, I don't know what will happen.' The Prime Minister had never expected to say those words to his accepted political enemy, the Leader of the Opposition, but they came from the heart and he knew he had no alternative. He had thought about it for a very long time.

'I know, Jim.' Beacon sounded sympathetic. 'The problem is that the British hate the Germans; it's one of the most basic things about us. We fear them, we call them rude names, we don't understand them and yet we are quite like them.'

The two men were sitting in armchairs facing each other in the Prime Minister's room at the Commons. Each had a whisky and water in his hand and they looked, for the moment, like the closest of allies and conspirators, jointly plotting.

'It's atavistic, something in our blood,' Beacon went on thoughtfully, 'a throwback to two world wars.'

'No, it's more than that,' Bishop said. 'We distrust the French as well. We're an island race, like the Japanese, and we don't get on with our neighbours. The Japs have never got on with the Chinese, or the Koreans, for that matter.'

Beacon got up from his chair, walked to the window and looked across the cobbles and the carefully trained lime trees in front of Westminster Hall. 'Strange,' he said, 'when you think that that building was built by Norman kings and we have part German blood on our throne now, mixed with Greek. We could hardly be more of a mongrel race, but you're right, it's a gut instinct. Shakespeare appealed to it with all his stuff about a scepter'd isle set in the silver sea, and it's never gone away. The funny thing is that we're only patriots for about three weeks in the year, during the Olympics or the World Cup. For the rest of the time, most Britons give the appearance of despising their country.'

Beacon drained his whisky. He knew the time had come to get to the point. 'Well, you want me to break up my party in order to help you out of a hole. Why should I?'

Bishop respected Beacon. He was a practical realist who had got to the top of his party by blunt commonsense and the ability to see both sides of an argument. There was nothing to be gained by beating about the bush. 'You're right, I'm in a hole, I'll not deny it, but then so are you. Your party is just as split on Europe as mine, and you don't want to win an election only to find Europe in tatters, Germany and France putting up trade barriers, interest rates and unemployment rising while new investment disappears. It could be like the thirties all over again. And so unnecessary.' He hesitated, then added, 'I don't want to teach you how to win elections, but you've a vested interest in keeping Europe prosperous and united.'

Beacon hated this sort of appeal. It passed over the politician in him and went straight to the heart. What did he think was best for Britain? He had always spoken up for Britain's membership of the European Union, but now he was being asked to sacrifice party unity on a European altar. He stalled.

'Be precise, Jim. Just what is it you have in mind? What's your timetable?'

'This is absolutely secret between us – Privy Council terms, and we don't even tell our chief whips?'

'Agreed.'

'I want us to pool our forces to join the single currency as soon as possible. If we do, France will stay in. If not, Germany will pull out, France will follow, there will be bitter hostility and the Union will collapse.

'I'm bound to be asked questions about this in the House next week. The Cabinet is split down the middle and I can't stall any longer. I'd like your personal backing, then I'll make a formal statement when I address the Assemblée Nationale in Paris the following week, and then face the House when I get back. That's when I'll need your votes.'

'A confidence vote?'

'Not unless you make it one. If you agree, I'll go for a free vote and together we'll get it through the Commons.'

'Christ,' said Beacon. 'Like the 1975 referendum all over again.'

'Yes.'

Silence settled on the room – the anxious silence of good people, accustomed to fighting but now searching together for a common solution.

Finally, Beacon said, 'You're asking me to do a hell of a lot. Do I get anything in return?'

'If it would help at any time, I'll say we're in this together because we believe it's the best answer. It's the only possible way forward for Britain.'

'That won't help in the tabloid press. They'll call me a traitor.'

'Some of my party,' a reflective smile twisted the corners of Bishop's mouth as he spoke, 'are calling me that already. I've learnt to live with it.'

Beacon shook his head as Bishop offered him more whisky. He still had a lot of work to do before catching the evening train to his constituency. 'I'll have to think about this, Jim,' he said. 'I'll come back to you Monday or Tuesday.'

'I hope you'll agree, Roger.' Bishop got up from his chair and escorted Beacon towards the door. 'It's much bigger than party politics.'

'Damn you!' Beacon's mouth widened into a broad smile. 'You're appealing to my nobler instincts.' He looked closely at the man by his side. His shoulders might be slightly hunched and his hair thinning, but there was a look of fixed

69

determination on his face. Here was a leader he could trust and respect. Several times in the past few years he had wished they were in the same party. Yet he sensed, too, a touch of the martyr in his opponent, a willingness to sacrifice himself in a cause he passionately believed in. Impulsively, he said, 'I think that if you were in a church procession, Jim, you'd be the one carrying the cross, fighting for ideals, campaigning for some impossible cause.'

Jim straightened his back and smiled at Beacon. 'You flatter me.'

Beacon wanted to end their meeting on a lighter note. 'I'm going to watch Manchester United play Spurs tomorrow. That'll help me forget your troubles for a few hours, and mine, too. What are you doing, Jim?'

'We're going to visit our son in Coventry. He's a music teacher there and it's his birthday.'

'A quiet family weekend,' said Beacon. 'Sounds like a good idea.'

After Beacon had left, Bishop picked up the papers on his desk but found it impossible to concentrate. Never before had he plotted with the Opposition against his own colleagues. It was going against the habits of a lifetime. He picked up the telephone, scrambled the line and rang Margaret.

'Darling,' he said as soon as she answered, 'I need comforting. I've just had the most unorthodox conversation with Roger Beacon. I've asked him to work with me on getting the Euro accepted in Britain. Graham Blackie and his friends will never forgive me.'

'Really, Jim, is that wise?' Margaret sounded distracted.

'I've no alternative,' Bishop said. 'I'm going to need a lot of his party's votes to get it through the House.' There was silence at the other end and he changed the subject.

'I should be ready to leave in about an hour. I'll come back to Number 10, change and then we can set off for Coventry.'

More silence. Bishop could picture his wife thinking hard and wondering how to deal with him. 'I'm sorry, Jim,' she said eventually. 'I've promised Angus Fyffe I'll join his bridge party tonight. He was desperate for another player. I'll drive down and join you both tomorrow. I'll be with you by mid-morning.'

'Damn,' said Jim. He felt the hopeful eagerness flooding out of him. 'I was really looking forward to a quiet talk with you as we drove tonight. I feel so anxious about this whole European business, and I want to talk it through with you. You're the only person I can really trust.' He paused and then said, 'Margaret, darling, couldn't you possibly get out of bridge with Angus? You see him often enough. You know, I'd love to have you to myself for a few hours. The pressure has been frantic and it's going to get worse.'

He sensed the frown, the determined tightening of the jaw. 'I don't often appeal to you, darling,' he said softly. But Margaret had made up her mind.

'I'm sorry, Jim, but I can't let Angus down. I'll be with you and Giles before lunch tomorrow.'

He heard the definitive click down the line. How absolutely and finally it cut off communication. And he remembered how, when he first became a Minister, Margaret had insisted on their having a drink together when he came home from the House with his red boxes. No matter how late it was, they had sat down together and he had told her of the rows and problems and occasional triumphs. But that was before he was Prime Minister and before Sally was killed. He thought for a moment of having another whisky but that would only make him sleepy. He put his glasses on and settled down to the papers stacked in orderly piles in front of him.

The Montclare was crowded. A high-pitched buzz – a mixture of excitement, alcohol and gaiety – rose from the long bar on the ground floor and spread out, through the open doors, into the billiard room and the coffee room. It had an infectious quality. Members arrived from St James's cold and ruffled, either by the November wind or by their day's work, but by the time they had taken off their coats, warmed themselves by the open fire and greeted a few friends, geniality was spreading through their bloodstreams. They moved to the bar, ordered a large drink from one of the three stewards in bottle-green coats with dark velvet collars and started to make a noise and laugh and salute acquaintances on the other side of the room.

Angus Fyffe did not follow this pattern. Ignoring the calls of two friends at the bar, he walked straight up the wide curved staircase to the first of the gambling rooms on the second floor, where Sheikh Matab and Harry Plank were waiting for him. With them was a brown-haired man with a heavy face dominated by a nose that veered off at a surprising angle towards the left-hand side of his mouth.

'Meet Tom Bobbins, Lord Fyffe,' said Plank. 'He runs my gaming operation in Britain. When we launch the Flute, he'll be responsible for the couriers going all over Britain to buy the two million tickets. We've already hired a warehouse in South London; next week he'll get the telephone lines and the jacks installed. We've got some spare staff – the casinos aren't too busy just at the moment – and we'll start to do some training.'

Fyffe looked surprised. 'You're moving that fast?'

'Sure thing,' Plank said. 'The disks you sent over have just the raw data we need; the number combinations and their different levels of frequency are very clear. I'm having them put on to spreadsheets by my number crunchers, and then allocated in blocks of hundreds for Tom's couriers. That way we'll get the men on the road just as soon as there's a roll-over of the jackpot.'

Bobbins nodded his head in agreement and slowly wiped his hands together as if rubbing out some insect that was caught in between. 'I can get about three hundred men out of the casinos and bingo halls at any time, and I'll recruit a hundred or two of their mates when I need them. They'll vouch for them . . . they'll have to.'

Fyffe felt the colour flooding into his face, and he ran a finger round the inside of his collar. 'Really,' he protested, 'I had no idea you'd move ahead so fast. I thought we were meeting tonight to discuss the details.' He realised how weak this sounded and walked over to the bar to help himself to a large vodka and tonic. There was silence while he tipped a spoonful of crushed ice into his glass and swirled it around. He dropped a fat slice of lemon on top, and some of the drink splashed out on to his Versace tie. 'Damn! I was only given this tie last week.' Sheikh Matab and Plank watched him in silence as he dabbed at the tie with his handkerchief. 'It's silk, a birthday present,' he explained.

'My dear friend,' Matab said expansively, 'you must not worry too much. No one will know where the . . .' He turned towards Harry. 'How do you call them? The combination frequency data, that's right. No one needs to know where they came from; that will be a secret between us.

'And, my dear Angus, think, if we buy two million tickets, how much we will be giving to good causes in your country and to your Treasury in taxes. Didn't you find the figures that Harry gave you very interesting? Double your money in under four years and a seventy per cent annual return on capital – isn't that very interesting indeed? You won't do nearly as well as that on the Stock Exchange.' Matab joined Angus at the bar and poured himself a glass of sparkling Curlew Spring water. 'You know, Curlew Spring is owned by a friend of mine, a good businessman. He wants to put a million into our venture, our Magic Flute, he thinks so highly of it, but I told him I could only allow him half a million. We will have too many subscribers.'

Angus knew he was being pushed over the edge. Unusually for him, he had woken during the night, his stomach drawn tight with worry and his body drenched in sweat. He had walked back and forth from bedroom to bathroom to living room. In the end he had taken two sleeping pills and been lured back to an uneasy sleep. Greed was conquering honesty, he saw that all too well, but it was the only chance he had of getting the bank off his back.

Harry Plank looked at him as though he could read his thoughts. 'I've told the Ambassador of the five per cent I promised you from our jackpot winnings. He thinks I'm being too generous but I'll stick by our deal. We'll need you to update the data from time to time but that shouldn't be difficult for you. It's great to have you with us.' He reached forward as if to shake Angus' hand but then seemed to think better of it.

'Six per cent,' Fyffe contradicted him without thinking, 'we agreed on six per cent. You remember I wanted ten and we settled on six.' He saw the knowing smile pass fleetingly over Matab's face and realised his error. Now he was compromised. 'There is,' Matab said, 'the Chinese ambassador in London tells me, an old Confucian proverb: "Many offer flowers to those caught in snowdrifts, but few bring burning charcoal." We are offering you, my dear Angus, a piece of burning charcoal. I am sure you will find it useful.'

The white telephone at the end of the bar purred quietly. Matab picked it up and listened for a few seconds, then told the others that Margaret Bishop was on her way up to the room. He suggested that they keep quiet about where the frequency data had come from. If she pressed them, they would just say that they had managed to acquire them but it was better for her to know as little as possible.

Margaret seemed to glow with self-assurance as she walked into the room and offered her cheek for Matab and then Angus Fyffe to kiss. She was wearing an off-the-shoulder black dress that seemed moulded round her breasts and the curve of her bottom. Over it she wore a burgundy red silk jacket with gold and garnet buttons, decorated with a ruby and diamond brooch.

Matab looked at her appreciatively. 'I am flattered you have put on the brooch my brother gave you,' he said. 'It suits you very well. I will tell him that you are still wearing it.'

Margaret laughed. 'I'm so glad that when we came back from our visit to the Gulf I was able to hide it away from the awful Foreign Office. Otherwise they certainly would have made me give it up. Now,' she looked round the room and seemed put out, 'you're four already – have you been playing bridge for hours?'

Tom Bobbins was introduced, his role briefly explained and he then left the room without another word.

The four sat down at a green baize table, cut the cards for partners and Matab, who had drawn the highest, started to deal.

'What are we playing for?' Angus asked.

'Five pounds a point,' suggested Harry. He was Margaret's partner.

'Too much,' Margaret protested. 'That sort of stake ruins my bidding. It makes me too nervous to take any risks.'

'My dear, when you hear about the certain profits from Harry's lottery scheme, you'll play for ten pounds a point. If, of course, we let you join the scheme.' Matab smiled at her. 'We haven't decided yet whether you are a suitable investor or not.'

'My dear Sheikh, Angus has told me a little bit about your scheme, code-name, of all things, the Magic Flute. Rather a silly sort of name, I thought.' She looked across the table at Matab, opened her eyes wide and smiled at him as if they shared a special secret.

'It's an intellectual kinda name,' Harry interrupted. 'It'd throw anyone off the trail. And it's very appropriate. Mozart planned to make a lot of money out of the *Flute* to save himself from going bankrupt. Unfortunately, he died too soon and others made the money generations later. Now you've even got a chocolate liqueur called after poor Wolfgang. Well, we're going to join the gang of moneymakers.' He looked round the table. 'Now, for Chrissake,' he said, 'let's get on with the game. Angus and Margaret, I guess you'd be happier at two pounds a point.'

75

Three hours and three rubbers later, Harry and Margaret were ahead by eleven hundred points. They agreed it was too late for another rubber and Margaret asked Harry to explain all the details of his lottery scheme over a final drink. 'It sounds absolutely brilliant,' she said after five minutes of listening, 'just what my bank balance needs at the moment. But how did you get hold of these combinations of numbers that are so unpopular they're hardly ever bet on?'

'We have our ways and we keep them secret,' said Matab, leaning over the table and gently putting his hand on hers. 'Don't worry about it. But we're keeping the number of investors down – we want as few to know about our Flute as possible. I'm afraid, my beautiful Margaret, the minimum investment is fifty thousand pounds. Even so, I think we will be too popular. Half this club would want to join if I put a subscription list up on the notice board.'

Margaret swallowed and then picked up her glass and looked at it intently. 'Fifty thousand?' she queried as if repeating the words would make the sum rather less.

'Yes,' said Matab. 'I'll put up a million between my friend and myself, and Harry half a million. That's right, Harry, isn't it?' Plank nodded his head. 'We don't want more than another ten investors at the most. If there are any difficult decisions, we have to be able to take them without delay.'

'What are you going to do, Angus?' Margaret asked.

'I'll come in for fifty thousand.' Angus answered almost too quickly. 'I can't afford it but it's too good an opportunity to miss. I'll borrow it somehow, and I think you should do the same, Margs.'

Margaret winced. She hated being called Margs and knew that Angus only did it when he was trying to cajole her into some scheme or other. She took a deep breath. 'All right. After all, we might win on the very first roll-over, mightn't we?'

'A one in seven chance,' said Harry. 'Not bad odds, almost like playing dice. But what I'm offering you is really an investment, not a gamble at all. Something to keep you all in caviar and champagne in your old age.'

Angus laughed, There was a rather sycophantic undertone in his laugh, Margaret thought. She wondered whether Harry already had some sort of hold over him, gambling losses perhaps.

Matab interrupted her train of thought, handing her the cheque he had just written out for £2,200. 'Fortune is favouring you, Margaret. You win at bridge and you will win in Harry's little scheme. And now, can I drive you back to Number 10?'

Angus butted in before she could respond. 'No need for that, Matab. I'm driving Margaret home.'

Matab shrugged his shoulders, moved forward and kissed Margaret on the cheek.

Angus didn't speak to her until they were in his car and driving towards Whitehall. 'Are you worried about the size of your stake in the lottery syndicate, Margaret?'

'Of course I am,' she said.

'I hope I didn't push you into it.'

'You certainly did, but we know each other too well. Neither of us can resist a gamble.'

'It sounds a tremendous opportunity.'

'I just hope Harry's got the figures right.' Margaret felt herself bubbling with enthusiasm. 'If he hasn't, Jim'll never forgive me, but he seems fantastically confident.'

'You won't tell Jim, will you?' Angus asked anxiously.

'Of course not, he'd never understand.'

Angus started to say something and then checked himself. They drove in silence past Buckingham Palace and up the Mall.

Margaret undressed slowly. Naked, she turned and looked at herself in the mirror, and then ran her hands tentatively over her breasts and down her stomach. She turned sideways and examined the profile of her body in the glass. She thought her

77

stomach might be a little bit bigger – that was the trouble with all those pompous, five-course dinners – but it was hardly noticeable. Considering she had had two children, it was surprisingly flat.

She looked at the reflection of her breasts and remembered how embarrassed she had been when Jim had first unbuttoned her shirt and stroked her breasts. She had wanted them to be bigger to please him, but now she was thankful they didn't sag. They were as firm as ever – well, not quite as firm, perhaps, but that really wasn't surprising.

She peered more closely at the mirror. There were definitely crows' feet in the corners of her eyes and a few lines down her neck. The other day someone had given her the name of a plastic surgeon. Brilliant, they said, but hideously expensive. She wondered where she had put his card.

She got into bed naked, and looked at the radio clock. One twenty already. God, why was Jim never at home? She suddenly imagined his hands running gently over her, and her body becoming warm and liquid and ready for love. It had been months since they'd made love. At first, Sally's death had been a barrier and then, as the awful scar of that hardened, their lives appeared to part and they were unable to pick up from where they were before Sally was killed. Every evening now, it seemed, Jim worked and she gambled, and they barely spoke when they met in bed. Not that she didn't still love Jim; it was just that there was no passion left, no closeness, no solving of problems together.

She turned off the light, remembering the hurt in his voice when she said she wasn't going to drive to the country with him because she was playing bridge with Angus. He had really wanted her there with him. Still, the bridge had been worthwhile. She had won £2,000, and that had given her the courage to join Harry's lottery scam. What did he call it? His flute? A silly name. Really, Harry and Matab were just like little children playing secret games that the parents weren't to know about. Code words and all that nonsense. Of course, she had agreed to far too large a stake. She didn't know how she could afford it, but it was safe enough. If she could pay off her overdraft, perhaps she wouldn't feel so guilty towards Jim. As she drifted into sleep, she stretched out an arm, searching for the man on the other side of the bed, and her hand grasped and held on to a fold in the sheet.

CHAPTER SIX

Every day Brinks armoured lorries drive into Lothbury in the City of London, home of the Bank of England. Their police escort waits at the gates as they turn into Bullion Yard, which is shaped like a test tube, with a thin funnel leading into a rounded bottom. Dark passages, protected by a series of locked gates, lead into the yard from the vaults of the Bank. This is where Brinks load and unload one-ton pallets of gold bars on to compact wheeled trailers. The owners and the customers are the many foreign banks and refineries who store their gold at the Bank, and each pallet, measuring a mere three feet by two by two, is worth around £9½ million.

There is a constant coming and going, watched over from the windows that look down into the yard. The one store of gold that never moves is the nineteen million ounces that belong to the British Treasury and to the British taxpayer. Thanks to the heaviness of the metal, it is physically a small quantity. Stored on around five hundred pallets, it could easily be moved by a convoy of multi-axle lorries, but it has the significance of a tribal totem. When all else fails, people turn to gold for permanent value and intrinsic worth. In crises, gold becomes of paramount importance.

The Chancellor of the Exchequer was concluding his formal annual inspection of Britain's gold reserves. He walked up the winding staircase from the vaults, thanked the black-suited official who had conducted the tour and congratulated him on his thirty years of service with the Bank. As the two armed guards who had accompanied them slipped quietly away he commented on the weight of the bars. 'They're really quite small, aren't they? You expect them only to weigh a pound or two, and then you find you need both hands to pick them up.'

The official saw a chance to make the comparison that visitors always liked. 'The metal is so dense, sir, you could put all the gold that's ever been mined on to the floor of the Albert Hall, put the Royal Philharmonic Orchestra on top, and there'd still be room for the Orchestra to play to a full house.'

'Extraordinary,' said the Chancellor dutifully. 'I'll remember that when I'm next at a concert there.'

A few minutes later, he was in the office of the Governor of the Bank, sipping a glass of dry sherry and listening to the Governor explain that it was the weight of the gold, and its high specific gravity, that was currently at the heart of one of their problems. The Fed in New York, being built on rock, could stock pallets up to the ceilings of their vaults. 'Since we're on London clay, we can't, as you saw, stock more than six pallets high. It's a very inefficient use of space.' The Governor spoke as if the geology of London was a matter of personal irritation.

'We're getting more and more central banks,' he continued, 'from the old Soviet Union, for example, and from the Balkans, who find it safe and convenient to store their gold with us. And of course, they pay us, rather handsomely. So we're going to have to spend money on strengthening the foundations. We'll have to move the gold round a bit while the men are at work. Troublesome, expensive and necessary.'

Graham Blackie looked over his glass at Sir Geoffrey Williams. Pinstriped suit, stiff white collar, six-buttoned waistcoat, black shoes that shone like a beacon on a grey November day – Sir Geoffrey was the archetypal central banker. Blackie imagined he would hate any change in his bank, even in the depth of concrete below the floor of the vaults. After all, it was a historic building, a model for central banks round the world.

'Well,' he said, 'just make certain you don't lose any of my

81

gold. I wouldn't want to put you in the Tower.' Sir Geoffrey smiled thinly, and Blackie changed the subject. 'Look, you've got some members of the Court coming to lunch, haven't you?' The Governor nodded. 'I can't say this over lunch, then, but I want you to know that the Prime Minister is going to announce in the next week or two that we're going to join the single currency and the European Central Bank. It'll be the end of your independence,' he added with a touch of malice in his voice.

Sir Geoffrey's cheeks reddened and his hand trembled as he put his glass down on the edge of the mahogany partners' desk.

'He can't do it,' he said bluntly. 'It'll ruin everything I've worked for for the last thirty years. Hell,' he added with rare, outspoken bitterness, 'I haven't fought successive Chancellors to get more independence for the Bank only to see it all taken over by Germans and the French.'

He took up the decanter of sherry and poured some more into their glasses. His hand was still shaking and he overfilled his glass until the sherry spilt on to the polished table. 'Damn,' he said, pulling out an exactly folded handkerchief.

'What's sterling doing this morning?' asked Blackie as he watched the Governor dabbing at the little liquid pool.

'Down another twenty points against the dollar. It's all the uncertainty in Europe – it looks bad in the States and Japan. The traders are going short.'

'I wouldn't want to do anything at the moment to strengthen the pound.' Blackie gave a penetrating look at Williams and the Governor nodded his head. 'It would give the wrong signals. There's no question of raising interest rates. Your dealers might want to let the market know that.'

'It'll slide further.' Williams drummed the fingers of one hand on the desk as he spoke.

'Well, you always tell me that's good for our exports.' The two men half-smiled at each other and Williams was about to reply when an attendant in the pale pink tailcoat that is the

Bank's uniform announced that members of the Court had assembled for lunch.

On the way out of the Governor's room, Blackie stopped to look at a portrait on the wall of a soldier in white breeches, red jacket with white crossed belts and black busby. His right hand held a rifle with a short bayonet while his left was placed on his hip, lending a certain nonchalance to his pose. 'Who's this fellow?' Blackie asked.

'He's one of the Bank volunteers,' Williams said. 'They were formed in 1798 to protect the Bank. That was in case there was a French invasion and the gold reserves and banknote printing presses had to be removed to somewhere safe.'

Blackie laughed. 'You'd better start recruiting,' he said.

'All right, Jim. I've thought about it all weekend and it ruined my football match, but I've decided I'll be with you. It'll be a hell of a fight and I wouldn't do it for anyone else, but there's no going back on it now. The news over the weekend was ghastly.'

Roger Beacon assumed the telephone line was scrambled, though he had little confidence in the Government Communications Centre. Most confidential discussions between Ministers seemed to appear in the papers the next day. He was determined to impose a ministerial vow of telephone silence when he got into office.

'All the way?' Bishop sounded tentative.

'Yes, all the way. I've had both the Spanish and the Italian ambassadors calling on me, asking me to support you if you announce Britain's joining the Euro. They're sure that will help their governments, and they have vowed eternal friendship if I do.' Beacon laughed. He felt a heavy weight lifted now that he had made his decision. 'That'll be a useful card to cash when I'm in your shoes. Have you been lobbying them, Jim? They sounded a lot more friendly than my Shadow Cabinet.'

'Of course not.' The voice at the other end was pleased but weary. 'But you only have to look at the strikes and battles in Rome and Madrid to know why they desperately need a lead from the European Union. There's practically civil war in the Mezzogiorno, which only a massive injection of aid from the Commission can possibly resolve. But that's all another story.

'Thanks for your support, Roger, I'm very grateful. I know your convictions and I hoped you'd join me. Some day we'll both have our statues in Westminster Abbey.' He paused and then added with perceptible embarrassment, 'How many of yours will support you, when it comes to the crunch? Of course, it'll be a free vote and a very personal one. About half?'

'Yes, I should think so. Perhaps slightly more. Say, a hundred and fifty or sixty. Of course, I don't have as efficient a whips' office as you, so it's harder to know.'

'My lot are all over the place,' Bishop said, 'like ferrets in a sack, as we used to say when I was a whip years ago. I think I've just got a majority, but Blackie will declare against me. He'll fight dirty and a lot of our weaker brethren will follow him. And the constituency chairmen, the chairpersons . . . I daren't tell you, Roger, what they'll be like.'

Beacon laughed and they agreed to keep in very close touch.

'A coalition of like-minded people from different political parties,' Bishop said thoughtfully. 'It's almost like the war.'

The fifth floor of the Victorian warehouse in Union Street, SE1 was filled with row on row of metal chairs with canvas seats. Sitting on the chairs, some upright, others slumped, were some three hundred people, almost all men. Their common characteristic was an inquisitive look, a wariness of eye that anticipated trouble, but trouble at an oblique angle rather than directly ahead. The tall room in which they had assembled was dusty with heavy cobwebs on some of the windows, and there were uneven holes in the planks of the floor where rats had chewed their way through. The neat and careful dress of those present was in strict contrast with the dirty surroundings.

Tom Bobbins sat on a makeshift platform, looking down at the sea of faces below him. Most of those present had seen him on the gaming floor of their casino or walking through the arcade where their fruit machines were installed. One or two had been disciplined by him, lost a week's wages and told they were bloody lucky not to lose their jobs. When he rose to speak, everyone fell silent and one man hastily shoved a dog-eared pack of cards into his pocket.

Bobbins began by introducing himself as the General Manager of International Corporate Enterprises, or ICE for short. 'You've all been sent here by your local managers because they haven't got enough work for you. Rather than sack you, the boss has decided to give you a short-term job that'll take you round the country. It'll be for one week, possibly two. Almost a vacation, you could say. Usual wages, but your travel will be paid for. Every eight weeks or so, the job may be repeated.' Bobbins saw 300 eager faces, mostly white with dots of brown and yellow, staring up at him, full of questions. He took a piece of paper out of the inside pocket of his black leather jacket, enjoying the feeling of power as everyone in the room hung on his words.

'Now, listen bloody carefully,' he said. 'The boss has decided he wants to win the lottery.' Someone sniggered at the back of the room but stopped immediately as Bobbins glared in his direction. 'It's no joke. When he wins, and knowing him and his friends he will win, that'll keep all you wankers in work.

'This means that whenever there's a roll-over and the jackpot gets big, he and his syndicate are going to buy a helluva lot of tickets. You lot are going to do the buying for him.'

'I haven't got any money,' a voice said from the back and was greeted with a supporting murmur.

'You silly cunt,' Bobbins said. 'If you don't want the job, bugger off. Go on, bugger off now.' Nothing but silence greeted him.

'Now, listen very, very carefully.' He started to read from the paper in his hand.

'Each one of you will find a brown envelope on one of the tables up here. Everything is in alphabetical order, A to F at this table, G to M at the next, and so on. Inside you'll find a plastic folder with a map of the part of Britain you're going to, a computer printout of the shops, Post Offices and garages you'll go to to buy lottery tickets and a Casio digital notebook which has been programmed with the sets of numbers you're to buy. Every Casio has got a different set in it.' He paused, took out a large checked handkerchief and blew his nose like a trumpet.

'Now comes the difficult part,' he said with satisfaction. 'You'll also find a detailed list giving you precise instructions about what combinations you buy where. The lottery outlets you visit have been numbered and you'll call on them in strict numerical order. This'll enable us at Head Office to check on how you're getting on.'

He paused again and a brave voice from the back shouted, 'What about the money, the dosh, the moolah?'

'I'm coming to that.' Anger raised Bobbins' voice to shouting pitch. 'For crissake, listen. As soon as there's a roll-over, a courier will deliver you a series of what are called certified bank cheques made out to the lottery. So, in case you're feeling tempted, there's no chance of you cashing any of them yourselves.' His index finger came up and stroked the side of his nose, persuading it towards the centre of his face. 'Don't try it or it'll be the end of you.

'As soon as you've bought all your tickets, you'll come straight back to London. Here your receipts will be checked against the list you were given, and you'll then be paid a hundred-pound bonus, lucky buggers. But only if you've got it all right.' Bobbins looked down at the silent, glum faces in front of him and said, 'For God's sake, cheer up. Any questions?'

'There won't be much time, will there, I mean, if we only get the cheques on Monday, and we've got to get it finished by Saturday? I mean, we'll be running all over the place, won't we?' The question came from a small man, perched on the edge of his chair, a cigarette dangling out of the corner of his mouth. 'With all that hassle, I mean, we should be getting overtime, we should.'

'Don't be a nerd.' Bobbins did not try to conceal his contempt. 'It's all worked out on the papers we've prepared for you. You'll each be covering one small part of the country, calling on forty to fifty outlets a day. You should be able to do it in four days; we've allowed you five. If you get sick or something, call here immediately, tell us how far you've got, and we'll get a replacement on to your job. But, of course, you'll lose your bonus, and the boss wouldn't want to see you again.'

There was a dissatisfied rustle as legs were first crossed one way and then re-crossed the other. But no one spoke until the same little man with the pendant cigarette asked, 'What happens if we buzz off with the tickets we've bought? I mean, if we don't show up back here, trouser the tickets and,' he paused, looking for the right word, 'flit, scarper, sort of sugar off?'

'What's your name?' asked Bobbins. His voice was suddenly menacingly soft, and those who had been quietly scratching themselves or picking their noses felt the urge to put their hands placidly together in their laps.

'Phil Darby.'

Bobbins walked down from the makeshift platform and made his way to Darby's side. 'Stand up, Phil,' he said. 'Nice to meet you.' He extended his right hand and Phil, a foot shorter, tentatively rose to his feet and took it. He was immediately pulled violently to Bobbins' chest, the bones in his hand were crunched together and Bobbins' knee rose

87

straight into his balls. He screamed and as he bent forward, doubled up with pain, Bobbins' other arm encircled him, took hold of him by the collar, shook him backwards and forwards and then threw him on the floor. As Darby lay at his feet, Bobbins looked at him as though memorising his face and then, slowly and with precision, kicked him in the stomach.

Bobbins turned and walked back to the platform. 'You've all worked for ICE for some time. I don't think any of you would want to double-cross the boss, not considering the way he looks after his employees. Any more questions?'

There weren't any.

CHAPTER SEVEN

The electronic clock announced that the time was three fourteen in the afternoon. One minute to go before the Speaker announced Prime Minister's Questions, and still no sign of the Prime Minister himself. 'He's leaving it bloody late,' Wally Wallace growled to Doug Mesurier, sitting beside him.

'He always does,' said Mesurier. 'It's a sort of machismo thing, shows that he's not worried, but you don't want him to miss your first question.'

'He'd damn well better not. My constituents are at last going to see me on television in prime time. I've told the local press and telly.' As Wallace spoke, the Prime Minister glided past the Speaker's chair and towards the further end of the front bench. He had hardly sat down when the Speaker rose to his feet and announced, 'Questions to the Prime Minister. Mr Wallace.' The formal question about the Prime Minister's engagements for the day was quickly dealt with and then Wally rose to ask the supplementary question that he had worked on, word by word, with Graham Blackie.

'Can my right honourable friend assure the House that, when he goes on his important visit to Paris next week, he will not make any commitment that Britain will join the single currency?' Booming cries of 'Hear, hear!' surrounded Wallace, drowning his voice. But the television cameras were firmly fixed on him, and he was by no means finished. He made a sweeping gesture with his hand, silencing his supporters.

'Does he realise that he would make himself extremely

popular with his party and the country – indeed, he would be regarded as a national hero – if he insisted that Britain was going to remain a sovereign state, maintaining the pound and keeping the sole right to tax British citizens? Does he realise that Britons never, never want to find Euros in their pay packet?' The last few words, simple as a slogan, were shouted over the uproar around him.

Jim Bishop got to his feet but was faced with a solid wall of noise. 'Order, order!' shouted the Speaker, rising from his chair. 'The House must let the Prime Minister reply.' There was a momentary lull.

'I must tell my honourable friend that I cannot give him the assurance he seeks.' There were groans from both sides of the House. 'Far from it. And I think he is wrong to ask for it.' I am in active discussion with Cabinet colleagues and with the Leader of the Opposition at the moment.' A second of silence followed while these words sank in, and then a surprised yell rose from both sides of the House. 'Whatever intention I announce at my meetings in Paris will, of course, have to be agreed by a vote in this House. I assure the House of that.'

The crowded benches were suddenly alive with movement as everyone turned and asked their neighbour whether they had heard right. In discussion with the Opposition? It was impossible.

'He's gone mad,' said Spencer Gray. He was sitting on the other side of Wallace. 'Off his head. Or in the pay of the Boche.'

Roger Beacon was on his feet on the far side of the dispatch box, waiting for the row to subside. 'Mr Speaker,' he said, and then again, louder, 'Mr Speaker. May I congratulate the Prime Minister on his courage and foresight?'

An unbelieving hush fell over the Chamber. 'It's as bad as Saddam Hussein getting into bed with the Americans,' said Mesurier, and Wallace and Gray laughed.

'Can I assure him that, on this side of the House, we are aware of the difficulties of the Germans in supporting the

Euro almost alone? We believe that an effective economic and monetary union is essential if Europe is to survive as a world trading bloc. Of course, joining the Euro must be subject to a vote in this House,' Beacon paused and then spoke with deliberate slowness, 'but the Prime Minister will have our support. This is a historic moment. Britain must look ahead, not back to the nationalism that has caused so many wars.'

The House erupted. Bald elderly men three rows behind Beacon got up and shook their fists at his back. Three women, sitting neatly side by side at the back of the Chamber, cheered and waved their order papers. Graham Blackie rose ponderously from his seat next to Bishop, his posture emphasising that he expected attention. The cameras turned from Beacon and, once Blackie sensed they were fastened on him, he walked deliberately past the Speaker's chair and then out of the Chamber. His back spoke of his disgust.

The Press Gallery did not wait to hear any more. They started a mad dash away from their seats, up the raked aisles and towards the exit. There was serious money for those who got first to the faxes and phones.

As the Speaker clambered slowly to his feet, he felt a familiar pain spreading across his chest. He hated trying to control the Commons when it reached this violent, unpredictable mood, and he searched for the packet of Rennies in his pocket. Damn. He could feel his keys and some coins but no indigestion pills.

'Order, order!' he cried plaintively. 'The Prime Miinister must be allowed to answer the Leader of the Opposition. I have never heard the House in such a dreadful temper. This must stop immediately.'

But peace refused to break out. 'Immediately,' the Speaker repeated.

Suddenly, it seemed that six hundred Members were all on their feet, bawling across the Chamber or at their neighbours.

The Serjeant at Arms reached nervously for his ornamental

sword. In thirty years of military service he couldn't remember anything quite like this, except perhaps the riots in Berlin – but then Britain had just finished fighting the Germans; now Britain was doing something to help them.

The Speaker rose again to his feet, his wig and his black robe with its gold banding lending him an authority he did not feel. 'Order, order! This is a disgraceful occasion. The House does itself no good, behaving like this when the world's television cameras are on us. I shall suspend the sitting for the rest of the day.' He gathered his robes in one hand and almost stumbled as he walked down the three steps from his chair. He could feel his knees shaking in his thin black breeches and hoped that he, alone, was aware of this. He would hate his trembling to be visible to the world at large.

Silence fell on the Chamber and Members of Parliament started to gather their papers together sheepishly, like schoolchildren suddenly given an afternoon off lessons because their teacher has broken a leg playing football with them. As Wallace, Gray and Mesurier walked down from their bench, David Armitage handed them a note. It said simply, 'Meet in Room J in ten minutes.'

Blackie felt extraordinarily elated as he walked out of the Chamber. At last, the division between him and the Prime Minister was out in the open. He did not have to pretend any more. Five reporters, pencils and notebooks at the ready, swarmed over him like wasps on ripe fruit as he walked across the Members' Lobby. 'Mr Blackie, Mr Blackie, please, can you . . . will you . . . did you . . .'

'Yes,' he said curtly, 'I did it on purpose. I'll talk to you later.' As he moved towards the door behind the message board he was stopped by a uniformed messenger who handed him a folded piece of pink paper. The message was timed only a few minutes earlier and it was very brief. 'I am back in London. Call me. Marie Claude.' There was a telephone number at the bottom.

Blackie stopped as if hit in the stomach. Christ, he thought, her. Christ, that was just what he didn't need at the moment. He read the message again and shook his head in anger mixed with disbelief.

As he entered Room J, Doug Mesurier, Spencer Gray and Wally Wallace jumped to their feet. David Armitage followed rather more slowly. 'Hell,' said Blackie, 'this isn't an army orderly room. You don't have to stand to bloody attention whenever I come in.'

'It's discipline.' Wallace laughed as he replied. 'In the campaign to keep Britain sovereign and independent, you're the general; we're the staff. How long have we got?'

Blackie paused. The elation he had felt a few minutes earlier was draining from him. He had burnt his boats, that was the truth of the matter. He hadn't waved the mace about, or anything histrionic like that. But he, the Chancellor of the Exchequer, had walked out while his boss was speaking, all in front of the cameras. It would be headline news round the world.

Gray read his thoughts. 'Don't worry, Graham, you had to do it. You had no alternative. We can't all go on pretending we're one party. This is bigger than any of us. Here, we've made a list of people you've got to see as soon as possible. There are a hundred and two MPs on it, including thirty from the other side. We're booking halls across the country, and you've to meet the Consolidated club and the Hussars and the '95 group . . .'

Blackie started to get his breath back. 'Who the hell are the Hussars?'

'It's all-party. You remember, we formed a year ago in protest at Britain posting two regiments to the European army. Bishop did it as a trial but a mass of the ex-servicemen were against it. We'll call an extraordinary meeting.'

'Of course, of course, I remember. I was asked to join but I couldn't as a Minister.' Graham ran his hand through his hair. 'Anyone know what happened to the markets this afternoon?'

'Weak, dangerously weak,' Mesurier replied. 'I was at lunch with Persimmons. The FT index had fallen by seventy points during the morning, and they were talking about the Bank having to put up base rate. I said you'd be in favour but the PM was against. Then along came some minion from the Bank, announced that the Governor saw no reason for increasing interest rates, and the market immediately fell another fifty points.' He paused and then added cautiously, 'Persimmons thinks you should get Geoffrey Williams to take early retirement. He's been at the Bank for far too long and hates any sort of change. Dead wood, really.'

Blackie ignored the suggestion. 'We've got to have a battle plan. Spencer, you're in overall charge. Get the loan of a house or flat nearby; borrow some fax machines and photocopiers. I reckon we've two weeks till the vote. Wally, you'll look after the media. Doug, I want you to draft a manifesto, a simple theme, Britain First, that sort of thing. David, you're to run the diary. I want to see every MP of any party who's ever spoken up against Europe. It doesn't matter for what reason – size of condoms, fishing rights, straight bananas – grab them all. These are the people I've got to win over.'

'They're the ones we've already got on the list,' said Gray.

David Armitage had kept very quiet but now he nodded his head.

'Fine.' Blackie looked at his watch. 'God, I must run; I'm doing the five o'clock news. But . . .' he punched his fist in the air '. . . we're on our way.'

After he had rushed out of the room, Gray, Mesurier and Wallace looked at each other and laughed, feeling a surge of excited confidence.

Harry Plank had never been inside the Medevan Embassy before. He stared at the coffee-coloured panels on the walls,

HOSTAGE TO FORTUNE

wondering what wood they were made of. They had very little
grain and no burr. They were bound to be expensive, that
was the only certainty. The sofas, set against three sides of the
room, were covered in an elaborate blue and silver brocade,
and he ran his finger over the thick, raised pattern in the
material as he turned his attention to the solitary picture
hanging in front of him. The handsome, haughty face looking
down at him belonged to an Arab prince in his forties, with a
clear eye, a long nose and a mouth that was resolutely closed,
giving nothing away. He wore a brown camel's wool *bisht* over
his collared *thob* and a red *keffiya* wound round his head.
Plank thought it was the face of an adventurer at home on a
horse, riding over the desert with a falcon at his wrist, rather
than someone who had to argue with oil companies about
seismic surveys, extraction rates and market prices. But he
was fantasising.

The door opened silently and Plank turned to find Matab
watching him from the far side of the room, looking at him
speculatively, summing him up.

'My half-brother, the Emir, Sheikh Abdulla,' said Matab,
nodding towards the portrait. 'We are like each other, except
that he is the ruler and I am not. Our father was killed many
years ago in what I think you would call a palace revolution.'
Plank started to mumble his regrets but Matab brushed these
aside. 'It was for the benefit of Medevan. Sheikh Abdulla has
ruled well. Our state has prospered. We are now as rich as our
neighbours; we can afford to buy Tornados and Chieftain
tanks from Britain, and send our young men to Sandhurst for
training. Sit down, Harry.'

Harry sat uncomfortably on one of the hard sofas and
wondered how long it would take Matab to come to the point
of the meeting. He knew that, of all the Gulf States, Medevan
was still the closest to Britain, but that was about the extent of
his knowledge. He had no interest in the defence industry.

Matab saw the faint look of boredom cross Harry's face

95

and he put aside the courtesies. 'Harry, I asked you here as I want to know about your lottery scam. Is everything in place?'

'You mean my Magic Flute, that's going to make us a lot of money? I don't like the word "scam". It sounds dishonest.'

'All right, the Flute then. Have you got the couriers all lined up? Do they know what to do?'

'Yes, that's all in hand. Bobbins is an efficient devil. If there's a roll-over this Saturday, I'll want your million from you on Sunday, and we'll start buying tickets on Monday.'

'You've no worries about the data Angus Fyffe got for you?'

'Technically, it's just great. We've done several computer runs and they all check out. The combinations he's given us concentrate on series of numbers that have regularly produced high returns in prize money. They are exactly what we wanted and what they set out to be, the combinations that no one chooses. About Fyffe . . .' He tailed off, rubbing his hands together and obviously uncertain what to say next.

Matab walked slowly round the room until he ended up staring at his brother's portrait. 'I know it's a little risky,' he said, his back turned to Plank. 'If the source of our information gets found out, there will be trouble. If it's known that Margaret Bishop is involved, there will be even more trouble.'

'Ambassador, we used Fyffe because he was the easiest person for us to get the combination data from. Remember, it was your idea to approach him. Margaret Bishop, she's altogether a different matter.' Harry shrugged his shoulders. 'We could drop her now. I think she's only in the gang because she's an attractive woman. We both like her.' He looked across the room at Matab who was still gazing at the picture as though seeking guidance. 'And you like danger, it's in your blood.'

Matab was far away. He was remembering the early morning when the sky was scarcely pink and he and his brother had crossed the wide-arched court and gone to their father's quarters with pistols hidden in their woollen *bishts* and how the guard had greeted them with smiles, thinking they had come to celebrate their father's birthday. He and his brother had had so many private talks, secret discussions, steeling their nerves, thinking of every move. He shook his head in a gentle motion, forcing himself back to the trivia of the day.

'I don't know what makes you say that, Harry. Margaret is in your plan because we both wanted to help her. She needs the money. I think she needs it rather badly.'

Harry looked at him and a broad smile broke across his face. He was about to say something more but stopped himself and waited.

'But I do like some excitement,' Matab agreed. 'London is boring, so very boring.' A note of anger crept into his voice. 'All these diplomatic parties, night after night, with the same people, the same little pieces of food on sticks, the same sparkling wine pretending to be champagne, the same conversation . . . I need something to keep me awake.'

'You have your shooting,' said Harry quietly.

'Yes, I'm grateful for that. And it's well organised in this country. Over the next few weeks I will kill several hundreds of pheasants, but I need more than that.' He looked again at the portrait of his brother and then faced Harry.

'You are right, Harry – the Flute will give me some excitement. We will go ahead. I trust you, but you must keep your scheme secret. Make certain it doesn't get known.'

'Of course,' said Harry, 'that's the way I've made all my money.'

Marie Claude looked out at the neon lights on the other side of St George's Street. It was a pity that London had not kept its old lamps like Paris. The concrete columns were so ugly and the light was far too bright – the thin curtains in her room would never keep it out.

She rose wearily from her chair and started to unpack her

bag with its multitude of pockets and zips. Opening the mirrored door of the cupboard that reached to the ceiling, she found there were no hangers inside. She went to the telephone on the cheap wooden table by the bed and asked the cross voice at the other end for some coat hangers. She could not resist checking whether there had been a call for her from Mr Blackie. She was assured there hadn't. The mere suggestion made the voice sound even more cross.

Marie Claude started to undress. As she took off her dress, there was a loud knock on her door. She opened the door a crack and stretched out her arm, and a bundle of wire hangers, some bent, others rusty, was thrust wordlessly into her hand. She looked at the label on the dark green dress as she slipped it over the thin wire. Givenchy. She remembered Graham taking a rare hour off from work on her birthday to buy it with her. They had walked all the way up Sloane Street, calling in on the smartest shops. In one of them the assistant, dark-haired and very pretty, had shyly asked Graham whether he was a Member of Parliament. When he said he was, the girl had looked relieved and said she had seen him on television.

Marie Claude looked at her watch. It was only ten o'clock but there was no point in staying up. If Graham did not ring her tomorrow, she would certainly call him at the Treasury. No, tomorrow was Saturday, she would try to reach him at his constituency office. She would start a brouhaha; she had all his private numbers.

She went to plump up the two pillows on the bed and realised with irritation that they were both made of foam rubber. The one thing she had to have was a soft pillow, preferably stuffed with goose feathers, like the ones in her old bedroom at home in Normandy.

She ran her hands tentatively across her stomach. It was firm and seemed beautifully flat, flatter than the marble Venus Graham had admired so much in the Louvre last Christmas. But she was only three months pregnant. The doctor had told her that she was not likely to start swelling noticeably until the fourth or fifth month.

Marie Claude said three Ave Marias, crossed herself hurriedly and jumped into bed. The mattress was too soft, but the sheets were at least clean and cotton, not nylon. She detested nylon.

CHAPTER EIGHT

Sheikh Matab walked out of the double front doors of Strudwells and looked across the gravel sweep at the activity taking place around the three Land Rovers that were lined up in strict order against the service trees. There were seven guns on the gravel; four were talking to each other, two were busy putting shooting sticks and heavy leather cartridge bags into the back of the Land Rovers and one, Jim Bishop, was stroking a black Labrador's head as he talked to the keeper, Colin Old.

It was a scene that Matab loved. Quintessentially English. Disciplined and organised. Traditional and exciting. He was pleased, too, at the group he had got together for his first big shoot in his lease of Strudwells. Five ambassadors, the Prime Minister, Harry Plank and himself. Although he would not make any obvious comment, his brother would be impressed when he told him about it. Plank was the odd man out, but he had shot a lot in the States and Matab felt he needed to get to know him better.

There had been a heavy frost overnight and the gravel was hard underfoot. As Matab walked across the drive, he was conscious that his plus-fours were louder and brighter than anyone else's. He had chosen a large-patterned red and brown check which he thought modest, but it was bold, even garish, compared to the gently faded, watery greys and greens which the other guns wore. And they all seemed to be in neat, close-fitting plus-twos rather than plus-fours. Even Plank, wearing a Norfolk jacket, moleskin breeches and Hunter boots, toned in with the late November landscape. He must go to his tailor again.

'Good morning, gentlemen. Good morning, Old.' Matab looked up at the high clouds scudding across the sky. 'It looks like a nice day.'

'Yes, sir,' Old said. 'The forecast's good. No rain and a bit of wind from the West, which'll help make the birds fly.'

'We rely on you for that, Old, wind or no wind,' Matab said and two of the guns laughed dutifully.

Matab pulled a thin leather case out of his pocket and opened it to reveal eight ivory sticks inside, with a different number engraved at the end of each stick. He slid the sticks into slots sewn inside the case so that only the blank top of each stick was visible, and invited each gun to draw one.

'We're numbering eight,' he said. 'We'll move two for each drive, as usual, but I like the odd numbers to move down and the even to move up. One at the first drive becomes seven at the second, two becomes four, and so on. That way we all shoot next to different guns throughout the day.'

'*Mon cher* Matab, that is very complicated.' The French ambassador smiled as he spoke. 'How can one ever remember? I find it difficult enough when we are just moving two places all in the same direction.'

'That's right,' Harry Plank said. 'If you're shooting with a New York banker and you tell him to add two to four when he's forgotten his number in the drive, he always gets it wrong.'

Colin Old smiled. He remembered a shoot the year before when one gun complained bitterly that he had been on peg number eight for three drives running, because he couldn't remember his number and others kept on walking to the pegs in the centre of the line where most of the birds would fly. There had been a violent argument, and Colin had told the agent that he hoped never to see that syndicate at Strudwells again. Sheikh Matab's guests would, he was sure, be better behaved.

TIM RENTON

'I insist,' Matab said. 'This gives more variety and I rely on you to keep count. Now, no ground game, but shoot partridges as well as pheasants, and no pigeon please until the drive has begun. Old will blow his whistle twice at the end of each drive, and there will be pickers-up with dogs behind the guns.'

'No foxes?' asked Jim Bishop.

'No. I'd like to kill every one of them, but Lord Fyffe has persuaded me to let the Hunt come here until January, so we mustn't shoot their foxes. That's right, isn't it, Old?'

'Yes, sir.' Old looked at his watch. 'If you don't mind my saying so, sir, the beaters will have started blanking in five minutes ago. You should start moving to the first drive.'

A faint shadow of anger passed over Matab's face. He did not like being interrupted or hurried, least of all by an employee. 'Very well,' he said. He turned to the French ambassador. 'Bertrand, will you come in the first Land Rover with the Prime Minister and me? The rest, divide yourselves between the other two. We will not be coming back here till lunch, so bring plenty of cartridges.'

He turned to Bishop as Jim prepared to get into the Land Rover. 'What about Margaret?'

'Oh, she's driving herself down from London. She should be here in time for lunch.'

Jim Bishop arranged himself in his usual way. He screwed his shooting stick into the ground and sat on it to make certain it was firm. Then he opened his old cartridge bag – a gift from Margaret when they were first married – and put it a yard in front of him, well within reach in case his belt ran out during the drive, adjusted the muffs over his ears until he could only just hear the sounds from the wood and finally slipped two cartridges into his gun.

He had had a marvellous morning, particularly in the second drive in the Mains wood. There he had been almost at the end of the line, at peg seven, but the westerly wind had pushed the birds towards him and for twenty glorious minutes they had flown over him, in ones and twos, just above the tops of the ashes and sycamores. There was enough clearance for him to see their dark shapes coming from forty yards away, and his gun was up and into his shoulder as the birds flitted into range. On to the head of the bird, move forward, swing in front of the bird, keep swinging, fire, break the gun and reload as the bird moved instantly from rapid life to death, tumbling heavily on to the ground twenty yards behind him.

Bishop found the cares of the world slipping away from him as his shooting got faster and his reactions quicker. He finished the second drive with two successive right and lefts, the last two birds falling together through the Sussex sky.

Harry Plank walked up to congratulate him as they moved to the next pegs. 'You were really fast, Prime Minister. I was on your left and you left nothing for me to shoot. You were on to the birds real fast.'

'Well, I was lucky. I was in a good spot,' Bishop said modestly.

'That's as maybe, but it takes years of practice to shoot the way you did.' Harry changed the subject. 'You may not know this, but I sometimes play bridge with your wife. In fact, we've made a foursome with Matab and Fyffe. I wondered if she'd be here today.'

'She will be, later on,' said Bishop. 'She's bringing our spaniel down with her and she'll be picking up in the afternoon. She loves picking up. It makes shooting much more fun for her than just watching me firing away.'

Some time later, Bishop reached the third peg for the last drive of the morning. The guns had come down from the woods on the hills in the heart of the estate and were to shoot the Home wood, which stood on a narrow ridge a few hundred yards from the house. The wood was V-shaped and ended in a point, towards which all the birds would run.

Bishop was on the edge of the wood and there were two guns in the field outside, standing on the steep slope below him.

Colin Old, determined to make the birds fly high over the guns, had strung two lines of white plastic strips between the trees in front of the guns, but Bishop could now see a dozen hen pheasants running over the ground, turning nervously in different directions. He heard the noise of the beaters' sticks in the distance and the occasional yapping of an excited terrier. Suddenly, governed by the same instinctive reaction, the hen pheasants took off in one flush, flew out of the wood, saw the guns and turned back towards the beaters. Bishop rested his gun on his forearm and watched.

The man next to him did not bother to put up his twelve-bore but the gun on the extreme right swung at the birds, firing two shots. A hen fell, picked itself up and started to run energetically towards the wood. Broken wing, thought Bishop, and he wished Margaret's dog was there to mark exactly where the bird went back into the trees.

Then birds started to fly over him and he stopped thinking about the wounded bird and concentrated on his shooting as pheasants streamed towards him, first singly and then in twos and threes. There were branches hanging over his stand and he had to be very quick, snap shooting in front of him, if he was to have any chance of getting his gun on to the bird before it was hidden behind the autumn remains of brown leaves and bare wood. The barrels of his gun became so hot they were hard to hold and his cartridge belt was soon empty. He was sweating with energy and excitement as he found himself diving quickly into the bag on the ground in front, as bird after bird slipped through the sky.

'You didn't have much time, did you?' the owner of the three large spaniels said to him as Colin Old's whistle sounded twice and his dogs, let off their leads, bounded away to start picking up the dead birds. 'But you did all right. I counted sixteen – nine hens, seven cocks.'

'Thank you,' said Bishop. 'I thought it was fifteen. I missed quite a few.' He laughed. 'I was in such a hurry, I got into a muddle with my cartridges.'

'One of the cocks came down way back, right at the end of the wood. You wouldn't have seen it fall, but it was a dead bird all right. A lovely shot.'

Two of the spaniels came back, tails wagging furiously, each with a pheasant held gently in its mouth. 'Good dogs, good dogs,' said their owner, picking up the birds after they'd dropped them on the ground, 'hilost, hilost, back you go.' As he gestured into the trees, Bishop was surprised to see Colin Old running towards him, his Labrador at his heels.

'Excuse me, sir, but have you seen Sheikh Matab anywhere?' Old's face was twisted with worry and Bishop felt an instant surge of pity for him. He had known Old for many years and respected him as a steady and friendly person who could be relied on to keep his temper even on a day when the rain poured down and the guns missed everything in sight.

'What's wrong, Colin?'

'It's bad, sir, a beater's been hit. It was that early flush of the hens that went out over the field; they were a bit too low for the guns on your right.'

'God, how dreadful! Is he badly hurt?'

'Hard to say, sir. There's a lot of blood on his face, but his eyes are all right.'

'Thank goodness . . .' Bishop was interrupted by the appearance of Sheikh Matab, walking rapidly towards them.

'What is it, Old? Is something wrong?'

Old pulled nervously at his cap. 'I'm afraid so, sir. It's one of the beaters, Tom Ruster. He got some shot in his face early on in the drive. I've put him in my Land Rover and I'll take him to the doctor in the village immediately, while you're at lunch.'

Sheikh Matab turned to Jim Bishop. 'I suggest you go with the other guns to the house, Prime Minister, while Old and I work out how we can help Ruster.'

Bishop repeated his regrets to Matab and moved away towards the picker-up and his spaniels.

As soon as Bishop was out of earshot, Matab spoke again to Colin Old. 'Who is this Ruster?' he asked. 'Is he going to die?'

'Oh, nothing like that, sir. The gun who shot him was thirty yards away, but he was below the line of beaters, and the hens were low. It was no one's fault. I think Tom'll have to have some shot taken out of his cheek, that's all. I've known him for years; he's worked on the farm since he came out of the army.'

Matab pulled a crocodile leather wallet out of his pocket and took out ten £50 notes which he pushed into Old's hand. 'Give these to Ruster, and tell him to keep quiet. There's to be no talk about this from him or any of the beaters. Do you understand?'

Old nodded his head slowly.

'I'll look after Ruster,' Matab continued. 'I'll see he gets any treatment he needs but . . .' He paused. '. . . I don't want any news of this to be passed around. If anyone asks, Ruster got just one pellet in his cheek. It was – what would you call it? – bad luck, and no one is to blame. One pellet can produce a lot of blood. Is that clear?'

Old's face did not show a trace of emotion. 'Very clear, sir.' He stood quietly, his tweed cap in his hands, waiting to see if there were any further instructions.

'If Ruster talks, I will ask Lord Fyffe to dismiss him, and I am sure he would follow my request.'

Old began to reply but stopped himself. Instinctively, he bent down and stroked the head of his black Labrador, whose tail wagged like a metronome.

'I want to start again at two fifteen sharp. I would like to get in three drives in the afternoon, if the weather holds.'

'We usually only do two, sir.'

'But that is because lunch lasts for too long.' The usual studied calm in Sheikh Matab's voice cracked. 'I ask my guests here to kill birds, not to sit at the dining table. What was the bag this morning?'

'Two hundred and seventy-five in the first three drives, sir, a hundred and fifty-three hens and a hundred and twenty-two cocks. The dogs'll pick up a few more. And seven partridges. I don't know about the last drive as I came straight to see you after . . .' Old paused, searching for the right word '. . . the accident, but I should think it was around seventy.'

'Excellent. The birds were well driven, Old. If we do as well this afternoon, there will be a good bonus for you and the beaters. Tell them that.'

Matab turned and strode off, his gun over his forearm. Old looked pensively at his back, stroked Zeppelin for several seconds and then walked through the trees to the path where the beaters had gathered.

Margaret Bishop insisted that the television be switched on before they went in to dinner so that they could watch the lottery draw. The Prime Minister protested, saying that the last thing Matab and his guests wanted was to watch a busty starlet performing her Lucky Winner routine, but the other guests expressed no opinion and, to his surprise, Matab supported Margaret.

The television at Strudwells was normally kept in the library, a long, cold room with heavy, inefficient radiators and a small electric fire, but Matab had the set moved in to the drawing room. As the lottery draw started, the whole party, champagne glasses in their hands, gathered in front of the screen. They watched the balls first churning around in their giant transparent mixer and then sliding, tantalisingly, one by one, down the transparent shute, to be greeted by Streppie Pepper, the blonde comedienne who was established as the regular star, the anchor of the evening.

Streppie ogled her nationwide audience in the manner that had brought her fame and fortune. 'Look,' she cried, 'eighteen!' She pointed at the first blue ball as it came to rest at the end of the shute. 'Just my age!' She fluttered her false eyelashes at the camera and the studio audience laughed dutifully.

Margaret Bishop looked at the clutch of tickets in her hand.

'Eighteen!' she exclaimed. 'I know I've got it. I've got it in lots of them.' Her hand quivered as she thumbed through the tickets and Jim felt a surge of embarrassment for her. He stared at the pile of logs glowing in the fireplace.

'Forty-three,' cried Streppie, 'my granny's age.' And the audience's laughter turned to a repressed groan. The forties were never popular; there weren't many forties in birthday dates. But this was to be their night. Forty-five followed, then forty-seven.

'Damn, damn,' Margaret said, 'I never back those two. They don't do anything for me.'

Jim raised a foot and kicked hard at one of the logs that threatened to slip forward out of the grate.

'Thirty-nine, that's sure to bring some of you some happiness.' Streppie greeted the green ball as though it were a personal triumph, a ball that she herself had chosen rather than the random churning of the draw-machine. Some of the audience clapped and others shifted uncomfortably in their seats. Forty-one followed and was again greeted with polite groans.

'Speed it up,' the producer muttered from his cubicle into the little microphone hidden in Streppie's ear, but she was powerless to do so as the slowly spinning wheel turned for an unconscionable time and the bouncing balls seemed held inside by a magnetic force. At last, one rolled out and slid slowly down the shute and into the eye of the television camera. 'Two!' she cried, relief that she had personally produced a low number evident in her voice. 'That's your lovely, special bonus number.'

Someone in the audience laughed, and suddenly everyone was laughing and a grin spread over Streppie's face.

'Anyone in the audience become a millionaire?' she cried.

A collective 'No' rose from the crowded seats.

'Never mind, I expect you've got lots and lots of numbers right, lucky you. You're a brilliant, lovely audience.'

Sheikh Matab gestured to the butler, who moved forward and pressed delicately at a black button. The screen went blank, and Matab got to his feet and suggested they go in to dinner.

Jim looked across the room at Margaret. All the colour had gone from her face and she stood staring at the fire, her hands hanging loosely by her sides. Her lottery tickets were already torn up and the pieces piled into an ashtray.

'Are you all right, darling?' he asked, moving over to her side.

She shook her head as if summoning herself back into the real world. 'No,' she said, 'don't you see? I had the first two numbers, eighteen and, for once, forty-three. I don't usually back forty-three. If only I had won . . . If *only* I had won,' she repeated slowly, 'everything would be all right. For a moment, I thought I was going to. And then it all went wrong again.'

Jim smiled at her and linked his arm through hers. 'Come on,' he said. 'It can't be that serious. No one expects actually to win the lottery. We'd better make a move. Everyone else is going in to dinner; they'll be waiting for us in the hall.'

After dinner, they played roulette. A green baize cloth marked with the roulette numbers was placed on the billiard table with the ebony wheel in the middle. Harry Plank offered to act as croupier and bank, and Margaret bought a pile of chips from him.

'Don't worry if you lose all of those,' Plank said. He gestured at the stacks in front of him. 'I've lots more.'

'That's all very well, but I've no more money in my purse,' Margaret said.

Plank laughed. 'You can give me an IOU. I know you'll be able to pay me back. I'll kinda add it to the backgammon.'

Bishop had declined an invitation to join them, and now he

looked around the room and saw the French ambassador standing by himself. He went across and suggested they go and talk in the library. The small electric fire had been replaced by a large pile of blazing logs, and Matab had provided port, whisky and cigars. Both men stood silently in front of the fire with glasses in their hands.

They knew each other well. Bertrand de Toussaint had served in London twice before, first as a second secretary and then as the Minister. His father had been a colonel in de Gaulle's Free French forces, and had insisted that English be spoken during at least one meal a day in their household, and that one holiday a year be spent in Britain. De Toussaint sometimes felt he understood the British better than they understood themselves. He appreciated the reserve and understatement that made them essentially different to his own hyperbolic countrymen.

His glass half-full of port, the Prime Minister said he was looking forward to his visit to Paris. De Toussaint laughed.

'I cannot believe that, Prime Minister. It will be critical for your country and mine and,' he shrugged his shoulders, 'for the whole of Europe. One cannot enjoy such occasions; there's too much at stake, even when one is as much of an expert as you.'

Bishop did not reply immediately, but crossed the room to a bookshelf and pulled out at random a leather-covered volume. He blew the dust off the top of the book, opened it, looked with unseeing eyes at the Fyffe bookplate on the first page and then replaced it on the shelf. 'Is that just an elegant formula, Bertrand,' he asked, 'or are you saying it because, for once, for the first time since nineteen-forty, your country really needs mine?'

De Toussaint hesitated in turn.

'*Allons, mon ami*, we have known each other for years.' Bishop's voice was determined and yet persuasive. 'We cannot go on fooling each other about this. As you say, it's too important. For me, I'm not just putting my career at risk, I'm splitting my party. It may take a generation to recover. And then there's Europe . . .'

The French ambassador appeared to take a deep breath. 'I paused,' he said, 'because I have to convince you, and we diplomats are not naturally given to conviction. We spend our lives putting over other people's points of view rather than our own passion.' He drained his glass of whisky.

'If you join with us in the single currency,' he spoke slowly, as if proclaiming a creed that was very close to his heart, 'we will know that this is not about economics, but is an act of political conviction, an assurance that Britain does indeed see her future within an ever closer Europe, a Europe where Europeans are determined not to fight other Europeans but to succeed together. And that will give new heart to the Germans and ourselves. And then I think Spain and Italy will join as well.

'If you don't join,' he shrugged his shoulders, 'who knows? But I think it will cause us to leave – the pressures will just be too great. After that, Germany will turn her eyes to the North and the East; she will slowly become the master of Central Europe. Will she remain peaceful? Who knows? That will depend on economics, on trade, on jobs. And on who governs Germany.' He walked slowly to the rosewood table in the corner and poured himself another whisky.

'It all depends on vision and leadership, Prime Minister. You have an opportunity now to save Europe. It will never happen again.'

It was the Prime Minister's turn to walk to the rosewood table. He ignored the whisky tantalus and refilled his glass with neat soda water. 'I was afraid you would answer like that, Bertrand,' he said. 'It's really the same age-old question, isn't it: do we hang together? If we don't, we'll hang separately.' He shook his head thoughtfully. 'You were quite right. I'm not looking forward to the Paris visit. In fact, I'm not looking forward to the next two weeks. It's all going to be horribly critical.'

111

*

Margaret was furious. She had hoped that, for once, Jim might sit with her and enjoy a bit of quiet gambling on the roulette wheel. After all, here they were away for a shooting weekend, just the sort of thing he most enjoyed. There were no civil servants around, not even another politician; surely he could forget about the red boxes for a few hours. But no. He had disappeared somewhere with the Frenchman, and was probably on the telephone to Graham Blackie now, talking about exchange rates. Damn, damn.

She took it out on the roulette table. She lost all her first little pile of chips in the first ten turns of the wheel and then quietly asked Harry Plank to lend her another £500's worth. He pushed a much larger stack of square and round chips towards her and cautioned her with a smile to make them last throughout the evening. She felt her cheeks colouring in front of the other guests and replied, indignantly, that everything depended on her luck.

At first the luck was with her. Every time the wheel was spun, she placed her chips on zero and the first dozen numbers, and they came up with monotonous regularity. 'I just wish the lottery was like this,' she said to Harry as she raked in ivory counters worth £180 in return for a successful £5 placed *en plein* on zero.

'It was to save themselves from women like you that casinos invented wheels with the double zero,' Plank replied. 'You know, some casinos in the States even have a triple zero. It's called Eagle Bird, I guess because it has so many innocent little victims. They don't know they've been gutted until it's too late.'

Margaret felt her humour returning. 'Do I come in that category?' she asked with a smile.

Before Plank had time to reply, Jim came into the room with the French ambassador and stood behind Margaret's chair. He placed a hand on her shoulder and very gently squeezed her collarbone, then kept his hand there, his fingers lightly tapping on her creamy silk shirt. 'Are you holding your own against these sharks?' he asked. 'Or are they bamboozling you?'

Margaret's better temper evaporated like a whiff of faint perfume. She had wanted to impress Harry and the others with her skill; now she was, as usual, being patronised, treated like a little girl.

Harry picked up the little white ball from the metal slot below zero and gave the wheel a gentle push. '*Messieurs, dames, faites votre jeu,*' he said.

Bertrand de Toussaint leant over from the far side of the table and congratulated him on the accuracy of his French accent.

Margaret was determined not to be outdone. She pushed her winnings back towards the centre and then added the pile of chips in front of her. She stacked them all neatly on the intersection of the lines between zero, three and *manque*, and announced, loudly and with a touch of professional pride in her voice, '*Les quatre premiers.*'

Sheikh Matab and the other players round the table stopped talking, counting their chips and drawing on their cigars, and looked at her. Bishop instinctively tightened his grip on her shoulder.

'That's a helluva lot of chips, Margaret,' said Plank quietly. He leant over and did a quick calculation. 'You must have nearly a thousand pounds there at eight to one. Matab, is that above the house maximum?'

'Of course not,' Matab replied quickly, as though his honour was at stake, 'but, Harry, you are the banker. If you lose, are you happy to give Margaret eight thousand pounds?'

Plank shrugged, then gave the wheel a further clockwise push. Pressing his index finger hard against the ball, he waited for a few seconds while he stared at the numbered compartments turning gently and silently in front of him, and then flicked the ball counter-clockwise against the movement of the wheel.

Jim Bishop stooped forward as if he were going to whisper an urgent message in Margaret's ear but seemed to think better of it. He straightened up and watched the little ball spinning round under the lip of the black wheel.

'*Rien ne va plus*,' Harry commanded as the ball dropped and started to bounce over the ribs of one metal slot to another.

Matab looked across the table and saw Jim's hand on Margaret's shoulder tighten until the knuckles were white.

Margaret had started to stretch her arm towards the table as if to take away some of her chips but, on Harry's order, she pulled back and let her hands drop into her lap.

The patter of the ball rippled across the room and stopped. Everyone was silent. Margaret held her breath as the ball hung indeterminately for a second or two over zero, slipped past to three, and then, settling back again, slid against the turn of the wheel into the black compartment between three and zero.

Margaret shut her eyes and leant back in her chair.

Harry stopped the wheel, stooped forward and picked the ball up. '*Vingt-six, noir, passe*,' he announced and then added conversationally, 'hell, were you close, Margaret.' A rare grin split his face. 'Luck's sure my lady tonight.' He reached for the croupier's rake and started to pull the pile of chips towards him.

'Darling Margaret, wasn't that very, very silly of you?'

Jim was sitting on the edge of their six-foot-wide four-poster bed pulling off his black silk socks. His shirt was undone and his black tie hung loosely out of his collar. He felt tired and unhappy.

'You know, we really can't afford to lose that sort of money at the moment,' he went on. 'Apart from anything else, we've really got to try and help Giles buy a flat in Coventry. And I may be out of Downing Street any day.'

'Oh, don't moan, Jim.' Margaret sounded cross as she

came out of the bathroom. 'It wouldn't have happened if you and Bertrand what's-his-name hadn't disappeared out of sight. I imagined you'd be talking on and on about Europe, although God knows there's nothing you can do to make Europe popular.' She took off her black and white dressing gown and slid between the linen sheets. 'I'm sorry. But I got so bored and there was nothing else to do but gamble. Harry was a sport; he lent me five hundred pounds.'

'That American lent you five hundred pounds?' Jim sounded deeply shocked. 'I know you've played bridge together a few times, but, really, you hardly know him. You'll have to pay him back immediately.'

'Don't worry, don't worry. It'll be all right. I'll find the money from somewhere,' Margaret said dismissively. 'Actually, I know Harry rather well. Not only have we played bridge together, but he has . . .' she appeared to search for the right words '. . . lots of good ideas. I think he could be a very useful friend.'

Jim knew he was getting out of his depth. He went through to the bathroom and grimaced at the mirror before cleaning his teeth, then walked back into the bedroom and tried again: 'Margaret, darling, on Monday I'll ring Angus and . . .'

But Margaret was lying on her side, her eyes tightly closed, her face, Jim thought immediately, looking young and amazingly unwrinkled.

He bent down and kissed her. 'Good night, darling.'

'Don't worry, Jim, it's just not worth it,' she murmured back.

But Jim lay on his back on the other side of the bed, listening to her slow, regular breathing, and found it impossible to get to sleep. He could not drive from his mind the picture of the garish, multicoloured pile of chips in front of Margaret on the roulette table and Harry's thin black rake reaching over to pull them all in.

He turned on his side, trying to concentrate on the maze through which he had to weave in the days ahead. Eventually he fell into a tangled sleep, full of worried dreams in which he ran around, pursuing, pursued, and always thwarted. He woke early, slipped out of bed without waking Margaret and started to work on the heavy red box, full of papers, that stood on a desk in the corner.

CHAPTER NINE

The courier delivered the sealed envelope to Phil Darby at ten on Monday morning. He was sitting in a shabby chair, cigarette drooping out of his mouth, watching a children's programme on television when the doorbell emitted its three-note jangle. Agnes started to move to the door from the kitchen but Phil beat her to it, despite his bruises.

He signed for the package, opened it and gasped.

'What is it, Phil? Tell us,' Agnes' querulous voice behind him demanded.

'It's what I told you last week,' he said. 'Here's all the cheques for the scam that Bobbins and his boss 'ave set up. I mean there was no jackpot winner on Saturday, so now we're off.'

He pulled one of the bundles out and looked at the top cheque. It was made out to the National Lottery for one hundred pounds and had a reference on the top right corner: 3MANB17. He took his instruction sheet and the map out of their plastic folder and checked. B17 was the grid reference on the map for the third store on his Manchester list. He looked at the other cheques in the bundle. They were all identical, except for the varying reference in the corner. Bloody neat, he thought.

'It's a dilly, Aggie,' he shouted towards the kitchen, 'but there's a lot to do in five days. I mayn't get back till very late Saturday. Look after yourself'.

As he drove north up the M6, Phil spent a comforting ten minutes inventing new tortures for Bobbins. He chose a red-hot poker but had not decided whether it should go into

Bobbins' mouth, ear or arse when he realised that Bobbins had, in fact, done him a favour. He had been hanging round home for too long waiting for a call back to the bingo hall. It was good to be back on the road again, even if it was only for a week or two, and, who knew, he might pick up a bit of stuff somewhere along the line. He had studied his route carefully. Stafford, Stoke, Newcastle-under-Lyme, Stockport, Manchester – lots in Manchester. Then over to Warrington, Liverpool, Bootle, Wallasey, and back to Chester, Wrexham, Shrewsbury and then over to the motorway and back to London.

Christ, he had to call on a total of 200 lottery outlets and buy 100 tickets at each. The people who had planned it had kept it as simple as possible, clever bastards. He had to be back at headquarters by Saturday night to hand over the tickets, he'd get Sunday at home, and then he'd start it all again on Monday if there was another roll-over.

He had £20,000 worth of cheques on him. Twenty bleeding thousand. Sod it, he hoped he wasn't robbed. Bobbins would never believe him.

A fifteen-ton six-axle lorry passed him on the inside lane. Darby swore, pressed his foot down on the accelerator of his Ford Escort and slowly inched his way back in front of the lorry. 'Got you, you bastard,' he muttered.

The Prime Minister picked up his private red telephone and had started to dial Angus Fyffe's home number when he heard a voice already on the line. Without thinking, he put the handset to his ear and heard Margaret saying shrilly that fifty thousand was what she needed.

'Fifty thousand, Mrs Bishop?' I'm afraid I'd have to ask you to cover that with a mortgage on your cottage in the country. I couldn't authorise that kind of sum without some collateral.' The voice was deferential and apologetic.

'All right,' Margaret said after a long pause, 'if you insist, I'll give you the mortgage, but I need the money quickly.'

Beneath the firmness, there was a noticeable quaver in her voice. 'I'd like to fix it all up today.'

The Prime Minister put the handset down and stared blankly at the files stacked neatly around him on his desk.

Marie Claude had a vivid memory of her first encounter with Graham Blackie. She had been at a party for Sorbonne graduates at the French Embassy when she'd heard Blackie, many glasses of champagne inside him, busily denouncing the perfidy of the French in tones which reached the furthest corners of the ambassador's salon. She'd joined in and argued with him, and after a while he had seized her by the arm and taken her on a tour of the heavy Gobelin tapestries hanging on the walls. He had explained the mythical scenes woven into the tapestries and dallied with pleasure over Leda's seduction by Zeus transformed into a swan.

Marie Claude, three glasses of wine inside her, had giggled quietly. 'That must have been difficult,' she had said, only to be assured that it was technically easy and sexually effective. She had laughed out loud.

A week later she received a formal invitation to a dinner at Number 11 in honour of a delegation of French deputies, and a week after that she was in the Chancellor's bed, happily enacting the role of Leda. Graham was tireless, demanding and brutal, and she was overwhelmed. She had had many lovers but she had never fallen in love before.

A corner was found for her in the Chancellor's private office as a European research assistant and interpreter. Armed with her pass, she came and went through the heavy gates between Downing Street and Whitehall, and the policemen fell for her smile and her pretty open face and the way she always talked to them and told them where to go to when on holiday in Paris. She met the Prime Minister and Margaret Bishop at the Chancellor's Christmas party and heard her boss being congratulated on having a French girl in his office. Very practical, the Prime Minister had said. But that was where matters went wrong.

Loyalty to France ran thick in Marie Claude's veins. As Graham Blackie's stand against the European Union hardened and his speeches became more and more hostile to the French and the Germans, Marie Claude found herself in bitter argument in bed and in the office. 'Christ,' he had said early one morning in September, 'I want a fuck, not a French lesson.' And Marie Claude had left that day for her parents' house in Quinnehou.

Marie Claude waved her out-of-date pass at the policeman at the gate.

'Have you come back, love?' he asked. 'It's great to see you again.'

She gave him her broadest, most dazzling smile, and walked quickly past the Cabinet Office. She told the attendant at the door of Number 11 that she had arranged a personal, private and very important meeting with the Chancellor.

'It's not on the list,' he said, looking at the typewritten paper in his hand. He was assured that it could only have been left off because of its highly confidential nature.

'Well, you're lucky he's in,' he added and was rewarded with such a big smile that he found himself smiling back.

A few minutes later Marie Claude was seated in one of the deep, low red leather chairs that had caused her embarrassment before. She had always been worried that too much of her leg was showing when she sat in them, and had constantly pulled down her skirt. She repeated the gesture now as Blackie marvelled at her ability to get into his office with an out-of-date pass.

'It's that fatal Gallic charm of yours, Marie Claude. Even the policemen fall for it.' He shook his head and looked at her with a mixture of wonder and apprehension. 'Why have you come back?' he asked. 'I don't think it's a very good idea.'

She gazed at him as she folded her hands over her stomach in a gesture that was strangely protective.

'*Je suis en cloque,*' she said quietly. Her English had a habit of deserting her in time of stress.

'*En cloque?*' Blackie sounded mystified.

'*Enceinte* – how do you say it? – pregnant. *Tu es le père.*'

'Oh, my God.' Blackie looked at her, appalled, and then buried his head in his hands. 'That's not possible.'

'Why not? *Topez la, tu dois assurer.* We made love often enough. And that can lead to babies, even in this modern age.'

Marie Claude had started by feeling very brave as she walked into the Chancellor's study but now the bravery was running out of the soles of her feet. She wanted to be held in Graham's arms and cosseted, but she knew that wasn't going to happen.

'Are you sure it's mine?' Blackie's face was still hidden in the palms of his hands, and he sounded throttled. 'I always had on one of those bloody condoms, we made certain of that.'

'*Espèce de salaud, tu m'emmerdes!*' The tears began to roll down Marie Claude's cheeks. '*Vous putain de roastbeef, vous ne pigez jamais rien,* how can you talk like that? Don't you want the baby? Our baby?'

She got up and put her arms round Graham's neck. 'You must remember, *mon mec*, the night in August? You were going on holiday the next day, and your red boxes, you said, were finished. We went out to dinner in Chelsea, we drank too much, the two of us, we came back here and made love here, here on the floor. *C'était peu banal, ça.* I still remember the tickle of the carpet on my back . . .' She laughed through her tears. 'There was no *capote anglaise* in your bureau, and we hoped it would be in order.'

She removed her arms from his neck, walked back to her chair and sat as upright as she could, trying to control the scene, to impose her love on Graham. '*Bien*, we took a risk, both of us. It didn't work: now we have to pay for it together. We have to find an amiable solution.' She paused, took a blue packet of Gitanes from her bag and lit one. She seemed to draw the smoke into the very bottom of her lungs and then blew it in a hazy stream that passed slowly across the room.

Immediately, Graham sat up, took his hands away from his face and said, 'God, I wish you wouldn't do that. It makes this room smell like a French brothel.'

Marie Claude leant forward and tapped her cigarette so that a long end of ash fell on to the carpet. She knew her courage was coming back. *'Mon chéri, j'en pince reél pour toi. Tu peux pas l'intégrer ça.* I'm not going to go away. I shall need your help, and I love you too much. Of course, you need time to think about our baby, and what would be the best for us three.'

Looking embarrassed, Graham had started to mutter that he was, of course, very, very fond of her when the telephone rang on his desk. Snatching it up, he listened for a few seconds, then turned to Marie Claude. 'Life is catching up with me in more ways than one. The Governor of the Bank of England has arrived for his weekly session. I must see him. But . . .' he got up and helped Marie Claude to her feet '. . . I'll be in touch, and . . .' he scratched his head '. . . we'll see what I can work out. Trouble is, I'm terribly busy at the moment.'

Marie Claude interrupted him. 'I know, darling, I read about you in the papers. You seem to be worse than ever, pulling Europe to pieces. You should read some history.'

Before Blackie could reply, the door opened and a private secretary appeared and politely suggested to Marie Claude that he show her the way to the lift.

Next door, at Number 10, Downing Street, Angus Fyffe was finishing a difficult interview with the Prime Minister. Jim Bishop had told him – in strictest confidence, of course – of the phone conversation he had overheard and asked if he could think of any reason why Margaret should suddenly need £50,000. Fyffe appeared to be completely mystified.

Both men sipped their coffee in embarrassed silence, then Bishop changed the subject. 'How's the lottery going?'

'Very well,' said Angus eagerly, relieved that they had moved on from the awkward topic of Margaret's financial position. 'Sales this week will be more than eighty million, probably nearer ninety, thanks to the roll-over and the extra money on the jackpot.'

A secretary brought in a handful of stiff folders, containing letters to be signed. 'I'm sorry, Angus,' Bishop apologised. 'These are very urgent.'

Fyffe got up and stared out of the window at St James's Park. It was raining and every bench was empty. Even the ducks on the ponds had a bedraggled look. Fyffe wondered for the umpteenth time whether there was any way out of what he was doing. He had made mistakes before, misjudged people, gambled too much, but he was crossing new boundaries now.

He heard the secretary thanking the Prime Minister and the door shutting. Then Jim said quietly, 'Look, Angus, you're one of our oldest friends. I've got to talk to you frankly. I just don't understand it. I can't think what terrible scrape Margaret has got into that would make her need all that money so suddenly. I know you go out on bridge evenings with her. Can you explain it at all? Does she play for hideously high stakes?'

Angus' face reddened. 'Well,' he began, 'the stakes are steep, but nothing really out of the way . . .'

'I know she gambles too much,' Jim said frankly. 'It's partly my fault. It happens when I'm busy night after night, and she gets lonely and needs a distraction. You'll understand that, Angus, of course, but I worry that she may be losing control. I couldn't get her away from watching the lottery at Strudwells on Saturday night.'

He looked again at Angus who nodded his head in apparent

sympathy. 'Could someone be blackmailing her for not paying her gambling debts? Is that a possibility?' Jim probed for a clue that would help him resolve the crisis in Margaret's life, but the telephone rang before Angus had a chance to reply.

As the Prime Minister conducted a brisk conversation with an unseen colleague, Angus reviewed his options. He knew this was the crossroads. If he went on, he would be so steeped in scheming that going back would be impossible. He bent forward to put his coffee cup on the table with a shaking hand. Cup and saucer teetered on the edge of the table, then fell to the floor and the cup broke, spilling black coffee all over the faded greys and blues of the carpet.

'I'm so sorry, Jim,' he said as the Prime Minister put the receiver down. 'Terribly stupid of me.' He got down on his knees and pulled the silk handkerchief out of his top pocket.

'Don't do that, I'll ask one of the secretaries to help.' Jim picked up the telephone again and, before Angus had finished his ineffective dabbing, a girl in a white shirt and black skirt was in the room with bowl, hot water and detergent. 'I was about to ring you, Prime Minister,' she said as she worked on the carpet. 'Your next visitor has arrived. The French ambassador with the chef de protocol. You remember, they want to talk through the details of your visit to the Assemblée Nationale. I've got the Under-Secretary from the Foreign Office here to check on their plans.'

'Thanks, Miranda. We must get on.' After she had left the room, Bishop seemed to hesitate a moment, then he spoke with an intense urgency. 'Angus, I know I can rely on you. I know you'll remember what I said. If you hear anything, just anything that could be of use, for God's sake let me know immediately. I'm afraid Margaret won't talk to me about it and I don't want to have to alert the security boys. It might come to that, but it'd be a last resort. It could be very embarrassing, as I'm sure you know.'

Outside, Fyffe's driver held open the door of the navy-blue

Jaguar. Angus stumbled as he got into the car and the driver moved quickly to catch him by the elbow. His thoughts were in turmoil: the security boys, MI5, Scotland Yard . . . It was an appalling prospect. Fyffe's thoughts raced around in turmoil, and he allowed the driver to get entangled in a traffic-jam in Piccadilly without rebuking him for not going through the Park.

To the outside eye there is no obvious division between Number 10 and Number 11 Downing Street. It is impossible to tell where one ends and the other starts. And, inside, a connecting passage enables the Chancellor to stroll from his first-floor study to the Prime Minister's office, or down the stairs to the Cabinet room, without being noticed by the curious eyes of the government drivers parked in the quadrangle of the Foreign Office. But, in times of strife, proximity becomes an embarrassment.

Jim Bishop and Graham Blackie were now so opposed that it would have been better if the River Thames and the Elephant and Castle had divided their offices. Meeting even by chance in the corridor was an awkwardness.

Certainly, as Blackie listened to the Governor of the Bank of England unveil his plans, sitting in the same deep chair that Marie Claude had occupied a few minutes before, he had a sense of unreality bordering on treason to his next-door neighbour. He had encouraged Geoffrey Williams in his opposition to a European Central Bank, but he had not been prepared for such a raw and ready nerve. The Governor was responding with extraordinary enthusiasm.

'All is going in the markets as we expected. Sterling is weak; share prices are falling again – they're already down another twenty points this morning – and the story that the PM will block any interest rate rise is bound to lead to a lot more trouble.'

Smiles did not often bend Sir Geoffrey's thin lips but the

125

usual straight line below his moustache gave way to the hint of a curve as he spoke.

'Because of the domestic troubles in France and Germany, the Euro is already weak against the yen and the dollar. The market expects us to join at around one-thirty to the pound. In fact, our economy is so strong that I think we could go in at one-forty Euros to the pound. But I suggest that we let the market think one-thirty may be too high. One-twenty-five, or even one-twenty would be more realistic. That will really put the cat among the pigeons.

'You know the form, Chancellor. All we need is one of your off-the-record lunches in Millbank, then something said in anger, a little over the top, in response to the usual barrage on the "Today" programme. We can follow up with a casual remark at a press briefing by the Bank. Nothing really indiscreet, of course, breaking no confidences. That would be quite against the tradition of the Bank.'

He paused and then added as a grudging afterthought, 'And, of course, the tradition of the Treasury, too. But I have another idea, Chancellor, that I want to try out on you. Of course, it's only for these very extraordinary circumstances that we find ourselves in.' He waited for Blackie's reply.

'Geoffrey, I had no idea you were such a Machiavelli. Go on.'

'It's to do with the gold,' Williams continued. 'You know I told you that we were going to have to reinforce the floors in the vaults, which would require some moving about of the stocks? That's going to start within the next two weeks.' He paused and then went on, very precisely, 'I have arranged, subject of course to your approval, for the British gold reserves to be moved out of the Bank and to be stored in a secret location while the work is going on.'

'*What?*' Blackie shook his head in horrified disbelief. 'You must be out of your mind. You can't do that.'

'On the contrary, Chancellor, you and I can do just that for the sake of Britain. It will be stored in a totally safe place. You will be able to announce, in the crucial debate in the House, that you have saved the gold for Britain, and the Prime Minister will not be able to transfer our nineteen million ounces to the Europeans. Without that gold, we can't meet the Central Bank's terms for joining the Euro. Ten per cent of the reserves transferred have to be in gold – those are the Central Bank's minimum terms. At a stroke, we will block our entry into the single currency system.

'The press will love it,' there was now a note of triumph in Sir Geoffrey's voice, 'and the House will love it. And you'll be a national hero, Chancellor.'

Blackie had never heard such excitement in the Governor's voice. Gone were the cool statistics, the monotonous figures, the dry economics. Here was Williams speaking from the heart, ready to break all the rules for a cause he believed in. Blackie remembered the portrait of the soldier in white breeches in the Governor's office. He laughed. 'You have a precedent – 1798, of course. The threat of invasion by Napoleon.'

He sensed Williams relaxing. 'Exactly, Chancellor. In the Bank, times don't change.'

'Where are you going to store the gold?'

'Lancaster House. It has very secure vaults, you know. After all, it's where the Government wine stocks are stored – close to a hundred thousand bottles, I believe, some of it priceless. The chairman of the Government Hospitality Fund is an old friend of mine, we were at Cambridge together.

'He gave me lunch at Lancaster House the other day. It was an excellent lunch, I must say.' Williams smiled reminiscently. 'Latour '51 and a very old Yquem, quite gold in colour . . .

'Anyway, he showed me the vaults afterwards. There is plenty of room, and of course the whole building has very strict security – it has been used for summit meetings. Better, if anything, than the Bank.'

Blackie started to laugh, rocking back in his chair. 'Geoffrey, you astonish me. Here you are suggesting that you and I, the Governor and the Chancellor, should engage in the biggest robbery of all time: the removal of Britain's gold reserves, all nineteen million ounces of it. Worth, let's see . . .' He pulled a calculator across his desk. 'At four hundred dollars an ounce, around . . . around five thousand million pounds. I can't believe my ears.' He looked at the calculator and started laughing again. 'Or is it five hundred million? I can never work out the noughts.'

'Five thousand million. Nearer five and a half thousand at today's exchange rate; sterling's been so terribly weak.' A reproving note entered Williams' voice. 'There is no question of us robbing anyone, Chancellor. You know that. The bullion lorries will load the gold in full daylight, and the gold will be held for a few hours in the lorries, with their armed guards. Then it will be delivered at night to Lancaster House and the police, I am sure, will be able to block off all access by St James's Palace, so its destination can be quite secret. It will all be totally secure of course. Otherwise I would not authorise it.

'In the meantime, you will be able to announce in the Commons debate that the gold is safe for Britain.' Williams' voice started to tremble. 'Safe for the Constitution. Safe for the Monarchy.' He clasped his hands together, almost as if he was praying. 'We've got to do it, Chancellor. It may be our only hope. Remember those wise words in the Bible: "ask for the old paths, where is the good way, and walk therein".'

Blackie swallowed twice, walked to the window and stared out at the bare prospect of Horseguards Parade. It was empty except for three dark-suited men scurrying along the cobbled path in the centre, briefcases in one hand, umbrellas bent against the wind and the rain in the other. He wondered momentarily whether they were worth saving.

What Williams was suggesting was a hell of a risk, but it could just swing things in the debate. It would certainly make for a splendid, dramatic speech.

He swung round to face the Governor. 'Are you sure the gold will be secure?'

'You have my word, Chancellor. After all, no one cares more about the safety of our gold than I do. That's why I am suggesting this action to you. Once the crisis with Europe is over, and the foundations have been strengthened, the gold goes back to the Bank, our Bank.'

Blackie walked back to his chair and doodled in silence on the pad in front of him. Williams sat motionless, his jaw clenched and his fingers interlocked, waiting for Blackie to reach a decision.

Eventually the Chancellor broke the silence. 'Very well, Geoffrey. You do it. It will certainly put us in the history books.'

For once, the day had passed quickly for Margaret. She went to her bank in Pall Mall and was greeted with oily deference by her branch manager, who ushered her personally into his elegant first-floor office and then spent five minutes showing her coloured prints of Pall Mall and St James's in Regency days. Margaret guessed he was nervous that she might criticise him to one of the bank directors whom she regularly met at official dinners. She rose to the occasion by suggesting that the limit on her new overdraft should be £100,000 rather than £50,000. After all, the cottage she was pledging to the bank was really a small house: it had three bedrooms and two bathrooms, and came with an acre of land. It was, moreover, in a very favoured part of Oxfordshire, made more accessible by the improvements to the M40.

The bank manager looked at the photographs of the cottage that Margaret had brought with her, hesitated for an appropriate time, and then agreed to her request. The newly typed loan documents were taken away, altered while they drank tea and refused biscuits, and then signed and witnessed. Margaret congratulated the manager on the speed with which their business had been concluded and he sighed with relief. He was very fond of the Pall Mall branch with its long roll of important customers, and he dreaded being transferred to Oxford Street or, worse still, Tottenham Court Road just because of a casual criticism dropped into a very important ear.

'When can I draw on the account?' Margaret asked as the manager helped her into her coat. 'Could I write a cheque this afternoon?'

'Yes, of course, Mrs Bishop. Everything is in place.'

He started to accompany her towards the curved marble staircase, but she stopped him, thanked him warmly and said she would find her own way out. As he went back to his office, he reflected it was lucky she had only wanted £100,000. That was within his own personal limit. Any more and he would have had to refer to Region. They would have wanted a surveyor's report, and it would have taken them days to reach a decision. He squared his shoulders as he returned to his desk. It was important that managers should be able to take quick decisions, on their own responsibility, with customers whom they knew and could trust.

The rain had temporarily stopped. Margaret sent away the government driver and walked down the Duke of York steps to the lake in the park. The ducks swam hopefully in front of her, but she hardly noticed them. The meeting with the bank manager could not have gone better, and she congratulated herself.

As she walked through the park, she made some calculations, based on the figures Angus Fyffe had given her. Every roll-over week, even without winning the jackpot, they should get 40–45 per cent of their money back from the small prizes. Call that half her money back. £25,000. She would now be able to join Harry's Magic Flute at least four times.

Angus calculated they had a one in seven chance of winning the jackpot, so she was more than halfway there. Fantastic. When she won the jackpot, it really would solve all their problems. Perhaps she would go on a cruise, or on a long safari to game parks in Africa.

She had left the park almost without realising it, and now she found herself at Westminster Central Hall. There was a poster on the wall advertising an exhibition by the Society of Women Artists. She might as well have a look now she was here.

She was examining an oil of a harvest scene in Suffolk, executed in bold brush strokes of red, yellow and blues, when she felt a gentle nudge on her elbow.

'It is Margaret Bishop, I mean Mrs Bishop, isn't it?'

She looked round and saw the wrinkled, smiling face of the president of the Society.

'It's lovely to see you here again,' the president said warmly. 'It's been years since you put in one of your own pictures.'

Margaret kissed her on the cheek. 'I was just walking by and saw your poster. I couldn't resist dropping in.'

'We're honoured. Shall I walk round with you and show you some of the new entries?'

Margaret would have preferred to look at the pictures by herself but she knew she had to accept.

As they toured the rooms, the president asked Margaret about her own painting. 'You used to be so keen, sending in pictures every year. And the Hanging Committee thought you were getting better and better. As I remember, your work was getting bolder, more impressionistic, all the time.'

Margaret laughed. 'But you never accepted any of them.'

The president paused to point out a small bronze statue from a new recruit, and then said, a note of apology in her voice, 'I am sure we'd accept a picture from you now.'

Margaret was surprised how embarrassed she felt; it was like explaining a failed exam to her parents. She gazed fixedly at the statue. 'I've given up painting,' she said finally. 'I gave it up a few years ago.'

'Why? I remember when I taught you – what was it? for a year – you were so keen.'

Margaret picked up the statue and started to pass it from hand to hand. 'I don't know . . . Well, yes, I do.' She felt her face flushing as she put the words together. 'You'll probably remember this; it was in all the papers. My daughter, Sally, was killed in a car smash three years ago. When that happened, I just didn't feel I could go on with anything. I gave up painting, the lot. In a funny way, I didn't want to create anything any more.'

The president of the Society put a hand on her arm and then took away the statue and put it back on the table.

'I do hope you'll come back to painting. You've far too much talent not to use it, and . . .' she shrugged her shoulders in a gentle, deprecating way '. . . even in the busy, busy life you lead, I'm sure you could find painting a sort of release. It could even help you forget, and rebuild.'

Margaret's mind was on those last words as the black door to Number 10 swung open. She was greeted by one of the guards and then by a worried-looking secretary, who hurried up to her in the hall, clutching a handful of files.

'The Prime Minister would like to see you immediately, Mrs Bishop. He asked if you would go up as soon as you came in.'

'Where is he?'

'In the first-floor study.'

Jim stood up to kiss his wife when she came into the room and then sat down again in his favourite high-backed chair between the fireplace and the window. He frowned, and the lines crossing his forehead deepened. 'Darling, I've been so worried about you all day. I couldn't wait for you to come back.'

Margaret felt the sense of calm that she had experienced ever since the exhibition in Westminster Hall suddenly leaving her. 'Why on earth?' she snapped. 'It's not as if I've done very much. I've just been to the Women Artists' show in Central Hall. I don't think there's any harm in that.'

She hadn't wanted to sound aggressive, but she couldn't help herself. She felt horribly nervous. She sat down in the chair on the other side of the fireplace and tried to compose herself.

'Darling, I simply don't understand it, or rather I just don't know what to think.' Jim looked and sounded utterly miserable. 'I picked up the private phone this morning by mistake and heard you borrowing fifty thousand pounds from the bank. I just can't believe it. What do you need the money for? You haven't mentioned anything to me. I . . .' His voice tailed off and he gazed across at his wife, willing her to speak to him.

She kept silent, and he went on imploringly, 'Why on earth didn't you talk to me if you're in trouble? You know I would do anything I possibly could to help. But, please, please, tell me about it.'

Margaret felt her heart racing. She was angry, and frightened, and ashamed all at the same time. She looked at Jim as if he were a total stranger, and then she stared over his head at the evening sky, yellow with the reflected light of London. She just wanted everything to go away.

'Are you being blackmailed? Or is it the lottery? Perhaps you've borrowed from some gambling friends, tried to get it back through the lottery and then lost a lot more?' Jim shook his head from side to side, in a slow, painful protest. 'What I mind most is that you didn't tell me about it, darling, whatever it is. We could have sorted it out together.'

Margaret still didn't reply, and Jim tried another tack. 'I talked to Angus about it this morning. I wondered if he had heard anything about it.'

'Angus? Angus?' Margaret's voice rose in panic. 'Angus is just a friend. How could you?'

'Don't worry, darling. He knew nothing and I'm sure he'll

be discreet.' He paused. 'I was so unhappy; you were out, and I had to talk to someone.'

'But you had been eavesdropping, Jim.' Margaret's voice became shriller. Fear started to subside and indignation took its place. 'That's a beastly thing to do and then you discussed it all with Angus. I just don't see how a decent person could behave like that.'

'Margaret, please, come off it. You know I didn't mean to listen to your conversation, I'm not that sort of person. It was a pure accident, but you must tell me now what trouble you're in. That's the only way we'll work things out.'

But Margaret had suddenly seen her way clear. 'I'm certainly not going to tell you anything if you eavesdrop. I assure you I can sort things out myself. Don't worry about the bank, I'll handle them. It is my cottage after all.' The anger in her voice was pronounced and clear. 'I can do what I like with it.'

She rose from her chair and walked towards the door, then turned round for a parting shot. 'And I'll go on playing the lottery.'

After she had left the room, Bishop continued sitting in his chair, staring unseeingly at the fire. Then, slowly, tears formed in his eyes and spilled over, down the lines in his cheeks. It was many years since he had cried.

CHAPTER TEN

The house was in a narrow street of tall, thin Georgian houses, two minutes' walk from the television studios in Millbank, and a minute from the cameras and microphones on College Green. It was a rabbit warren of small rooms, leading off twisting stairs that climbed up to attic rooms where housemaids had once slept and which were now jammed with files and photocopiers and typists absorbed in computer screens.

Only the old senior partner's room on the ground floor, panelled and lined with shelves, was of a decent size. Here Spencer Gray had installed himself behind a vast folding table with an armoury of plastic filing trays and telephones, and pens and pencils scattered about like confetti. He could hear Wally Wallace's voice through the half-open door from the next room.

It was eleven in the morning and Wally was doing his daily round of the political correspondents. 'Graham Blackie is speaking at one at the Mad Duck . . . you must know the place, there's a private room on the first floor . . . yes, Marsham Street. . . . he'll give his summary of the costs to Britain of the EU, trade deficit of eight billion a year, three p minimum off the basic rate if we come out, brilliant . . . it's tomorrow's headlines. Tonight he's speaking at eight at the Chamber of Commerce at Queens Flushing . . . can't come? . . . OK, I'll fax copies of both speeches to you . . . lots of coverage and I'll buy you lunch next week . . . it's going fantastically . . . huge support . . . Did you see the piece in today's *Tribune*?'

Spencer shut his ears and turned his attention back to the crumpled many-paged list in front of him.

ADAMSON	YES
ADSETTS	YES
AINGER	DOUBTFUL GB TO SEE
ALDRED	PROMISES BUT DONT TRUST
AMBRIDGE	HOPELESS
ANCLIFF	YES
ANGELL	FORGET HIM
APPS	GOT HIM! GB MUST SEE AGAIN
ARMITAGE	SHIT OYSTERS FOR LUNCH BUT NO GOOD
ARMSBY	WONT TALK
ARMSON	YES OFFERS TO HELP
ARON	TALK AGAIN PROBABLY WASTE OF TIME
ASHE	YES
ASHWOOD	NO
ASPINDALE	GB MUST SEE NEXT WEEK
ASTON	YES IF HE GETS A JOB LORDS?
ATTEW	WONT TALK SEE AGAIN
ATWILL	BASTARD LEAVING US GB TO SEE?

Two telephones rang simultaneously in front of him. He pushed the sheaf of papers away from him, picked up the further phone, listened for a few seconds, then said, 'Very sorry, no, it's impossible. No, not today, he's absolutely full up. We'll try tomorrow? Great, OK.'

He picked up the other phone. It was David Armitage, complaining that he had been at Central Hall for an hour and Graham Blackie had still not turned up. The twenty Commonwealth correspondents who had been there had now all disappeared. He had given them the press release but he had seen half of them put it in the wastepaper basket as they left.

Spencer Gray felt he had to apologise. 'I'm very sorry, David, but I told you the Commonwealth lot weren't a first priority for Graham. He had that breakfast in the City which the Bank had organised for him. It was important for him to be there, the way sterling is going. I expect he's overrun and the traffic is awful today. You will be at the Mad Duck at one, won't you? And then there's this meeting at four with Opposition MPs. I don't know how many will turn up but you'll grab each of them after Graham has spoken.'

He heard the sigh at the other end of the line and frowned as he put the telephone down. The fax rang and started to spill out pages in an indiscriminate heap on to the floor below one of the sash windows. An average sort of morning.

Harry Plank found the brocade sofa in the Medevan embassy as uncomfortable as it had been the week before. It tilted him backwards as he spoke and he found himself constantly adjusting his position as he and Matab talked. It made him feel nervous, an unfamiliar sensation. Matab sat opposite him in a gilt chair with armrests, his back ramrod straight, his face expressionless.

'Yes, it was after midnight when he rang,' Harry said. 'I guess he had had a few drinks.'

'Drunk?'

'No, frightened. Bishop had scared him. He's certain Bishop knows something about Margaret and a lottery scam. Bishop overheard her on the phone, borrowing money from her bank manager.'

'Foolish woman.'

Harry shrugged his shoulders. 'These things happen,' he said. 'Neither Fyffe nor Margaret will talk; the money is too important to them. They've both paid up their first fifty thousand.'

'What about Bishop?'

'You know him, ambassador; I've just met the guy. Would he call in his security police on a suspicion like this?'

Matab said slowly, 'He could. He is a very upright man but, of course, he will want to protect his wife.' He gazed at the portrait on the wall as though seeking inspiration. 'When eyes meet, the tongue becomes shy,' he said suddenly, dropping the words into the silence in the room. 'The Emir wants me to see the Prime Minister. He is very concerned about the fall in sterling. It costs Medevan a great deal of money. He is becoming angry. He has told me to make our views known.' A half-smile broke across his face, lightening it. 'I have to make what in diplomatic terms we call a very strong protest.'

An Arab servant, in plain white *dishdasha*, came quietly into the room, carrying a silver tray set with an ornate, heavily decorated metal jug and two white china cups. Both men took a cup. For a while they sipped in silence at the sugary sweet coffee.

Matab spoke first. 'Your Magic Flute. It makes progress?'

'Sure. The couriers are all on the road. Bobbins reports to me twice a day. There are a few problems, the main one being blocks on the motorway, which make the couriers get behind schedule. I wish to hell the British would build a proper system – they're still in the last century. But, in spite of that, we'll have all two million tickets bought by Saturday. If not, Bobbins is out of a job and he knows it.'

The servant came back into the room, picked up the metal jug and poured more coffee into their cups. 'That's a strange shape, that jug,' said Plank. 'It looks as if he were pouring from an eagle's beak.'

'It's traditional,' Matab replied. 'We are a hunting people and we take these jugs everywhere with us in our saddlebags. You make pretty china figures of people – princesses and lovers. We are like the old cave-dwellers – we fashion our pots like the birds we know in the desert, the birds that can kill, the hawks, the falcons and eagles. We respect them.'

The servant returned, this time carrying a silver salver with a card on it. He bowed low as he put the salver in front of Matab. 'My next visitor,' Matab said as he looked at the card, a note of anger coming into his voice, 'is a director of a famous British arms manufacturer. He wants the next large order from Medevan but he wants to be paid in dollars, not sterling. He says that sterling is too weak. Is that my fault, Harry?'

Plank was surprised at the passion in Matab's tone. He had never heard anything other than quiet diplomatic politeness in the ambassador before. 'Not my business,' he said, then added, 'Look, what about Margaret Bishop?'

The shutters closed again and Matab seemed to withdraw into himself. 'We must protect her,' he said. 'Of course we must. We may have to worry about Bishop, but not yet.' He thought for a moment and then said, 'We will see how we do this weekend when we put your theories to the test – at a cost, dear Harry, of two million pounds.'

'Not theories . . .' Plank started.

But the Ambassador had already risen to his feet and was moving towards the door, leaving Plank no option but to follow in his wake.

The Embassy Rolls-Royce, flying the royal pennant, passed the church of the Madeleine, crossed the Seine, turned into rue de l'Université and entered the maze of neo-classical buildings that is the Palais-Bourbon. At the far end of the Court of Honour, the President of the Assemblée, the tiny red bud of the Légion d'Honneur decorating the lapel of his coat, formally greeted the Prime Minister. The two men then walked solemnly between the Corinthian columns of the cradle-vaulted Vestibule.

Bishop turned to the Frenchman by his side. 'For an elected and democratic parliament, Monsieur le Président, this setting is exceedingly grand. Certainly grander than the Palace of Westminster.'

The Frenchman smiled. 'That may be so, but Napoleon, after adding to the original *maison de plaisance*, so disliked the result that he wished his artillery would blow down the whole complex.'

As he spoke, an order was barked, swords were drawn, and they passed between the ranks of the black-and-gold uniformed Republican Guard. In the steeply raked semicircle beyond, 550 deputies waited.

Men and women, they all rose to greet the British Prime Minister, and then, spontaneously, they clapped. The clapping grew steadily louder and lasted until their President held up his hand from his rostrum and, as a conductor guides his orchestra, led them gently to silence.

The President introduced Jim Bishop with kind and friendly words, then invited him to address the French Assembly. Bishop spoke a few informal sentences in French, remarking how honoured he was to be speaking from the famous orator's seat, the heart of debate, the symbol of the dialogue of the French nation with itself, and how greatly he had been looking forward to this occasion, and then with apologies he turned to his English text. The interpreters, sitting in a glass box at the back of the chamber, cleared their throats.

Bishop wasted no more time. 'I am here to announce a historic decision to you,' he said. 'I, as the Prime Minister of the United Kingdom, have decided to ask our Parliament to vote in favour of our joining immediately the European economic and monetary union and the single currency. The decision will be put to a free vote . . .' He got no further.

Deputies on all sides of the semicircle in front of him were on their feet, cheering and waving papers. Only the French Nationalist party sat gloomily on their hands, ostentatiously shaking their heads in disapproval.

The President had to gesture for silence three times before he managed to quieten his colleagues.

The Prime Minister, conscious that his every word would be reported in the world's press, spoke for twenty minutes giving his detailed reasons for his decision. If the single market was to succeed, it needed monetary stability, which could not be achieved without a single central bank and sole monetary authority. He already saw the dangers for the Euro, that those outside with weaker currencies would devalue those currencies to obtain more competitive advantages, while those inside would be led on to protectionism. This way the

European Union could fall apart. Britain therefore must now accept the challenge and join France and Germany in giving a lead to the rest of Europe.

The deputies knew the economic story well but they listened enraptured. They had never heard a British Prime Minister speak with such fire and conviction in a cause which the vast majority of them supported wholeheartedly. And then Bishop turned to his finale.

'I have heard two Presidents of your great country speak to our Houses of Parliament in the Royal Gallery. Each time our Lord Chancellor, introducing them, has mentioned, half-joking, half-embarrassed, the vast pictures of Waterloo and Trafalgar that hang on either side of the Gallery.

'Here I see no pictures of Austerlitz or the Battle of the Nile surrounding me and in that you represent the future and we the past.'

The deputies looked on in amazement. A British Prime Minister accepting that, two centuries later, perhaps the British should stop glorying in the defeat of Napoleon? *Épatant.*

'In the new millennium, we have to have a vision of a new place for Europe in the world. A Europe that is at peace with itself, of course, a Europe where living standards are high, a Europe that holds its own in international trade, but a Europe that, using our age and experience and civilisation, can actively bring peace and prosperity to other parts of the world. We cannot for ever ask the United States or the United Nations to do all of this for us.

'This is not a role that any one of us, as an individual country, can take on. It is a role made for the four hundred million citizens of Europe. It is the great challenge that we Europeans have to meet.

'Jack Kennedy, visiting East Germany before the Wall came down, shouted out *"Ich bin ein Berliner"*. Here, in Paris, in this historic building a generation later, I take up the cry. *Moi, je suis européen.*'

As he sat down, the Assembly erupted. The front rows of delegates surged forward, anxious to touch Jim Bishop, to shake his hand and kiss him on the cheek. The President stepped down from his podium, put his arms round the Prime Minister and said, 'Today, you have spoken for the future of Europe. How can we ever thank you enough?'

On the way back to the Embassy, the Prime Minister, exhausted from shaking hundreds of hands and being kissed time and again by enthusiastic lips, kept silent until the Rolls had crossed the Place de la Concorde and swung towards the Faubourg Saint Honoré and the Embassy. Then he turned to the ambassador, correct and upright by his side.

'I thought that went quite well, Roderick. Don't you agree?'

Sir Roderick Carmichael pursed his lips together and looked straight ahead. 'You departed quite a lot from your text, Prime Minister.'

'Yes, of course.'

'The French press will love it, but I'm not certain about ours.'

'Why?'

'That reference to the House of Commons representing the past; I didn't see that in your text.'

'No. It was an impromptu line. I've always been embarrassed by Presidents of France having to make their great orations in front of dying Frenchmen – on canvas, of course, but still dying, and with blood all over the place.'

Sir Roderick frowned. 'It'll be picked up, I'm afraid. It's just the sort of thing they'll go for.'

Bishop felt the energy and excitement draining out of him.

'Christ,' he said, 'I said a lot of things a hell of a lot more important than that.'

The late edition of the *Evening Herald* carried a front-page report of the Prime Minister's speech in Paris. Its banner headline read 'BISHOP TOADIES TO FROGS'. The story underneath bitterly criticised Jim Bishop for even bothering to address the French Assembly, a powerless parliament made up of mayors and ex-ministers, a bunch of elderly nobodies who met in a palace built by a French king for his mistress and her bastard daughter.

Bishop, the paper said, was trying to curry favour in Paris for his disastrous decision to take Britain into a single currency, but French support for this meant nothing. It was only the voice of the British people that counted, and they were a hundred per cent behind the Chancellor of the Exchequer and his campaign to keep the pound for Britain.

Wally Wallace laughed as he showed the article to Doug Mesurier in the Commons tea-room. 'You must write Graham Blackie a speech on this,' he said. 'It'll go down brilliantly. Telling the Frogs their parliament is better than ours – that'll win us some more votes; it'll make all the old boys and girls at Westminster furious.'

Mesurier put his glasses on and read the paper carefully. 'You're right,' he said. 'There's nothing makes us more cross than being told we're not the best parliament in the world. Bishop's made a mistake there.' He looked at the headline again. 'Toadying to the Frogs – lovely, we'll use it.'

CHAPTER ELEVEN

Graham Blackie stared in surprise at the Penguin 60p classic that had slipped out of the envelope marked STRICTLY PERSONAL AND URGENT. One of his secretaries had brought it in to him in his Treasury room, along with the daily bulletins from the Bank and the Stock Exchange. He held the little book in his hand and looked at the front cover. It showed a pretty girl lying in the bath, one of her breasts half out of the water, her left hand cupping the back of her head, her right holding a white rosebud over the edge of the bath. The picture was both prim and faintly provocative, and something in the position of the girl was familiar. Or was it her profile?

Curious, he turned the book over and read the blurb on the back page.

BOULE DE SUIF
A merciless exposé of human nature
by a master storyteller

He shook his head, puzzled.

Guy de Maupassant achieved instant fame with *Boule de Suif*, his first published story, set during the Franco-Prussian war . . . A group of travellers are fleeing occupied Rouen by coach to Dieppe. Forced to accept the courtesan in their midst, their baser instincts are brought to the surface when they are faced with a terrifying dilemma.

What the hell . . . who was mucking him about? He bent the paperback open and saw the inscription on the inside page,

144

written in the familiar handwriting that still made his heart turn:

> *To my darling Graham*
> *from*
> *his French Tart*

Oh, Christ, he must ring Marie Claude. He really wanted to help, if he could just find the time – and think of some sort of solution.

At that moment, David Armitage came into the ornate heavily decorated room, carrying a brown file crammed with papers. He sat down opposite the Chancellor at the centre of the absurdly long table that he had come to know so well from so many meetings. 'I've done your diary for next week,' he said, pushing some sheets of paper across the table.

'It's crammed to the gills – you've got an average of seven political meetings, meals or speeches a day. One day you've got to eat three lunches, I'm afraid, all buffet, finger food, standing up.' Blackie winced as Armitage continued, 'And, of course, there are countless one-on-one sessions with the waverers. I've allowed them a maximum of fifteen minutes each.'

'Too long,' Blackie interjected. 'If I can't convince them in five minutes, they're wasting my time; they're Bishop's.'

'Well, it's the last week, and most of them will rabbit on. I'll probably have to squeeze in another twenty or so in the final days. The whips are planning to have the great debate on the following Monday. The one day I've kept free for you, as you said, is next Saturday.'

'That's right. The Medevan ambassador has asked me to shoot that day, and I want to go, if possible. It'll be a break before the debate and a day in the country'll freshen me up.' He added with a hint of guilt, 'I don't get many chances, and it's a great shoot, I'm told. Keep it clear, if you can.'

Armitage had bent his head over and was gazing across the

table at the cover of the Maupassant story. 'That's *Boule de Suif*, isn't it?' he asked. 'That picture of the girl is in the Musée d'Orsay in Paris. I took my family there last summer. I didn't know you read Maupassant.'

'I don't. D'you know the story?'

'Yes, I did it years ago at school. It's brilliant – it's all about the German troops taking over Rouen in the 1870s, and a famous French prostitute who saves . . .'

'OK, OK, David,' Blackie interrupted. 'Let's get down to the nuts and bolts. How's it all going, d'you think?'

Armitage knew the Chancellor wanted good news. 'Well . . .' He paused, choosing his words carefully. 'Pretty good, I think. Spencer Gray reckons it's neck and neck. You've won some, lost some, but you're just ahead.'

The tautness went out of Blackie's face and Armitage heard him take a deep, relaxed breath.

'Next week will be decisive, of course, and then there's the debate itself.' He paused again, hesitating, and some instinct told Blackie that Armitage had problems.

'What about you?' he asked. 'You're my lieutenant in all of this; you bloody well can't let me down. I want your vote.'

David Armitage studied the elaborate plasterwork in the ceiling, then he admitted, 'Yes, you're right. I have got problems.' He pointed at the newspapers lying all over one end of the table. 'I just hate all this rabbiting on about Frogs and Huns. It's so . . .' he searched for the right word '. . . demeaning.'

Blackie exploded. 'You must see, David, that that's just the surface stuff. You can't stop the tabloids having a go. But that's fundamentally unimportant; it doesn't make any difference. The real issues are life and death for our country. Nothing more or less. Do we get lost in Europe or not? Submerged until Parliament and our law courts disappear into the European Court, the European Commission, the European Council of Ministers?'

He hit the table with his fist. 'I'll stop at nothing, bloody nothing to win that argument.'

David did not reply and Blackie noticed there was something wistful in his face as he gathered up his papers. A lost disciple, perhaps. The thought slipped through his mind and out again.

The moment Armitage had left the room, Blackie picked up the reports from the Bank and the Stock Exchange. Bishop's Paris speech had been very badly received. Equities were down nineteen points and gilts a point and a half. Good. The Bank had had to accept a rotten price at the morning's tender for gilts. Gold was up five dollars, a sure sign of worry in world markets. Blackie smiled to himself. That would make Britain's gold reserves even more valuable.

And sterling had gone over the precipice since his talk with the Governor. The Euro had gone from one-thirty to the pound to one-twenty-four, the lowest for two years. Holders of sterling must be shitting in their pants.

Blackie pushed back his chair. He and the Governor must get sterling down to one-fifteen to the pound, or even one-ten, before the great debate in the House. That would be a crisis point. There would be a sort of tidal wave of chaos and frenzy in the markets and that would show how vulnerable the Eurosystem was. Importers would panic at the thought of the increasing cost of their raw materials, and it would be just like the 1970s all over again.

Once confidence was lost in one market, it was lost in all. The disease spread from one end of the world to the other. They called it globalisation, a grand word. In fact, it was plain old panic – people acting shit scared, trying to protect their business and their cash.

Blackie pulled a blank sheet of paper towards him and started to sketch in his ideas.

Phil Darby was a worried man. He was half a day behind in his journey round the lottery sales points in the west

147

Midlands, thanks to two mile-long tailbacks on the motorways and road repairs in Manchester. When he called to make his evening report, Bobbins was furious. 'You meet your schedule or I'll personally carve you up. It won't just be no bonus, it'll be no teeth.'

Darby spent a bad night tossing and turning in a small, hot room on the second floor of a Liverpool pub. After his call to Bobbins, he had bought the landlady's teenage daughter a shocking number of vodka and lemonades, 'cheering myself up', he said, and she had allowed his wandering hand to stray over her knee and up her skirt.

As they sat close to each other at the dark end of the crowded bar, Phil told her the number of his room, and when he went upstairs he left his door unlocked. Several times during the night, he heard noisy creaks from the passage outside, and he imagined his door opening and the blonde nymphet who'd excited him so much after the third vodka – he didn't know her name, but that didn't matter – opening his door and slipping into his bed.

But nothing happened. He dozed fitfully and then woke to find the morning light, clear, cold and unpleasant, filtering through the thin curtains. He rolled over on his side and tried to fall asleep again, dreaming of the soft curves of the little blonde he had touched and stroked so hopefully a few hours before. Through the thin wall, he could hear the couple in the next bedroom starting to move about. Their bed bumped against his wall and for a moment, he envied them. They were banging away. But then he heard one of them get out of bed, and the sound of water running into a basin, and his vicarious enthusiasm disappeared.

Phil looked at his Mickey Mouse watch and scratched the back of his neck ruminatively. His skin felt dry; he hoped he wasn't coming out in one of his attacks of eczema. When it was bad, his whole body seemed to be on fire and it was hard to concentrate on anything other than an urge to scratch.

The wallpaper was starting to come off the edges of the

ceiling, and he imagined climbing up and tearing strips off it, peeling it back to the plaster below. It would be satisfying, like stripping off bits of one's skin and scratching through to the flesh below.

Phil's eczema always broke out when he was tired and worried. That's what his wife, Agnes, always said to him. If you didn't worry, she said, if you were at home more regularly, you wouldn't get that nasty skin disease. If he had time, he would call in at a chemist and get some ointment to rub into his neck and the backs of his hands, which was where the red patches always started to appear. The sooner he got some ointment into those bits, the better.

Christ, he had such an awful day ahead of him. Ten lottery retailers in Liverpool still to cover, dotted all over the city. A hundred boards at each.

He had a large street map of Liverpool in his car on which all the retailers were marked. He just hoped he would get the one-way streets right and not end up stuck in a traffic jam. He must catch up with his schedule. He had to get to Chester tonight, and then on to Wrexham and Shrewsbury tomorrow, before driving down to London with all the tickets. It was going to be a hell of a rush. By five on Saturday evening, he'd have finished, and then he'd drive straight back down the motorway to Bobbins and Agnes and beans on toast for supper.

It was a shame he hadn't got anywhere with the little blonde. Perhaps he could come back here after his next lottery trip, tell Agnes that Bobbins wanted him to do some more work in Liverpool and have another go. A Lolita. That's what she was. Nothing could be neater than bonking with Lolita, he sang tunelessly. He was sure that she wanted it really, even if she hadn't come to his room last night.

He looked across the room at the bundles of lottery tickets, a hundred in each, piled in the corner. He wondered if he couldn't trouser just one lottery ticket without Bobbins noticing. Or two or three. It would be a hell of a risk, but worth it if he won.

Stimulated by this thought, he got out of bed, stumbled across the floor and pulled back the flimsy curtains. He stared out at the Liverpool sky, full of a dreary promise of rain and wet streets and thin shoes getting soaked. Christ, he thought, just my luck. I bet I'll have eczema plus a cold by this evening.

Looking down at the cobbled courtyard immediately below, which acted as the pub's car park, he picked out his grey Ford Escort in the row of cars. Hang on. What was that man doing, bent over on the far side? He had something in his hand and Darby suddenly saw the windscreen turn into a pattern of cracks and then fall away on to the bonnet.

'Fucking hell,' he muttered, 'what's he bloody doing? He's stealing my radio.' He got hold of the window, which was loose in its old frame, and started to shake it and bang on the glass in order to attract the stranger's attention.

'Stop it!' he shouted. The man paid no attention, so Phil redoubled his efforts, rattling the window. Anything to stop this man breaking up his car. His pyjamas flapped open, then suddenly the window pane broke and his hand shot through into the cold air outside. As he pulled it back, his wrist grazed against the top of a broken edge. His skin peeled back as cleanly as if it had been cut with a surgical knife and blood started to surge out all over his arm.

Phil looked down in horror. He hated the sight of blood. Shuddering, he clasped his wrist tightly with the other hand, but this only made the blood pump out more quickly, all over his pyjama trousers and on to the floor. It's my artery, he thought, feeling sick with fear. I could die in a few minutes.

'Help!' he shouted at the top of his voice. 'I'm bleeding! Help me, someone!'

Suddenly, the whole hotel seemed totally quiet. The owners of the voices next door must have already gone down to breakfast. He walked over to the bedroom door and tried to turn the handle but, by now, the palms of both his hands were covered in blood and the handle was stiff and slippery. He couldn't get it to move. 'Help!' he shouted again. 'For God's sake, I'm dying!'

There was the sound of someone running up the stairs. His door opened and there was the blonde girl from the night before. With one glance, she took in the middle-aged man gaping at her, his face full of fear, pyjamas wide open and, for some unaccountable reason, blood all over one arm and trickling down his fingers.

'I'll get me mum,' she said. 'You lie down on the bed and stay quiet. Mum'll be here in a minute.'

CHAPTER TWELVE

This Saturday there was no shoot at Strudwells, so Colin Old had the day off. After feeding the pheasants and checking that there was enough water in the drums, he set off in the Land Rover for the local town.

His first port of call was the supermarket. He wandered round with a list in his hand, picking packets off the shelves with hardly a glance at the labels. Shopping he regarded as a boring necessity, something to be done once a week at the most. Then he walked along the High Street to the gunsmith to collect his second gun, a Wesley Richards twelve bore given him by Angus Fyffe. The firing pin on the left barrel had jammed when he was shooting jays and magpies, and the gunsmith had made a new one.

Colin looked round the shop as if he had come home. There were the familiar rows of guns locked by chains into the walls, each with a grubby white label tied round its barrels, and the pervasive, faintly sharp smell of gunpowder mixed with cleaning oil. He sighed with relief as he put his shopping bags down on the counter and started a long, pleasant discussion about why the pin had gone on the left barrel rather than the right, when the right was used more. Then the gunsmith showed him some new cartridges. 'Just in from Belgium, lead-free, one and an eighth-ounce load, but I can tell you, Colin, they'll kill a pheasant at forty-five yards. Never mind the choke on your barrels, it's the new packing in them, a new design of the plastic cup that holds the shot together in the barrels. I've sold hundreds in the last few weeks.'

Colin did not believe in new inventions, but the gunsmith

had been a friend for twenty years, so he took two boxes to keep him quiet.

His last stop was at the county hospital on the edge of town. The wound in Tom Ruster's face had taken much longer to heal than Colin had expected. Tom was still suffering from shock and his hands trembled as Colin talked to him.

'Trauma,' the nurse told him in a confidential voice, and Colin looked suitably wise. 'But he should be well enough to leave us on Monday,' she added brightly.

'We've a big shoot next Saturday,' Colin said. 'I'll want all the beaters I can get. Will he be ready to join us?'

'Oh, I should think so. It will probably do him good to get back to his usual routine.'

Jim and Margaret Bishop sat facing each other at the long oak refectory table. The waitress came and went, offering them more food, filling their glasses, removing their plates. They each thanked her formally and then sank back into silence as she left the room.

Jim normally looked forward to these occasional quiet days at Chequers. No visiting Ministers, no ambassadors, no fellow politicians. They gave him a chance to catch up, to walk with Margaret through the fields, to talk together. Sometimes, Giles would come down from Coventry and spend a few precious hours with them.

But today was different. Since their row earlier in the week, Margaret had not spoken a word to him except on routine matters of diaries and appointments. Now they were alone in the country, the silence seemed particularly oppressive.

Jim felt tortured in himself. He wanted to share his excitement about his Paris visit and his rapturous reception in the French Assembly and his huge doubts about the days ahead. He needed to talk through his plan of campaign, the maze of action ahead of him, the reliability of friends. In the crises of the past, it was on Margaret's instinct that he had most depended.

He pushed away his coffee cup and cleared his throat. 'Darling,' he said, 'it's ridiculous us sitting here, just not talking to each other. We must sort something out.'

Margaret picked up one of the spoons in front of her, turned it over, examined the hallmark and put it down again. Then she looked across at him. 'I don't know that we can, Jim. I think that maybe it's gone too far. I don't know what we've got left in common. That's the real trouble.' She picked up the spoon again and played with it.

Jim smiled. 'You're nervous, aren't you? You always fiddle when you're nervous.' He stretched out his hand towards her across the table but Margaret ignored the gesture.

'Of course, I'm nervous,' she said. 'I've a lot at stake.'

'What d'you mean, a lot at stake?'

'Well, you, Giles, our future . . . the lottery.'

'Damn the lottery,' Jim said suddenly. 'I wish we hadn't started the bloody thing.'

'But you did,' Margaret said.

'And you're hooked?'

Margaret thought for a long time before replying. 'You could say that, I suppose. It means a lot to me. I haven't got much else left now, you know. And you're always so busy.'

'I know I am,' Jim said sadly. 'But that'll pass, darling. Then we could start again. Being Prime Minister isn't a life sentence. You know I'll help you any way I can.' He poured a spoonful of sugar into his empty coffee cup. Looking down at the little pile he had created, he said, 'I realise you must be in big trouble of some sort. You've got to get out of it, darling. It could break us.'

'I know. If only it were that easy.' Margaret stretched out a hand and called the dog that was lying at Jim's feet. She wandered over and Margaret gently scratched her ears.

'Tell me,' Jim said.

'I can't, Jim, I really can't. It's too . . .' Margaret searched for the right word '. . . complicated.'

Jim shook his head and poked violently at the half-melted sugar in his cup. 'I'm worried for you,' he said. 'I've got to try and do *something*. I can't just stand by and accept your getting into such a mess.'

Margaret said nothing.

Silence fell, weighing on them both like a heavy blanket on a summer night.

'Do you remember that poem we used to quote to each other?' Jim said suddenly. 'How did it go?' He paused and then started to recite: ' "The old couple in the brand-new bungalow, drugged with the milk of municipal kindness, fumble their way to bed. Oldness at odds with newness, they nag each other to show nothing is altered." Couldn't we do that? Nag each other to show that nothing is altered? We used to. Silence, not talking, is the worst possible thing.' He stopped and looked across the table at Margaret.

She carried on stroking the dog's head. 'Possibly, Jim. It depends.'

'Depends on what?'

'How things go.' She looked up and saw the sadness in Jim's face. 'I'm sorry, Jim. We've both had to grow up.'

Phil Darby seemed to be out of breath as he handed his bundles of lottery tickets to Tom Bobbins at seven on Saturday evening. 'Christ,' said Bobbins, no trace of sympathy in his voice, 'I thought you'd never arrive. You're the last one to get back.' He looked at the sling round Phil's arm and the plaster on his wrist. 'What the hell happened to you? Did you slip on a banana skin?'

'Sort of,' said Darby, determined not to be drawn. 'I mean, I had to work bleeding hard to get round all those fucking shops. Started at seven this morning, I did, been at it ever since.'

Tom Bobbins gave him a look in which contempt had the

upper hand over distrust, then passed the bundles over to one of the line of shirt-sleeved men sitting in front of a row of computers set on wooden trestle tables. 'Wait here while your tickets are checked against the master list.'

Darby sat down and waited while his bundles were opened and distributed along the line and a matching series of numbers called up on the computer screen. It was like watching a bank clerk counting notes, they did it all so bloody fast, but then they did nothing else all day.

He felt his eczema tickling inside his collar and stretching down his neck to his chest. He longed to open his shirt, have a good scratch, and then light up. He started to fumble in his pocket but he noticed Bobbins staring at him and he quickly put the crumpled pack back into his pocket.

'Looks all right, boss,' said the overseer at the end of the row, the only one wearing a tie. 'The numbers tally with the computer list. We'll go over them again but it seems OK.'

'Come here, Darby,' Bobbins said.

Phil walked slowly and reluctantly up to the tall desk in the middle of the makeshift platform.

'I know your type,' said Bobbins. 'You'd like to pocket a few tickets if you thought you could get away with it. But you're just too scared: you haven't got the guts to do it.'

Darby could see his right hand clenching and unclenching, the fingers folding into the palm and then, thick and powerful, opening up like the release of a spring. He wondered whether he was going to be hit and instinctively he put his hands in front of his chest.

Bobbins sneered at him. 'Little coward, aren't you? Don't worry. I'm not going to hurt you this time. You're not worth the trouble.' He reached into the drawer below him and threw a slim bundle of £10 notes at Darby. 'There's your bonus,' he said.

Three of the notes fell on to the floor and Darby scrabbled to pick them up.

Bobbins laughed. 'That's all you're good for – mucking

156

around in the dirt. Now listen. If there's no winner of the jackpot tonight, come here Monday at eight, and don't be fucking late. If there's a winner, don't bother. Stay at home and wash the dishes.'

Back in his Ford Escort, Darby unlocked the glove pocket and pulled out twenty lottery tickets. They were duplicates of combinations from the list given him by Bobbins and he had bought them with his own money at a garage shop in Walsall. He lit a cigarette and laughed aloud as he fingered them. It was worth spending £20 to annoy Bobbins. If he won and shared the jackpot with Bobbins' boss, he guaranteed it would annoy Bobbins a very great deal.

He scratched his neck thoughtfully as he put his car into gear.

Harry Plank and Sheikh Matab both arrived at the Montclare Club at a quarter to eight. They went to the smallest of the gaming rooms on the second floor and watched as Streppie Pepper, the princess of the lottery, radiant with the good health that unexpected riches bring, went through her routine and charmed her live studio audience. She told them that ticket sales had reached ninety million and the roll-over jackpot – the queenpot, she called it – could be over £30 million. *Thirty million*, she repeated. The winner would be richer than his wildest dreams. And the audience whistled and cheered and imagined a fantasy world in which the mortgage was paid off and the only worry was how to spend the money.

And then, sharp at eight o'clock, the coloured balls started to roll out one by one. Plank put his martini glass down on the card table and stared at the screen. Thirty-nine. Thirty-six. He took a sip of the ice-cold drink. Forty-three.

'You know, Matab, no one likes those numbers,' he said. 'They don't figure in anyone's birthday calendar, that's for sure, and the lottery computer didn't like any of them, either. In the first eighteen months, thirty-nine only figured in three jackpots. We could be on to a winner.' His usual control had slipped; he sounded almost excited.

Matab said nothing and went on quietly sipping at his glass of champagne.

But then the scene changed. Low, popular numbers rolled out. Seventeen, eleven. 'Damn!' Plank exclaimed. 'That could have fucked it.' There was a long pause as the giant wheel turned and the balls seemed reluctant to leave their hive. Finally, one detached itself and trundled down the shute.

'Sixteen!' exclaimed Streppie proudly. It was quickly followed by another. 'And the bonus number is . . . eighteen. Eighteen and never been . . .'

Matab made an impatient gesture towards the screen and Plank quickly walked across and switched it off.

Matab sat silently for a moment, staring at his glass. 'This is called a flute, isn't it, Harry?' he asked. 'A champagne flute.' He held it up to the light. 'The same as your code-name, Magic Flute. One Saturday we'll drink a toast to the lottery but not tonight, you think?' There was no emotion in his voice, merely a hint of impersonal enquiry.

'I guess that's right,' Plank replied. 'Those numbers in the teens are all popular, and sixteen and seventeen have often won. I'd be surprised if that was one of our one-in-fifty-million combinations. We'll know in a few minutes; I've told the office to call us here.'

He picked up his martini glass, took the olive out of the bottom and started to chew it slowly. Then he looked at the piece of paper on which he had written down the winning numbers: 39, 36, 43, 17, 11, 16, bonus 18. 'I guess, though,' he was thinking aloud, 'we may have done pretty well on the other prizes. People just don't like backing on sequences. Sixteen, seventeen, eighteen – they just find it very hard to write that down. It's the same in the States.'

He poured himself another martini and started to pace up and down the small room, but Matab sat motionless in his chair, looking ahead of him at the Victorian portrait of the

Club's founder, saying nothing. Plank wondered whether to go on talking and speculating about the result and decided against. He sat down at the card table, put his glass by his side and started to deal himself a hand of patience.

Eventually, the telephone rang. Plank jumped up and reached for it. He listened for a few seconds, shaking his head, then issued a few curt instructions. Putting the phone down, he turned to Matab. 'We didn't win the jackpot.'

Matab's gaze did not shift from the picture but he cocked his head slightly to one side.

'But at first sight we'll have done well on matching five, and on the five plus bonus as well. They'll go on working on that, and I'll be in the office in the morning myself. I'll call you.'

Matab nodded quietly, then suggested that they play a hand of two-pack bezique. To his surprise, Plank noticed that Matab's hand was shaking as he dealt the cards.

Marie Claude ran her hand over her stomach as she lay in bed. For the first time, she felt it was beginning to swell, and her breasts were definitely bigger. Her bra had felt really tight as she walked round the Tate that afternoon. She must have another talk with Graham. She couldn't just go on hanging round London, calling up her old friends, asking them to meet her at a Prêt-à-Manger for a croissant or to have a drink in a pub. Soon they'd all notice she was getting fatter.

She had to bring Graham to a decision – but the right decision. Lovely man, bloody man – she loved him so much despite his moods, his anger.

She stared up at the patterns in the ceiling and then turned the light off and fell asleep, dreaming of her home in Normandy.

CHAPTER THIRTEEN

'It looks fantastic, just fantastic!' Harry Plank shouted down the telephone, his excitement driving all caution away. 'It's worked out exactly in line with my calculations. That shows we're on to a sure-fire winner.'

'But we haven't got the jackpot.' By contrast, Matab's voice reflected his normal self: quiet, cautious and hiding his feelings.

'No. But then no one has. I've heard it on the news. The jackpot has been rolled over again. It'll be massive this week – forty million plus. They're all getting excited about it already. The queenpot has become the kingpot.'

'So the syndicate's in action again this week?'

'You bet. As agreed. We'll put the money together today and get the couriers out again tomorrow. I've already alerted Bobbins.'

'How much will you need?' Matab asked.

'That's the great news. On the match three – three numbers right and an automatic ten pounds – we got just slightly under my calculation, three hundred and forty thousand pounds. But on all the others, the fours, the fives and the fives plus bonus, there were fewer other winners because it was an unpopular combination. Not quite unpopular enough for us to win the jackpot, but still unpopular. So the prizes were higher, nearly three times the past average. We've won close to seven hundred thousand, not the five hundred and twenty-seven that I used in my note to the syndicate.

'It just shows that my theory about significantly higher

prizes on the lower frequency combinations is right in the ballpark. We're going to hit a lot of home runs.' Harry's words were tumbling out. 'We'll make ourselves a fortune, Matab, an absolute fortune. My Flute's going to be magic, real great magic, for us all.'

Matab looked across his study and the picture of his brother distracted his attention. It was slightly crooked. Perhaps a servant had moved it when dusting the heavy gilt frame.

Memory of the telephone conversation with his brother early that morning came flooding back to him. He had never heard Abdulla sounding so angry. He had ordered Matab – there was no milder word for it – to stop delaying and to call on the Prime Minister immediately to protest at the damage the fall in sterling was doing to Medevan.

Unless the fall was stopped, Abdulla had threatened, he would personally cancel the British defence contracts and call Matab – the most senior member of the diplomatic corps – back from London. This would be the ultimate humiliation for Matab. He could never face all his old friends again, friends of twenty-five years' standing. He would have to give up the shoot at Strudwells, sell his house at Ascot and the horses. He would be a laughing stock in the Arab world.

Yet all the time Medevan's financial reserves were falling, Matab felt in some deep, unexplained way that it was his fault. His brother had always been his guiding star and now, in a moment of great crisis for their country, he was failing him.

'Matab, are you still there? Did you hear what I was saying?'

'Yes, yes, I did.' Matab pulled himself back to the world around him. 'You were saying . . .'

'The total we've won from all the small prizes,' Plank repeated, 'comes to just over a million, a hundred and forty thousand more than I anticipated in my note to investors. If anyone had doubts, that'll sure cure them. So ahead we go. On to next week and the second roll-over.'

A matter-of-fact tone came into Plank's voice. 'I'll keep thirty thousand back for Bobbins' expenses and the couriers,' he said, 'and I'll call for just a million more from the investors. Then we buy the two million tickets again. Half a million pounds from you, please, fifty per cent of last week's stake.'

Matab paused before he replied. 'Even I can't get you half a million every Monday morning, Harry,' he said. Pride stopped him saying any more. 'I'll see that you have a banker's draft by Wednesday.'

'All right, but it can't be later. I have to get the certified cheques distributed round the country. We'll follow exactly the same pattern as last week, that makes it simpler.'

'What about Margaret and Angus?' Matab asked.

'The same as for the other investors. They'll each put up another twenty-five thousand if they want to go on.' Plank laughed. 'I guess they'll find it somehow, Matab. They're both greedy. And, after all, they've each won more this time than they had reason to expect.'

Matab cut off the conversation without comment and walked over to the picture. He straightened it and gazed reflectively at his brother's face, wondering what Abdulla would do if he were in his position. He stared out at the blank street, with its leafless plane trees and empty pavements. He hated London on a Sunday morning when all the life had left and, suddenly, he longed to be away, shooting, riding, living with danger, silent but active, using his eye and his nerve and his body. Anything to be rid of the diplomatic world, the polite conversation, the pretence.

Margaret drove her car straight from Chequers to Angus' flat in Albany. She found him watching a video of a Masters golf match. The Sunday newspapers were scattered all over the carpet.

'I got your message,' she said, talking fast as he bent to kiss her. 'I didn't want to telephone in case anyone heard me. So, how did we do? I haven't slept all night thinking about it.'

'No jackpot winner, you'll have seen that in today's papers.'

Margaret nodded. 'Can't you switch that thing off?' She gestured towards the picture of a golfball soaring through the blue Florida sky. 'It's distracting.'

Angus pressed a remote control and the screen went blank. He started laughing. 'My beautiful Margaret, I, by contrast, find golf very relaxing, watching grown-up, very rich and presumably intelligent men trying for hours to get a little white ball into a hole in the ground. Marvellous. I wonder what the Martians must think of golf as they watch us from their space satellites.'

'Now you're making me angry, Angus. Don't keep me waiting. Tell me, how did we do last night?'

Angus reluctantly became serious. 'All right,' he said. 'Harry rang me at some ghastly early hour this morning when I was hardly awake. We did much better than he had calculated on the small prizes, five plus bonus and all that lot. The syndicate's made just over a million on them.

'But, of course, there's another roll-over this week. There'll be a huge jackpot – over forty million, Harry says – and the syndicate's going straight on. They're calling for fifty per cent of our stakes; that means another twenty-five thousand from each of us.' He paused. 'Harry wants it by tomorrow, or Tuesday at the latest.' His face suddenly went bleak. 'Difficult, isn't it?'

'Christ,' said Margaret, softly, under her breath, almost inaudibly. It was all happening too quickly. 'Harry won't let us stay in for less? Simply carry forward our winnings and invest those?'

'No, he's insisting that the minimum stake must stay at fifty thousand. He doesn't want to bring in other investors. To be fair, he said that right from the beginning.'

'And if we don't go on?'

Angus shrugged his shoulders. 'I haven't asked. I guess we just lose what we put in last week.'

'Oh, my God!' Margaret screwed her eyes up and then stared out of the window at the stone walls on the other side of the covered walk. 'We're caught, aren't we, Angus?' she said quietly.

He did not reply immediately, but walked over to a cupboard in the panelled wall, took out a bottle of wine and poured her a large glass. As he handed it to her, he leaned down and kissed her on the forehead. 'Of course we are. But look on the bright side – we've done much better in the first week than we might have done; we can go into the next roll-over at half cost. The only thing is that it's all on top of us at once. We expected a gap, and some time, to get ready again, and there isn't one. But the jackpot is even bigger, the odds are just the same, and if we win we'll be just that much richer.'

He raised his glass. 'Come on, darling, a toast to our bank managers. I'm sure we can get them to put up the ante.'

Margaret found herself smiling against her will. 'I admire you, Angus. You can always cheer me up. And, yes, I've squared my bank manager for the time being, but I didn't expect it all to happen so quickly. At this rate, I can manage two or three more weeks, but then I'm finished and the cottage will be gone.'

Angus thought of the mortgage on Strudwells and the letter he had received from Crane's ten days before. His position was far worse than Margaret's; he just carried it off more lightly. He was used to living on the dangerous edge.

He finished the wine in his glass. 'Listen, Margaret. Jim told me he had overheard you borrowing fifty thousand. He's convinced you're caught up with some great gambling losses, so you're being blackmailed, and buying too many lottery tickets to pay off your debts, or whatever. And, being a very decent guy, he's terribly worried about it.' Margaret started to interrupt but Angus pressed on. 'No, Margaret, you must let me finish. This could be very serious for both of us. He hinted he might even have to alert the security people to find out what was going on. That'd certainly be the end of the road for me.' Margaret frowned and again tried to interrupt but Angus went on doggedly.

'I'm going to have to tell Matab and Harry Plank about Jim's worries. Frankly, it's getting a bit too hot. I don't think it's fair not to tell them. I've got to warn them in case the police start nosing around.'

Margaret did not like the prospect of letting Matab and Plank into the secrets of her and Jim's life. 'Do you really have to do that? It seems . . . sort of private to me.' She remembered the anguished look on Jim's face and she shook her head as if in pain. 'No, Angus, I'd much rather you didn't. I don't want Jim hurt; things are bad enough between us.'

Angus sat down beside her and put an arm round her shoulders. They sat in silence and then she rested her head on his shoulder and ran a finger lightly down his cheek. 'It's difficult, isn't it?' she said.

'Yes,' he agreed, 'but we do need the money. Then, we might be able to start something new, do something different.'

Margaret hesitated and then, reluctance evident in her voice, she agreed. 'All right, if you think you must, but don't tell them too much about the differences between Jim and me.'

Angus gave her a gentle hug. 'Thanks,' he said. 'Of course I won't.'

The Hussars had been summoned to a special dinner meeting. The ground-floor room at the back of Saint George's tavern was full, and two extra chairs had been crammed in at either end of the table. Spencer Gray, as president of the club, had had a special dinner menu printed:

VE DAY minus 8

DINNER BEFORE THE BATTLE

SCOTCH SMOKED SALMON
MORECAMBE BAY SHRIMPS

ABERDEEN ANGUS ROAST BEEF

Yorkshire Pudding
King Edward Potatoes
Welsh Leeks

WELSH RAREBIT
or
STILTON CHEESE
or
DOUBLE GLOUCESTER

COX'S ORANGE PIPPINS
KENT COBS

WINES
SUSSEX DOWNS SPARKLING BRUT
BOADICEA RED RESERVE

GUEST OF HONOUR:
THE CHANCELLOR OF
THE EXCHEQUER

'So we're boozing for Blighty now. Great, but am I allowed a cappuccino before I speak, or do I have to have Earl Grey tea?' Graham Blackie asked towards the end of the meal.

Humour was not Spencer's longest suit. 'Of course you can have coffee. I don't think I've ever seen you drink tea.' He looked round the room. 'Marvellous turnout tonight. Extraordinary, considering it's a Sunday.'

'I don't think it's extraordinary at all. It shows how seriously our members are taking it. Quite right, too.'

A few minutes later Spencer gave the club's traditional toast – 'The Queen and the Constitution' – and then Graham was on his feet. He thanked the club for its hospitality and remarked how pleasant it was to see so many friends.

He picked up the pamphlet lying on the table in front of him. 'This,' he said, waving it in front of him, 'is our manifesto. As you see, there's a Union Jack on the front and it's addressed simply to THE BRITISH with two headlines, PUT BRITAIN FIRST, and, further down the page, YOUR COUNTRY NEEDS YOU.

'Inside are two lists of short but detailed points. The first shows the costs and dangers of our membership of the European Union. For example, the cost of membership equalling eight pence off income tax. Or the danger that in a federal Europe our politicians will no longer have the legal power to govern. Or the fact that we'll pay huge sums in subsidy, not just to the Irish and the Portuguese – we're almost used to that – but to the Czechs, the Poles and all the other poor countries that want to join.

'On the other side is a list of the immediate benefits if we leave the EU. We will control our own beef and fish again; British law will be supreme, not European; we can choose our own working hours and wage rates, and so on. You all know the arguments and I needn't rehearse them.

'On the back is a membership form. We are calling ourselves the British Alliance. Now, this is the heart of the matter.' He paused for effect and looked around the room.

Everyone's eyes were fixed on him, waiting for the next words.

'The challenge that Spencer and I are setting you is to distribute thousands of these manifestos in the next seven days before the Commons debate. And I mean literally thousands: through your firms, associations, schools, families, in factories, on the underground and at railway stations. We want you to get as many members as you possibly can.

'There's no charge for membership; just the opposite as far as you all are concerned. A kind friend, who wishes to remain anonymous, will give ten thousand pounds' – he stopped before repeating the words, emphasising them slowly – '*ten thousand pounds* to the Hussar who produces most signed forms by next Sunday night.'

A charge of excitement ran round the long table. Ten thousand pounds – that made pounding along the pavements in November rain worthwhile.

'In the debate next Monday, I want to be able to wave this manifesto in Bishop's face and tell him that the British Alliance has got a million members.' He paused, and his voice rose as he repeated the words: 'A million members, and growing all the time.

'From tomorrow, we're advertising in all the tabloids, paid for by a great patriot, and we'll print this leaflet and the membership form in all the ads. By the end of the week, our Alliance will be better known than the lottery.' He stopped and waited for the buzz of conversation to die down.

'For you and all your friends, and those like you and me who want to save Britain and to stop us being swallowed up in Europe, this is the week when we can save our country by our efforts.' There was a long silence as he looked round the room.

'And we'll win. We'll win.' Blackie raised his arms as he shouted these words, and suddenly all the Hussars were on their feet, cheering and waving their manifestos.

Wally Wallace got up from the far end of the table and

walked over to the upright piano in the corner of the room. He opened the cover and started to thump at the keys. 'Rule, Britannia,' he sang at the top of his voice and the refrain was immediately picked up.

Rule, Britannia, Britannia rules the waves
Britons never, never, never shall be slaves.

They sang till their voices were hoarse. *Rule Britannia* was followed by *Land of Hope and Glory*. Blackie, in a powerful baritone, quietened the Hussars for a few minutes as he sang, solo, 'I vow to thee my country'. And then it was *Rule Britannia* again, and the National Anthem. And more toasts to the Queen and the young Princes.

The crowd round the bar in the front of the pub heard them and agreed they were a noisy lot, but they seemed good sorts. The publican produced a copy of the manifesto that Blackie had given him as he walked through to the back room. It was handed round and the general verdict was that it made a lot of sense. An elderly customer asked for another pint of Bass and said that he had never liked Europe, not since the war. He had never been there since.

CHAPTER FOURTEEN

Graham Blackie woke with a headache. He had drunk too much whisky at that damn dinner the night before. Still, it was worth it. Spencer had told him as he left that the Hussars had loved his speech and they would be working like fury all week.

He hastily shaved and got dressed. Waiting for him downstairs in his study was the usual tray with a mug of black coffee, orange juice and a small bowl of cereal. The day's papers were stacked by the side and, on top, the typed list of his engagements for the day. He went down the list quickly. All morning in the Treasury, a speech at lunch, meetings with back-benchers in the House from half past two onwards. An all-party European Affairs meeting at five.

Then he groaned as he saw that his diary secretary had arranged for him to go to a concert at St John's, Smith Square that evening in aid of World War veterans. However, he calculated he need only spend half an hour there. He made a note to check that the Press Secretary had told the media. If he got there at six, it might make the evening news.

As he drank his coffee, the headline in the *Financial News* caught his eye. 'STERLING WEAK IN TOKYO' it announced in bold type. He was still reading the details when his telephone rang. The Downing Street exchange told him the Governor of the Bank was on the line.

'Put him through on the scrambler,' he ordered and a series of telephonic barks and grunts followed. Then he heard a surprisingly cheerful Geoffrey Williams.

'Morning, Chancellor. It's a bit early but I thought I should let you know sterling slid another three and a half points against the dollar in Tokyo and Hong Kong. It's bound to be weak here when our market opens in half an hour.'

'What about the Euro?'

'Just as you'd expect. It's just about followed the dollar. It was one-twenty-four to the pound; it's now . . . I'm just calling it up on my screen. Yes, it's now one-twenty-two point twenty-five. I should think the market will push it down to one-twenty-two or even one-twenty-one during the day. It's never been so low. This is new territory.'

Blackie sat back in his chair, thinking. 'You won't do anything, will you, Geoffrey?'

'Not unless you instruct me.'

'What about your gold?' Blackie asked.

'That's going ahead just as planned. The bullion vans will be here at two thirty next Monday afternoon.' Graham heard a strange noise from the other end of the line. The Governor of the Bank was chuckling. 'You'll like this, Chancellor. We've given a code-name to the removal of the gold. We're calling it Operation Napoleon.'

The fifth floor of the Union Street warehouse was again crowded. There were grunts of recognition as couriers greeted each other and exchanged stories of difficulties they had had in meeting their daily deadlines. Two, sitting next to each other, had got parking tickets while outside lottery retailers and were complaining loudly of their difficulty in getting that bastard Tom Bobbins to refund their fine.

Phil Darby sat at the end of a row, his arm still in a sling. He was showing off to his neighbour. 'Yeah,' he said, accepting a cigarette without thanks, 'he was a big guy, I mean three inches taller than you, and heavy, very heavy, but I was buggered if I was going to see my car smashed up. I picked up this old spanner from the floor and I grabbed and hit him until . . .' The conclusion was never revealed. Tom Bobbins walked on to the platform and everyone fell silent.

Phil thought he looked even more menacing than he had on Saturday.

Bobbins, for the benefit of the few newcomers, went through the same drill as before but stressed that, as it was already Monday morning, they had some hours less than the previous week. No excuses were acceptable. The couriers must start each day earlier and finish later. The first batches of certified cheques were waiting for them with their plastic folders on the tables at the back of the hall; the remainder would reach them on Wednesday or Thursday at the pubs and bed and breakfasts where they were to stay.

'Those of you who did it last week, you'll call on just the same lottery outlets in just the same order. So even the most nerdish among you –' he suddenly caught sight of Phil Darby sitting near the back and glared at him, 'and that's you, Darby, you little shit – you can't have any fucking trouble this time.'

He walked down from the platform, pulled Darby out of his chair and held him out like a rag-doll for all the couriers to see. Phil's feet were a few inches off the ground and some of the couriers sniggered as he struggled. They had all had hard lives and it was pleasant to see someone other than themselves being screwed.

'This little bastard didn't get his tickets back here till after seven on Saturday evening. That's too bloody late.' Bobbins had his hand on Darby's collar and he shook him back and forth as he spoke. 'This week's the big one. The boss wants to win, so no fucking mistakes.' He emphasised each syllable by a violent jerk on Derby's collar. 'There's a two-hundred-pound bonus for everyone back here by five on Saturday, all tickets in order. You're all to phone in every evening to confirm you're up to schedule.' Bobbins threw Darby back into his chair and went back to the platform.

'I'm a kind-hearted guy,' he said, 'but the boss doesn't put up with mistakes.'

Driving through Brent Cross on his way to the M1, Darby

ran a finger tentatively round the inside of his collar. He knew his eczema would start again but, at least, he had his ointment and pills with him this time. He thought about Bobbins all the way to Spaghetti Junction.

'You're going to have to do something about him. We can't let him screw it up.' There was fury in Harry Plank's voice.

At lunchtime the Montclare looked like a woman who had only recently got out of bed. It was faintly bedraggled, a gentle smell surrounding its grand rooms, a memory of luxury from the night before and a promise of pleasures to come. Meanwhile, cigar smoke clung to the burgundy red curtains and the silver ashtrays looked as if they had not been emptied, even though they had all been cleaned and buffed

There was, however, a crispness about the atmosphere in the small gaming room on the second floor, where Lord Fyffe had met Sheikh Matab and Harry Plank for a working lunch. Fyffe had handed over his and Margaret's cheques for £25,000 each, then broached the difficult topic of the Prime Minister's suspicions. 'My worry is,' he concluded, 'that he'll get the security services to check on us.'

'Why would he do that?' asked Matab.

'Well . . .' Angus looked embarrassed. 'Because he wants to protect Margaret from her own actions, I think. And, even more than that, he wants to save their marriage.'

Harry Plank angrily pushed away his plate of smoked salmon. 'Get her out of the Flute, Matab. This could ruin us.'

Matab refused. 'She needs us,' he said simply.

'In that case,' Plank urged, 'you've gotta do something about the big guy, about Bishop himself.'

Plank's thoughts turned to his companies, grouped together under the grandiose title of International Corporate Enterprises. Only he and his accountant knew how much their profits from bingo halls and casinos had fallen in the last two years, thanks to competition from the lottery. He had expanded at precisely the wrong moment, borrowing money to buy up a rival chain in the north just weeks before the effect of the lottery on the business became obvious. Turnover in the last few months had fallen disastrously.

He had maintained appearances, gambled at the Montclare, made new friends like Matab, but the success of the Flute was vital to him. And the results of the first week showed it was going to be a far greater success than he had dared hope. But he knew they had to hang in there. It could be a week or a year before they won the jackpot. Other people's nerves might break; his wouldn't.

Plank guessed that what Fyffe had done was probably illegal – conspiracy to fraud or some shit like that. If they were broken by the police now, if the police used the law to stop them . . . Christ, he wouldn't let that happen. He had been a mean fighter years back in Baltimore. He had not forgotten.

Sheikh Matab and Angus Fyffe were silent, playing with their plates of food. 'Come on, Angus, you're not at a funeral.' Plank stood up and his tall body dominated the room. 'We're celebrating,' he said. 'We're going to make much more money out of my Flute than I had dared hope. But we may need time. We can't let the police or anyone stop us. You'll just have to put Bishop out of action.'

Fyffe quivered. 'Put him out of action?' he repeated tentatively, as if trying out the words for effect.

'Yeah,' Plank said, 'get him out of the ring for a good long time. He's the only one who might put the police on to us.'

'You're out of your mind. I can't do that,' Fyffe protested. 'He's my oldest friend: we've known each other for years. He trusts me, that's why he told me his worries about Margaret.'

'You can't do that? That's great.' Plank bent down over the table where Angus was sitting until his head was only a few inches away from Angus' face. Then he spat his words straight at him. 'Just think what would happen if your police received a little note saying how a certain group of investors had got hold of the low frequency combinations. And a copy of that little note found its way to your dear Jim Bishop's desk.

What's your job called? Special adviser? That's great. That's really funny. How long d'ya think you'd remain special adviser for?'

Angus Fyffe went grey and his jaw sagged open. Then he shook his head in disbelief and tried a half-laugh. 'You couldn't do that,' he stammered, 'you just couldn't.'

'I could and I will.' Plank sat down opposite Fyffe. His hand moved forward as if he were tempted to take hold of Fyffe's collar and shake it. 'I'm not in this for kicks, Angus. Maybe you are. I'm in it to make serious money. I've got a tape of our phone conversations. You're the one who bust into the system at your Lottery Board to get us the numbers we needed, and we're paying you for that, remember? Five per cent of the jackpot, or did you bargain up to six per cent? I know you need the money.'

Plank looked across at Matab, who sat carefully stroking his chin, saying nothing.

Fyffe kept on shaking his head as if he could not believe what he was hearing. Then he turned to Matab. 'Matab, you must see this is all ridiculous. Tell Harry to come down to earth. I only wanted to alert you there was a possibility of Jim Bishop getting the police involved, but there's no certainty he will. It'll probably never happen.'

Matab looked at the heavy gold watch that nestled among the thick dark hairs on his wrist. 'I must leave you. I have many people coming to see me at the Embassy this afternoon; we have a few difficulties.' He paused and then said 'Some weeks ago, Angus, I asked the Prime Minister to come and shoot again with us at Strudwells this Saturday. It should be the best shoot of the season, and you are coming as well as my guest in your old house.'

Matab got up from his chair and started to walk towards the door. He walked like an athlete, with his small feet turning slightly inwards and his back beautifully straight. At the door he turned and spoke again, his words quiet commands.

'Harry will work out the details with you. It is regrettable but necessary. Saturday will give you a good opportunity.'

Angus bowed his head and brought his hands up to hide his face.

An image of Jim Bishop the first time he came to stay at Strudwells flashed across his mind. He must have been fourteen, rather small for his age, with a mass of curly brown hair. He was extraordinarily good-natured, always smiling and ready to join in any plan.

Jim had brought his twenty-eight-bore gun with him. He was so proud of that gun. He had just been given it as a birthday present, and they were allowed to go out together to shoot pigeons. Every afternoon they had walked round the estate as the sun disappeared, looking for clumps of trees covered in ivy towards which the pigeons would fly as they came in to roost.

One evening they shot nine pigeons, their record, and Jim wounded one that fell fifty yards away. They searched for it endlessly. Angus wanted to leave it and go home for tea, but Jim had insisted on going on looking. Eventually, they found it, stuck in a bramble bush with one wing broken, and Jim had quickly broken its neck and put it in his game-pocket.

By the end of the holidays, they had woven the sort of bond of friendship that, with ordinary luck, lasts for a lifetime. They had gone on to the Army and then to University together.

'I can't do it,' Angus muttered, his hands still hiding his face. 'I just can't.'

'You've no choice,' Plank said brutally. 'You'll make it look like an accident at the shoot. These things happen. Some days it's not only the birds that get hurt.'

The Georgian church of St John stands in the centre of Smith Square, an island of musical culture in a sea of politicians' houses and offices. Four evenings a week, chamber orchestras and choirs, some professional, some young, all sparkling with musical talent, play and sing, in the great body of the church, to a mixed audience of office workers, peers, secretaries and members of parliament.

Music was one of Marie Claude's passions and she had introduced Graham Blackie to the musical life on the doorstep of Westminster and persuaded him to become a Friend of St John's. Now his mail regularly included details of the concerts and his diary secretary, who lived for her hours of choral singing, occasionally committed him to go when there was a gap in the evening.

Marie Claude learnt from a friend in the box office that the Chancellor was coming to the concert on Monday evening and she waited, wearing her dark red coat and a scarf round her head, at the foot of the stone steps that led from the church into the square. She heard the choir inside the church singing the Bach Mass in B Minor, and she longed to be with Graham, holding his hand, sharing excitement about the baby with him. She felt cold and lonely.

The moment the Mass was finished, the door at the side of the church opened and Graham walked out quickly, between the heavy pillars and down the steps, humming to himself.

She moved in and slipped her arm through his before he had time to protest and together they started to walk along Lord North Street towards Westminster. Neither of them knew how to start the conversation.

Eventually Marie Claude said, 'I returned to my family in Quinnehou for some days last week. I told my mother and father that I was pregnant. They were shocked but excited. Of course,' she added, 'they're good Catholics; they go to Mass every Sunday.' Blackie said nothing. For once in his adult life he felt embarrassed and uncertain how to cope with the situation ahead. They passed into Great Peter Street and turned towards Millbank. Ahead was the looming grey tower of the House of Lords.

Marie Claude took a deep breath and asked, 'Did you get the copy of *Boule de Suif* that I sent you?'

'Yes.'

'Did you read it?'

'Yes, I did. Late one evening.' Graham thought for a moment and then added, 'I suppose it's true to human nature, the way the rich ones first eat the fat tart's food, then persuade her to sleep with the Prussian officer so that they can get on their way to Dieppe, then cut her and despise her. Typical bloody privileged middle class, I thought.' He paused again before saying, inconsequentially, 'It's a marvellous story.'

They crossed Millbank and started to walk across the Green to the Thames.

Marie Claude smiled and nodded her head. 'But, *chéri*, that's not why I sent it to you.' She pulled him closer to her as if for warmth and protection, using him as an overcoat against the cold, chill wind. 'It was to remind you that the Germans were in Normandy in 1870 and they occupied Normandy again in 1940. That's my home; that's where we have lived and farmed for years and years.

'Me, I was educated on memories of German invasion, of bodies floating in the river, swollen and bloated. They're all part of our history. I remember my grandmother telling me how she walked to church one Sunday morning and found two soldiers lying in the ditch. She turned one of them over and his head was broken in, but she recognised him. A month before, he had been billeted on them and had been kind and helpful, feeding the animals. He told them he came from a farm in Bavaria and all he wanted was to get back there.' She paused. 'From the way my grandmother talked, I think if the German had asked her to marry him, she would have.'

They walked under the row of skeletal trees, branches clawing at the dark sky above them, and gazed over the wall at the Thames. It was low tide and the oily mud stretched out in front of them, dimly reflecting the street lights.

Marie Claude turned and stared at Graham and wondered how she could persuade him to change his mind – about her baby, about Europe, about anything. She knew him so well, she could describe every centimetre of his body, and yet she didn't know him at all.

'You know,' she said, 'last week, darling, I walked to the end of the harbour in Barfleur. There is a stone there which marks the place from which William, Duke of Normandy, sailed across the Channel to become William, King of England.'

Graham had been silent for some minutes but now she felt him becoming restless. She could not let him go yet. 'Close to that stone is the war memorial. My family, Moisan, is on that other stone three times. There is a Pierre Moisan who died for France in 1916, a Jean, my grandfather, who died in 1943, and another, Yvette, who is called a "victime de la libération" killed on the seventeenth of June, 1944. I don't know what happened to her. I've often asked my parents but they won't talk to me about her. Something unpleasant, I suppose.'

Graham broke away and said angrily that this was all a very long time ago. It did not have any relevance in today's world.

Marie Claude felt her calm leaving her. She was going to cry and she knew Graham would hate that. '*Mon jules*,' she said, 'an instant more. Do you not understand, I just don't want the name of any baby of mine, of yours, ever to be on a stone war memorial. And that's the way I've been brought up, with memories all round me.'

Graham started to walk past the House of Lords. He was surprised at the feeling that those words about a baby of his produced in him. He was stirred in a way he had not expected and, yes, interested. 'Are you all right?' he asked Marie Claude as they passed the statue of Richard, Coeur de Lion. 'Have you got enough money?'

Marie Claude did not reply immediately. She was determined not to let Graham see her tears. They turned into New Palace Yard and the policeman greeted Blackie and smiled encouragingly at Marie Claude and she realised she was, in some way, gaining ground.

She would not let Graham see her hanging on him, waiting for favours. She looked at the great entrance on her right to Westminster Hall and found herself laughing. '*Tu n'es qu'un idiot. Nul en histoire*,' she said. 'You're so proud of that big old hall but you forget it was built by the Duke of Normandy's son. Really, you English owe everything to us French. If we had not been always threatening and fighting you, the Scots would have conquered you long ago.'

Graham shook his head. 'You're got it all wrong. Listen, darling, I've got a hundred meetings in the next week, but we'll definitely arrange something together soon.'

He kissed her on both cheeks and disappeared into the Members' entrance to the House of Commons.

CHAPTER FIFTEEN

The Prime Minister rose from his chair and greeted Sheikh Matab warmly. 'You have come by yourself?' he asked with a smile. 'No Commercial Counsellor? No secretaries?'

'By myself. I thought we could talk most frankly without secretaries taking notes.'

'Very well.'

The private secretary handed Matab a cup of coffee, then, at Bishop's discreet nod, picked up his notebook and left the room.

'This is unorthodox. The civil servants won't like us talking alone,' the Prime Minister said, 'but I know you have a problem.'

'A very serious one,' Matab replied. 'I am calling on the specific instructions of the Emir, Sheikh Abdulla.' There was silence while Matab sipped at his coffee and Bishop waited for him to continue.

'Prime Minister,' Matab began, 'you know how much we have always supported Britain. Medevan keeps almost all its reserves in sterling; we place our big defence orders here in Britain with your manufacturers. The Americans and the French would be very pleased to win those orders.'

'I know it well, ambassador,' Bishop said simply, 'and we are very grateful.'

'You must see then,' there was a sudden, restrained surge of anger in Matab's voice, 'what damage your policy of joining the European currency is doing to my country. In the last two weeks the fall in sterling has cost Medevan two thousand million pounds. I repeat, *two thousand million pounds*. And there is every sign of the fall continuing. Speculators all over the world do not like Britain being locked into the Euro. They are afraid for the future, and therefore they are selling the pound and buying yen and dollars instead.

'If we sell our reserves of sterling, we will – how do you put it? – knock the floor out of the market. And we, too, would lose a great deal more money.

'My brother . . .' Matab looked across the room at Bishop but saw him sitting silent, with an air of abstraction on his face. He cleared his throat and went on, 'Sheikh Abdulla formally requests you, Prime Minister, to abandon your policy of joining the European currency. He asks you this in the interest of Medevan and, he strongly believes, of Britain as well.'

Jim Bishop sat back in his chair and, for a moment, allowed himself the luxury of daydreaming. It would be so much easier if he changed his mind. Graham Blackie and he could be allies again; the newspaper barons would love him; he could unite the party; Margaret and he might even patch things up. They could go away on a long walking holiday, with Giles, perhaps, as a sort of peacemaker between them. Why on earth was he torturing himself, all for some great European ideal that had so many fearful obstacles in its path? He shook his head. He realised Matab was still talking to him.

'I cannot exaggerate the consequences if, on your advice, the House of Commons votes to join the single currency. But, Prime Minister, you have great personal authority. People trust your leadership. If you say you have weighed all the factors, seen the damaging effect on sterling and on your friends abroad, and changed your mind, that would totally alter matters.'

Bishop smiled and shook his head. 'You flatter me, Sheikh Matab. If only it was that easy. As you know, the issue is far bigger than me or my personal judgement.' He thought for a moment and then said he was very surprised that Medevan had lost as much as £2 billion in the last two weeks. That must, of course, be a matter of extreme worry to Sheikh Abdulla and he asked the ambassador to explain the figure to him.

Matab took a small notebook, bound in crocodile leather, out of his pocket and started to read off numbers. 'Sterling has fallen from a Euro exchange rate of one-thirty to one-twenty this morning, most of it since your speech in Paris. That's a fall of seven per cent. We now have thirty billion pounds of our reserves in sterling. Seven per cent of thirty billion is two billion. Two thousand one hundred million pounds lost, to be precise.' He paused. 'It's all too simple, Prime Minister, and very, very expensive for us.'

The Prime Minister looked at a sheet of notes in front of him. 'I didn't know your sterling reserves were quite as large as that.'

'They used not to be,' Matab admitted. 'But over the summer, we quietly converted most of our dollar reserves into sterling. I personally advised my brother to do this when the dollar was very high. At first, the market moved the right way for us, but now it is going disastrously wrong. We might well have to cancel our contract for the new British supersonic fighter, even though we believe we badly need this plane for the defence of Medevan. The threat from the fundamentalists on the other side of the Gulf is becoming more serious every day.

'Prime Minister,' Matab summed the matter up, 'I personally feel very responsible for our difficulties', he said.

He spoke in his normal quiet tone but Bishop sensed an undercurrent of anger that surprised him. He had grown to like Matab and respected his views on the complex Arab world, but he had always regarded him as a playboy at heart. Now he had struck a vein of pride, an obstinate determination that his small country should not be prejudiced in any way that Matab regarded as unreasonable.

'I can't change my mind, ambassador. You know that. There is far too much at stake. If I backed down now, the

whole future of the European Union would be at a risk.'
Bishop was aware that Matab was staring intently at him with
those extraordinary dark eyes of his. The man must be a good
poker player: his face never betrayed his thoughts. He would
like to discuss that with Margaret.

'Please tell Sheikh Abdulla that I personally very, very
much regret the fall in his sterling reserves.' The Prime
Minister's genuine concern sounded in his voice. 'I'm not a
market man myself – I leave that to the Chancellor and the
Governor of the Bank – but I have to tell you I think the
speculators have overdone their fears about sterling and the
Euro. I regard our joining the Euro as a source of future
strength, of great strength, not weakness.'

He paused deliberately, giving Matab an opportunity to
interrupt him. But Matab was silent, leaning slightly forward
in his chair with his hands resting on his knees.

'I really think the market can improve,' Bishop tried again.
'Once we have exchanged sterling for the Euro, the Euro itself
will be seen as much stronger, a better currency to hold
than either the dollar or the yen.' Still Matab did not
reply and Bishop found the continuing silence in the room
embarrassing.

'You kindly asked me to stay again at Strudwells and to
shoot this Saturday. So far I've managed to keep the day free,
but perhaps it's now inconvenient for you, Sheikh Matab. I
would quite understand that.' Bishop spoke gently, trying to
make it easy for Matab to cancel the invitation.

'No, no,' Matab said, rising to his feet. 'I insist on your
coming, Prime Minister. We should have a good day. Old, the
keeper, is optimistic. And I will, of course, pass your message
back to Sheikh Abdulla.'

Clearly Matab wished to end the meeting. The Prime
Minister rang a bell on his desk. The door was immediately
opened and Matab was ushered out.

Bishop rubbed his eyes wearily as Matab disappeared down
the passage, then picked up his daily diary. He had started to

look at it when the door reopened and David Armitage was shown into his study.

Armitage did not beat about the bush. 'Thank you for seeing me at such short notice.' He sounded nervous.

Bishop smiled at him and asked him to sit down. 'This is a surprise, David. Are you a messenger from the enemy camp?'

'No, not quite.'

Bishop leant back in his chair and waited.

Armitage took a deep breath and plunged in: 'I just wanted you to know, I've told Graham Blackie I'm not going on as his parliamentary private secretary. I can't take it any longer. I've told the whips, too.' He paused and then added with obvious embarrassment, 'I've brought our lists of all the MPs and how we think they're going to vote next Monday. Would you like to see them?' He started to open a slim black briefcase.

'No, that wouldn't be right,' Bishop said. 'And, in any case, my office have got lots of lists, too, and they don't mean much. Too many of our dear colleagues tell both sides they'll vote for them. That way, they hope whoever wins'll give them a job. No.' He looked thoughtfully at Armitage. 'What I'd like to know is just why you left the other side. After all, you've worked with Blackie for some time now. Is it that you think,' the Prime Minister contemplated Armitage carefully, 'he's going to lose?'

'No, Prime Minister, not that at all. I reckon it's neck and neck just now. Everything depends on what happens to sterling and the speeches you and Graham make on Monday.' Armitage paused, struggling to find the right words. 'There are two things I can't stand,' he said finally. 'One is the total conviction in Blackie's team that everything is right with Britain but wrong with the rest of Europe. They don't seem ever to have travelled to Paris, let alone Rome or Madrid or Berlin.' He fell silent, nursing a deep-felt grievance.

The Prime Minister pushed him on. 'And the other?' he asked quietly.

'The other is the economics. Of course, I know going into

the single currency is a leap into the unknown. But I was a banker before I came to the House. I know that there are huge advantages for the single currency if it works – lower interest rates, lower inflation, lower transaction costs. All the big international customers of our bank said they couldn't see Britain staying out of a single currency if France and Germany went in. We're just not putting over the economic arguments strongly enough. And I think sterling's being manipulated. It shouldn't have fallen to one-twenty-one. That's ridiculous.'

'One-twenty,' Bishop corrected him instinctively. And some of Armitage's tenseness left him.

'One-twenty. You're more up to date than I am, Prime Minister. All right, but that's even more ridiculous.'

The Prime Minister looked at Armitage and saw an eager, intelligent forty-year-old. His instinct told him that here was someone in the dirty world around him that he could trust, that he could use in the extraordinary days ahead. 'All right, David. I need you. I'll take you on myself as an extra parliamentary private secretary. It may be the shortest appointment in history, but I'll do it if it'd suit you.'

Armitage's face filled with surprise and he started to laugh. 'That's really not what I planned when I asked to come and see you this morning, Prime Minister. But I'd love it.'

The Prime Minister got up and put a friendly hand on his shoulder. 'Fine. It may not read that well on your CV: PPS to the ex-Prime Minister for one week. But who knows?' He walked over to his desk and picked up the daily report from the Bank. 'Now to business.'

Five hours later the Prime Minister went to committee room fourteen in the House of Commons to address a special meeting of back-benchers. As he walked into the long room, the bronze plaque on the panelling by his right shoulder caught his eye. He remembered noticing the dramatic wording on it when he'd done a tour with Margaret and their two children when he was first a member of parliament.

In this room Field Marshal Earl Kitchener KG
spoke with members of the House of Commons
on Friday, June 2nd 1916.
On Monday, June 5th, 1916 he died at sea.

It all seemed extraordinarily appropriate. His crucial debate was in four days' time.

David Armitage followed him into the room and sat beside him.

There was not an empty space in the rows of green leather chairs in front of Bishop. His parliamentary colleagues, men and women of all parties, sat facing each other while he stood at a sloping desk on the raised dais, and their chairs stretched away into the distance. It was like a court in which he was being tried by three hundred jurors.

For fifteen minutes he talked without a note. His voice was filled with passion as he spoke of his certainty that Britain had finally to forget its imperial past, stop behaving like a self-sufficient island and work with its European neighbours for a free and prosperous future.

He strained to catch the eye of individual colleagues and to carry them along on the great and hazardous adventure on which he was embarked. He reached out for his audience, letting his mind and his words wrap round them, ease their doubts and pull them in his direction. Like a man throwing a rope to catch straying cattle, he used every sense and skill in him to seize and persuade the hesitant.

He concluded simply: 'It will be a free vote on Monday – the Leader of the Opposition and I are agreed on that. If I lose I shall resign.'

There were no questions.

When he sat down, half the audience banged noisily on the

desks in front of him; the other half sat silent, hands in their laps, staring ahead.

'You were brilliant,' said Armitage loyally as they left the room.

'But did I win any votes?' asked Bishop.

'Some. Some were with you at the end that I didn't expect.' Armitage hesitated and then added, 'I'm very glad I've joined your team. I feel at home.' The Prime Minister smiled at him and then stopped to talk to the crowd of lobby journalists who were waiting to pounce on him in the long, dark corridor.

CHAPTER SIXTEEN

Phil Darby drove into the car park behind the Liverpool pub and parked as near as he could to the entry door to the main bar. He took his radio out of its slot in the dashboard and carried it into the pub with him.

'I'm not taking any risks this time,' he said to the matronly woman who handed him the key to the room he had had the week before.

'How's the arm?' she asked.

He thought he noticed a trace of a snigger in her voice and he answered with as much dignity as his small frame could muster that it was mending nicely, thank you.

He carried the neat bundles of lottery tickets, a hundred in each, up to his room, noticed the wallpaper was still peeling off the ceiling, and then laid out his detailed instructions and maps on the bed. By their side he put the pocket Casio computer which held the lists of the combinations he had to buy. He stared at the bed, seeking inspiration. There must be some way in which he could break the system. Even a small break would be better than just doing what bloody Bobbins wanted.

All week he had puzzled at it but he was damned if he could see the answer. So far this week he was strictly on target. Nothing had gone wrong, and he had reported back to Bobbins every night.

He unzipped his bag, took out his eczema ointment and rubbed some into his neck and the backs of his hands. Then he put on a clean cotton and polyester fawn shirt and went downstairs for a drink. His little Lolita was serving behind the bar and he sat on a bar stool in front of her and gazed lustfully at the curves straining at her white cotton shirt.

'Hello, my love,' he said. 'What'll you have? Mine's a gin and tonic.'

She poured him his drink, then said, 'I'll have a Fanta, thanks very much. That'll be four pounds.'

Darby winced with pain as he delved into his pocket.

'Hand better?' she asked. 'All mended? That was a silly thing you did.' She wandered off to the far end of the bar, served another customer, and then came back.

'How did you get on in the lottery last week?' she enquired. 'Are you a millionaire now?'

Phil remembered that he had boasted about the number of lottery tickets he had in his room. 'Not too good,' he said. 'In fact, bloody awful.'

'Shame. No point in my talking to you, then, is there?'

He ordered a pie and chips and offered her another Fanta, but their conversation had come to an end. A gang of tall, noisy young men in leather jackets and jeans leant on the far end of the bar and kept his Lolita laughing and running for drinks. She didn't look in his direction when he left the bar and went up the stairs to his lonely room with its narrow bed and thin, ill-fitting curtains. He switched on the electric fire at the wall, but the single bar remained a grimy black, and he felt too tired to go down and complain. He might just be laughed at.

During the night, the wail of an ambulance woke Phil and he started to puzzle again over Bobbins and the lottery tickets. Something nagged at him – what was it? Suddenly he remembered the girl downstairs asking how he'd got on last week. He got out of bed, dragged his bag across and unzipped the little pocket at the front. There were the twenty tickets he had bought the previous week for himself, matching combinations that he was buying on Bobbins' orders. He looked at them and remembered that he had got three numbers right:

thirty-nine, thirty-six and eighteen. But eighteen had been the bonus number, so he had won nothing.

Phil checked on his Casio. As he ran figures down the little screen, he saw that thirty-nine, thirty-six and eighteen were again appearing at frequent intervals. Of course, this week he was buying just the same combinations as the week before.

He picked up one of his tickets and studied it.

The Great British National Lottery

IT'S A ROLL-OVER WEEK:
JACKPOT EST 30 MILLION

---

18 35 36 39 45 46

SAT 17 NOV
FOR 01 DRAW

He was thoroughly awake now. He remembered the clerk in the Union Street warehouse feeding the lines of numbers into his computer at great speed, making certain that no combination had been left out, but he had not examined anything else on the ticket. Why should he?

Suppose he kept back twenty tickets from this week's draw

and substituted his twenty from last week's. The combinations of numbers would be all right and would tally with Bobbins' master list; only the date and the size of the jackpot would be wrong. It'd take hours, more like days, for them to notice that among two million tickets. If ever.

Of course, it was a risk. If it was spotted, he'd have to say he had somehow got the tickets mixed up. And he had hardly any chance of winning – about a million to one, he reckoned. But, if he did, Christ, he and Agnes would be off somewhere fast. And Bobbins would squirm. Perhaps the big boss would arrange some concrete boots for Bobbins, that's what they did in America.

Feeling happier, Phil slid between the nylon sheets on his bed and dreamt of Bobbins pleading for mercy while he sharpened a rusty knife and prepared to cut off the bastard's fingers one by one. Bobbins would never be able to shuffle a pack or roll the dice again.

A bell rang in the distance, and Phil groped his way back to consciousness, smiling to himself and feeling that, at last, he had some chance of revenge.

Angus Fyffe had never had three worse days in his life. He knew he was caught in a trap, in which his own greed had landed him, and he could see no way out of it. For three nights running he had woken drenched in sweat, haunted by the tail end of nightmares in which he chased Jim Bishop, or Bishop chased him. The pursuit was endless and there was always murder in mind, but neither man ever quite caught up with the other.

He thought of going to the police but instantly dismissed the idea. That would mean confessing to pirating the frequency combination data from the lottery computer, which could only lead to his losing his job. Several times he picked up the telephone to talk to Margaret and each time he put it down before it started ringing.

He received another letter from Crane's. This time the tone

was curt, bordering on angry. The letter expressed indignant surprise that he had issued a further cheque for £25,000. Because of his family's long connection with the bank, it had been honoured, but that was the last one. No further increase in his overdraft would be accepted and he was asked to call urgently to discuss a programme for reducing his debt. He noticed the letter was signed not by the manager but by one of the directors. He knew him personally, indeed he had invited him that summer to a pleasant afternoon at the Lottery Board's Wimbledon hospitality tent.

Angus was sitting looking in despair at this letter and wondering what pictures or furniture from Strudwells he could put up for immediate sale when the telephone rang and the porter from the Piccadilly entrance said there was a visitor to see him. He opened his front door and watched as Harry Plank walked down the covered passage towards him. He was carrying a long, heavy, well-balanced gun case. The leather was still new and the metal caps on the ends of the case shone in the dim light from the Albany lamps.

Fyffe had not asked Harry Plank round to his rooms; Plank had invited himself. 'I wanna have a talk with you, Angus,' he said the moment Angus had ushered him into the flat. 'I brought you these guns of mine; I thought I'd lend you them for the weekend. They're great guns, twelve bore, heavily choked on each barrel and, unlike your British guns, chambered to take a two and three-quarter inch cartridge. They were made for me by a great gunsmith in Philadelphia. I reckon the shot can kill a turkey ten yards further than your average twelve bore.'

Angus looked at him in horror. 'You can't be talking seriously.'

'I am, and you know it.' Plank looked around the room, as if he was making a quick inventory of its contents. He noted a Pembroke breakfast table in the corner, covered with magazines, the mahogany veneer broken in several places; an elaborately patterned silk carpet with two holes in it from burning embers; four family portraits, three old and dark, one brightly modern, hanging on the wall, and one discoloured patch on the wallpaper marking where a picture had recently been removed.

'Look, Angus, you can't get away from it. You need the money, and I'll screw you if you don't do the necessary.'

'The necessary?' Angus tried to make the question sound light, as if he were expecting an ordinary, commonplace reply.

'Kill Bishop. There's no other way you can protect yourself and make sure the Magic Flute keeps going. From all I hear, you sure as hell need my Flute.'

'What d'you hear?' Fyffe's question was both tentative and aggrieved.

'You're about to go bankrupt. I had my bank take out a professional reference on you. You've no credit rating at all; your net worth is zilch.' Plank piled it on. 'I'm amazed Bishop has let you stay on in that job of yours at the lottery – special adviser, or whatever the cute phrase is – for so long.'

'I can't kill Bishop; he's my oldest friend.' Fyffe spoke softly. It was difficult to say the words.

'Brother, you're going to have to. You've no choice. And that's why I've brought round these guns for you to try. It'll make the hit easier . . .'

Plank bent down and started to undo the straps on the gun case. Angus momentarily shut his eyes. He felt as if he was in a world that was spinning out of his control. Surely he could do something to bring it back to sanity – but what? He had no idea. He simply could not find another solution.

'Harry,' he said, 'I don't think you've any idea what you're asking me to do.'

'I sure have,' said Harry. 'You won't be the first person to take a shot at a president or prime minister. Just make certain you hit.' He pulled the stock of one of the guns out of the case and started to slide the hook at the end of the barrels round the knuckle-pin. 'Lovely workmanship here,' he said, 'as good as any of your Purdeys. I've had them for five years and I've never shot better.'

Despite himself, Angus' interest and love of firearms were aroused. He looked across the room at Harry's gun. 'I'd never shoot with that,' he said immediately. 'It's an over and under, dreadfully modern. I've never shot with one of those in my life, and I'll not start now. Jim Bishop would notice something strange the moment he saw me.'

Plank laughed mirthlessly. 'Bishop's going to have more to worry about on Saturday than your shootin' with an over and under. How far do your own guns carry?'

Fyffe shrugged. 'Forty, fifty yards. They're long barrels, thirty inches, half choke on the right barrel, three-quarters on the left. Come downstairs and I'll show you them.'

He led the way down the twisting little staircase to the basement. Unlocking a barred green door with an airhole at the top and bottom, he showed Plank into a whitewashed room with small brick buttresses on one side. Between the buttresses were wine racks, empty save for a few dusty bottles without labels and one magnum of champagne. On the other side was a gun cupboard built into the wall. The baize-covered curves in the shelves were all filled with guns.

'That's what I'll be shooting with on Saturday.' He pointed to two guns in the middle. 'William Evans, about 1925, at the height of their fame. They were given to me by my father on my twenty-first birthday. Lovely guns.' He took one out and handed it to Plank, who weighed it in his hand, then turned towards the door and lifted the gun to his shoulder.

'Very light, comes up easily,' Plank commented.

'Yes, makes me very quick. I can shoot a tremendous number of cartridges without getting tired.'

Fyffe took the gun back and went through the others in the cupboard. 'Those are my father's Bosses, single trigger, made before the First War. The only trouble with them is the trigger mechanism – it's worn and tends to fire the second barrel at minimal pressure. I still shoot with them from time to time. I should have them looked at, but that sort of repair is very expensive these days.

'There's the sixteen bore I bought for a nephew,' he pointed further along the line of guns, 'but he didn't like killing things and I took it back. And next is a twenty bore. The keeper at Strudwells taught me most of what I know about shooting on that gun.'

Plank interrupted: 'If you won't shoot with the over and unders, it'd be sensible to take one of the Bosses with you on Saturday. It could fit in well with what you have to do.'

Fyffe stared at him.

'You're no fool, Angus,' said Plank. 'You know what I mean. And you know the consequences.'

He looked at his watch and said abruptly that he had to leave. Bobbins had assured him all was up to schedule with the couriers but he intended to go round to Union Street and make an unexpected check. He wanted to leave nothing to chance.

On his way out, Plank took a tape out of his pocket and put it down on the crowded Pembroke table. 'I told you the other day that I had a tape of our phone conversation, the one when you asked for ten per cent of jackpot winnings and I agreed to six.'

He looked at Fyffe with no trace of humour. Angus read the cold calculation in his eyes and knew that here was someone who would not scruple to destroy him if he stood in his way.

'That was a business deal,' Plank continued, 'and I've brought you a copy. When we win the jackpot, perhaps this Saturday, you'll have your record of our agreement. That could mean a helluva lot of money to you – two million pounds if we are the only winner. You'll have calculated that yourself.'

He put on his topcoat and picked up the gun case he had brought with him. 'Of course, I've got the original tape. I can make other copies if we need them.'

After Plank had left, Fyffe went down to the basement to lock the cupboard and the door. He paused as he looked at the guns and then, on a sudden instinct, leant forward and took out one of the pair of Boss guns. He slipped two dummy metal cartridges into the breech, swung at an imaginary bird and very gently pulled the single trigger twice. The hammers clicked on to the dummies and Angus broke open the breech. Both cartridges shot out and fell on the floor by his side. He looked at the number engraved at the bottom of the barrels: two.

By Thursday evening 230,000 people had joined the British Alliance and the momentum was increasing daily. Several tabloids, running the Alliance's ads, told their readers that they expected the membership to be a million by the time of the Commons debate on Monday.

The team of Spencer Gray, Doug Mesurier and Wally Wallace met Graham Blackie late on Thursday night for a final weekend's briefing. They had with them early copies of Friday's papers. 'FIFTY MILLION LOTTERY KINGPOT' shouted the *Globe*. 'MILLIONS BACK BLACKIE' claimed the *Chronicle*.

Spencer Gray looked wearily at the pile in front of him in the Chancellor's office. 'I'm exhausted,' he said. 'I've never felt so tired in my life. We've flogged around, every meeting has been a success, yet we still don't know how the vote here's going to go. It's like the bloody lottery – you get millions backing you but you still don't know who's going to win.'

Wallace lit a cigarette and muttered his gloomy agreement. 'It's too close to call,' he said. 'Armitage joining Bishop certainly helped him; he knew where the waverers were.'

Blackie was surprised. He had expected to hear more confidence from his campaign team. He picked up a copy of the *Chronicle* and pointed out that it reported overwhelming support for the British Alliance. From the way their political editor wrote, Britain would be out of the European Union and income tax would be at fifteen pence by the end of next week.

'Yes, but we know that's all superficial, don't we?' Mesurier, as always, spoke thoughtfully and carefully. 'That's the froth. It may get a hundred thousand more recruits for the British Alliance but it doesn't convince anyone here. Suppose you win on Monday, and you become Prime Minister and you form a government . . .' He shrugged. 'Well, many of our colleagues here don't quite know what would happen then. They're frightened of plunges in the dark. They like Jim Bishop even if they're against Europe; they trust him. You're still an unknown quantity.'

'Hang on,' Blackie protested, 'I have been Chancellor of the Exchequer for three years . . .'

'Fact is,' Wallace interrupted, 'a lot of MPs think you're right about Europe but backing you still seems a bit of a risk. We need something more to convince them that it's a risk that has to be taken.'

Blackie felt his heart sinking. Somehow he had assumed the Commons were coming his way, that victory on Monday would be his. He was so totally convinced of the rightness of his cause.

'Christ, is that really so? In all my talks, one-on-one with colleagues, they all seemed to be with us.'

Spencer Gray sighed heavily. 'You're being a bit naive, Graham. Of course, they say that to you when they're alone with you. But they want to see how the debate goes on Monday before they make up their minds. Then, if you win, you'll have friendly memories of them and give them a job. But I bet a lot are saying just the same to Bishop when they see him.'

'The rats.' Blackie chewed at a fingernail for a few seconds. 'Should I try and see some of them again over the weekend?'

'No, forget it,' Gray advised. 'You've done all that. You go and enjoy your shoot on Saturday; that'll put you in good form for the debate. In any case, everyone'll be in their constituencies, listening to their chairmen and the ones who pay the big subscriptions.'

Gray started to scoop papers into his briefcase. 'What we need is something more, Graham – a major crisis in sterling, panic in the markets, a catastrophic run on the pound. Something that puts a real fear of the Euro into our hearts.'

Wallace took up the cry. 'Sterling's stood still in the last few days – around one-twenty Euros to the pound. That's not what we want. The idea of joining the Euro has got to frighten the balls off members of parliament on Monday.'

Mesurier stretched his arms and yawned, then got to his feet. 'I don't see how we can cause an earthquake under the pound at this stage. It's time we all got some sleep.'

After the others had left the room, Graham Blackie sat on at his desk, deep in thought. The leather on the desk's top was worn and fraying, and he picked absent-mindedly at the edges. He was not used to the idea of losing. All his life, fighting his way up from a poor mining background in Durham, he had set himself impossible targets, but he had had the will and self-confidence to achieve them. He had been elected a councillor at eighteen, a member of parliament at twenty-four. When he had become Chancellor at the age of thirty-two, he had been hailed as a young Lloyd George. And then he had been slowly sucked into the battle about Britain and Europe and he had put all those painstaking, agonising years of climbing up the ladder at risk.

He was suddenly acutely aware of the silence in the panelled room. Next door was the Prime Minister's office, so close that he imagined he could hear the clock on the wall ticking above the secretary's desk. That was the office he had always intended to occupy since he was a boy at secondary school. In four days he would know whether he was to achieve that ultimate ambition or sink back to where he had begun. He realised he couldn't stand the thought of failure.

Blackie took a bunch of keys out of his pocket and unlocked the bottom drawer on the right side of his desk. Inside was a pile of files and he took out the top one. The first paper in it was a list of the leading political journalists, together with their telephone and fax numbers. Below was a draft that he had started to work on the previous week. He looked at it and pulled out a pencil. Half an hour later he examined his handiwork:

STRICTLY PERSONAL.
FAX OF ONE PAGE ONLY

SATURDAY, NOVEMBER 24

TO: Selected Political Editors

FROM: Senior Treasury Source. Not for release before 0100, Sunday November 25.

The Prime Minister intends to announce in the Commons debate on Monday that Britain will join the European Monetary Union and the single currency at the rate of one-ten Euros to the pound. This represents a de facto devaluation of the pound of fifteen per cent from the rate ruling three weeks ago.

The reason for the devaluation will be given as the Government's anxiety to maintain the competitiveness of the British economy after joining the stringent disciplines imposed by the European Central Bank. It will be the last chance for a British Goverment to take such unilateral action.

The Chancellor strongly opposed the devaluation on the grounds that it was bound to be followed by similar action by other countries outside the Monetary Union (such as Italy and Spain). Thus, however justified in itself, it could only lead to further turbulence and anxiety in world markets that were already very unstable.

The Treasury's view was however overruled by the Prime Minister.

Not bad, thought Blackie, chewing his pencil. Not bad, but it needed some polishing, a bit more subtlety and a bit more anguish. He'd work on it again tomorrow, before going to Strudwells, and then he'd talk to Spencer Gray about where to send it from. Or to Wally Wallace. Yes, Wallace might be better. He was used to organising media leaks.

Blackie locked the file into his personal red box and carried it down with him to the courtyard, where the solitary figure of his driver stood waiting for him. All the other drivers had long since gone home.

CHAPTER SEVENTEEN

As they walked through the woods around Strudwells, Sheikh Matab kept on suggesting changes in the position of the pegs where the guns would stand for the shoot the following day. Colin Old was surprised. Matab had never interfered with the organising of the drives before, but today he seemed downright fidgety. Old put it down to the fact that it was the biggest shoot of the year and there were some grand and important guests coming. He wasn't happy about it. Old liked his employers' personalities to be like their shooting: steady and doing nothing unexpected.

For the first two drives of the day, where they first drove the top of the Old Plantings away from the release pen to the wartime water tower, and then blanked in the bottom half back to the pen and drove the birds towards the New Plantings, Matab insisted on having six guns in the wood instead of the usual five, and only one gun outside on each flank. Old thought this made the guns too close for comfort but said nothing. Matab watched carefully as he positioned another peg in the broad path through the wood and slipped a yellow card marked 6 into the cleft in the stick.

'In my country, Old,' Matab remarked, 'we do not bother with these niceties – drawing for pegs, numbers and the rest of it. The host places each gun where he wants him to be.' He laughed. 'That means he places himself in the middle, the guest of honour on his right, an important relation on his left. The unimportant guests are strung out where they will get least to shoot.'

Colin moved up the path, adjusting the position of the

other guns. 'I suppose, sir, we try to be fair to everyone here and see they all get a reasonable share of the shooting.'

'A typical British attitude,' Matab commented.

They reached the release pen and Matab watched with close interest as Old threw handfuls of mixed grains on the ground and then showed him a bin full of millet. 'I'll be putting quite a lot of this out early tomorrow to hold the birds on the high points where we want them,' he said.

'It hardly seems necessary,' Matab said, 'you have so many hundreds of birds. I congratulate you, they all look well grown.'

All around, cock pheasants were stalking like elegant courtiers over the ground, with the hens holding back more demurely in the low bushes.

'I think Lord Fyffe is coming,' Old said. 'You'll be wanting to show him our best birds.'

Matab understood the respect in Old's voice and forbore to mention that the Prime Minister and Chancellor of the Exchequer were coming as well.

The disagreement between Matab and Old came when they walked through the Home Drive and approached the spot where Tom Ruster had been shot two weeks before. The two pegs on the right of the line, numbers one and two, were in the field, below the wood, and Matab told Old to bring them fifteen yards closer to the edge of the wood. Old objected. He thought it was too near the line of beaters and he didn't want another accident.

Matab disagreed. 'Ten yards then,' he said. 'All the guns here tomorrow are expert shots, Old, there won't be any mistakes. But out here, where you've got the pegs, the edge of the wood is practically out of range. They won't be able to reach the birds that go back.'

Colin looked up and calculated that the edge of the wood was only about thirty yards away, certainly within range for a good shot. But it was impossible to contradict his boss. He tried another tack. 'Number one,' he said, 'will be walking up with the beaters for the first half of the drive; he'll have plenty of chance to get the birds that go back then, before he moves out into the field.'

It was no good – Matab insisted. Old moved the pegs in closer to the wood.

'How's Ruster?' Matab asked as they came to the fence at the edge of the Home Drive.

'Better, thank you, sir. I hope he'll be out with us tomorrow.' As Matab nodded his agreement, Colin saw the cock pheasant with the black head and the blue feathers on its back watching them. He pointed it out to Sheikh Matab. 'It's been around since last season,' he told Matab. 'It always seems to be nearby when I'm feeding. I hope it doesn't get shot tomorrow. It's become a sort of mascot. A good luck token, you might say.'

'Please do not talk like that, Old.' Matab sounded surprisingly cross. 'I do not like superstitions. For me, shooting mirrors life. There are only two kinds of birds: those that kill and those that get killed. Pheasants are, of course, in the second category.

'Nine o'clock sharp tomorrow, then, at the front door.'

'Very good, sir.'

Old walked back to the keeper's cottage with Zeppelin ranging around a few yards from him. He found himself strangely upset by Sheikh Matab's remarks. He had never thought of pheasants in any sort of way other than as part of his working life. He was pleased when they were born, pleased when they were free of disease and pleased when they were killed. It all paid his wages. It was just that he seemed to have got to know that Melanistic and Michigan blueback cross, and he looked out for him now as he walked around feeding the birds. Of course, it was inevitable that he would be killed sooner or later.

'Come here, Zeppelin,' he ordered as the Labrador raced away after a rabbit, and Zeppelin returned reproachfully to his heel.

★

Margaret rummaged at the back of the cupboard, looking for her favourite warm jersey. Her hand encountered a hard edge, and she found herself pulling out her old sketchbook. She had not looked at it for three years. She abandoned the suitcase she was packing for the weekend at Strudwells and opened the pages. There was a passable sketch of Jim in shorts on the beach at Taormina Mare and another of a younger, more carefree Angus Fyffe when they had all sailed together along the Turkish coast. That had been a marvellous holiday – fourteen days in a *gulet*, swimming before breakfast, visiting Ephesus, sketching the ruined amphitheatres and the Turkish boys who made up the crew, no telephones.

As she resumed packing, she wondered whether she and Jim could possibly go back to the closeness of those days. She thought not. Too much had come between them since Sally's death. She found her thick jersey and put it into the suitcase, along with a Damart vest and her brown tweed shooting suit. It wasn't just her gambling – though that had become very bad – or the fact that they didn't make love any more, though that didn't help, either. It was something more fundamental than either of those things. They had drifted apart and didn't seem to respect each other any longer. No. Respect was the wrong word. They didn't sympathise with each other.

What was she going to wear in the evening? Obviously Matab would have a grand dinner party. She looked at the outfits hanging in the cupboard and decided on her new cream satin trouser suit. After all, Strudwells was in the country; it wouldn't exactly be like a London dinner party. They would be sitting down at the table at eight, just the time of the lottery draw. What awful timing. But presumably someone – Harry Plank, probably – would telephone and tell Matab whether they had won. It would be fantastic if they did. God, it would change her world.

Margaret's mind raced ahead as she collected make-up, scent and her hair dryer and piled them into her suitcase. If they did. Please God. It would make such a difference to her life. If they didn't – well, she could manage another two weeks in Harry Plank's syndicate and then everything would have gone. Even the cottage in the country. Of course, it was her cottage, her father had left it to her, but she and Jim had always planned to retire there when he finally left politics. It represented their future. She didn't think Jim would ever forgive her for losing the cottage. He really had no capital of his own.

What else did she need for the weekend? Of course, her cap. Jim had given her a large, floppy velvet cap for her birthday, very smart. It looked the sort of thing Francis Drake might have worn when he told Queen Elizabeth of the booty he had brought her from the Spanish Main. If it wasn't too wet and windy, she would wear it out shooting. Matab and Angus would like it.

Margaret felt a twinge of pleasure as she took the cap out of a drawer and put it on the top of the suitcase, but it didn't last long. The familiar black cloud of depression settled over her. Everything ahead just looked so impossible. She couldn't see how she and Jim were going to survive, and she had staked so much, far too much, on the lottery. She couldn't undo that now.

She slammed the lid of the suitcase shut, then rang and asked for a messenger to take it down to the front door. She looked at her watch. It was eight thirty and Jim was still not out from his meeting in the Cabinet room. Typical. It would be horribly late when they finally arrived at Strudwells.

CHAPTER EIGHTEEN

Angus Fyffe fingered the white card in his pocket as he walked towards his place in the first drive. It had, on the inside, a list of the eight guns who were shooting that day and opposite, a series of headings – Pheasant, Partridge, Wood-cock, Duck, Pigeon, Rabbit, Various – for him to fill in the numbers shot. On the front was emblazoned the name STRUDWELLS, then the Fyffe family crest, the day's date and, below, the number he had drawn, FOUR. He privately wished that Matab would not use the Fyffe crest on his shooting cards but he did not know how to stop him.

Four. That meant he was in the very centre of the line for the first drive through the Old Plantings. He knew the precise spot where he would stand, his back to some tall sycamores, they made the birds get up well, in front of him the fifteen-yard-wide path that he had had cleared ten years before, and a scattering of well-grown oaks. He looked up at the sky. The wind was gusting from the west and there were heavy rain clouds around. He knew he would get a lot of birds over him at number four.

At the draw for numbers outside the house, he had heard Jim Bishop tell Matab that he had drawn number one. He and Jim would be far apart at the first drive, and he could just concentrate on shooting the pheasants, but he reckoned that Jim and he would be next to each other at the second drive. With Matab's system of odd numbers going down and even numbers going up, he calculated that he would then be six and Jim, on his left, seven.

Angus arrived at his peg and immediately noticed that it

had been moved a few yards to the right from where he was expecting. Number five was a bit close and he did not have too good a line of vision in front of him. That would make the birds more difficult. He took his Boss twelve bore out of its sleeve, opened up his cartridge bag and stuck his shooting stick into the wet ground behind him. As he did so, the keeper's whistle blew to mark the start of the drive and, immediately afterwards, a hen pheasant, a black silhouette against the sky, glided silently over the opening between the trees on his left. Angus saw the bird a second late but his gun slid up into his shoulder and straight on to the bird's head. He swung and pulled the trigger. The bird's head tucked back and it changed instantly from a living, striving creature to a bundle of feathers. Angus' movement was as quick and graceful as the pirouette of a ballet dancer.

For the next fifteen minutes he had no time to think about Jim. The pheasants, fully grown, had only been over the guns once before and the cocks had not learnt to fly back over the beaters or the hens to concentrate in one huge flush. The beaters moved steadily and silently, pushing their sticks into every clump of wild honeysuckle, their spaniels working through the bramble. Colin Old, Zeppelin and two other dogs with him, occasionally urged the beaters on the right to move a little faster; those on the left, who had less ground to cover, to go slower. The line moved forward with a remorseless sense of discipline and purpose, driving everything in front of it, and the birds got up in ones and twos, the cocks protesting, and beat their way heavily up through the branches and then, with the wind behind them, flew straight at the noise and the guns ahead.

Angus concentrated on the business of killing, as he had been taught to do from the age of twelve. The rhythm of his hand, moving from cartridge belt to breech of gun to trigger, was quiet and controlled. He picked up the birds, urging their way through the sky, as easily as if they were standing still, and they were no sooner in range than they were dead, the momentum of their flight carrying them past Angus and dropping them heavily on the ground behind. For fifteen minutes he thought of nothing else.

At the end of the drive, Colin Old blew his whistle and shouted 'All Out'. He walked up to Angus. 'You were shooting very well, sir. You were killing them all very clean from what I could see.'

Angus smiled with pleasure at the compliment. 'Thank you, Old. They flew well, and I was in a good place. And the beaters were good – no big flushes.'

'Thank you, sir.' Old paused and looked at Angus' gun. 'You're shooting with your father's old gun?' There was a note of respectful interest in his voice, and Angus felt all his elation suddenly drain away, to be replaced by the sick sense of dread that had haunted him since his talk with Plank and Matab at the beginning of the week.

Three Land Rovers drove the guns to the second drive, where the pegs were placed in a semicircle in the ploughed field around the New Plantings. The ground was hilly, on the steep edge of the Downs, and Angus remembered the farm manager telling him how difficult it was to plough. He was on the sixth peg, with Jim on one side of him and Graham Blackie on the other.

At the start of the drive, a solitary cock flew very high towards the line of guns. Angus muttered 'You're mine, you're mine' to himself and the bird, catching the wind from the west, turned away from Blackie and flew straight above him. Angus raised his gun to his shoulder, gave the bird a long lead and fired. Like a burst paper bag, the bird crumpled in flight and fell dead forty yards behind him. He moved to break open his gun and reload but the mechanism inside had jammed and the breech would not open. Bugger, muttered Fyffe, bugger. He turned and shouted first to Blackie and then to Bishop, 'Shoot my birds; my gun's jammed.' He looked at the number on the barrel of the Boss and noticed that it was number one.

209

Then he stood, a silent, irritated spectator, as the birds poured out of the wood over the guns. More seemed to come over his peg than any of the others and he watched as Blackie and Bishop swung, shot, reloaded and shot again. But I couldn't have done anything here, he thought – the birds are far too high, and it's all out in the open.

At the end of the drive, Colin sent a beater back to the house to get Angus' second Boss out of its case and Angus climbed into the Land Rover with Sheikh Matab. 'I'm sorry about that, Matab,' Angus began. 'You see, my gun jammed . . .'

'Save your energy,' Matab interrupted. 'You'll be next to the Prime Minister again in the fourth drive. It's the last one before lunch.'

The wind died down and was followed by rain, great, grey, driving sheets of it, soaking guns, beaters and birds. Angus pulled his cap down over his forehead, wiped the rain off the barrels of his second gun, turned up the collar of his Barbour and tried unsuccessfully to concentrate on his shooting. But the easy swing, the sense of being unable to miss, had gone and the bird that would have fallen dead in the first drive now passed unharmed through the sky. 'Damn, I've lost it,' Angus muttered under his breath, but the more he tried, the more he concentrated, the fewer the birds he hit. And despite the rain, despite the fact that he was at the far end of the line, the pheasants went on streaming over him.

As soon as the keeper's whistle blew twice, he sought out Colin Old. 'Old, I couldn't hit a barn door in that drive,' he apologised. 'I shot ten birds but I should have shot forty. I've almost run out of cartridges. Have you got a box or two to spare? I'll replace them after lunch.'

They walked back to the beaters' van and Colin took out two boxes. 'They're Belgian, sir, our local gunsmith got me to buy them. I hope they're all right. That's all I have with me.'

'Thanks. Anything's better than empty barrels. I'm not

having a very good morning, am I? Gun jammed, nearly run out of cartridges, and I can't hit your birds.'

Old pointed to the cock lying on the floor beside the driver's seat. 'There's one I wish you hadn't hit, sir. It's the only bird you killed at the second drive. It had become quite a friend of mine.'

Angus looked at the very dark body, the black head and the splay of blue feathers over the back.

'Unusual bird,' he commented. 'Sorry, Colin, but he was a high flyer. I was rather proud of hitting him, one of my better moments of the morning.' He looked at the other guns assembling by the Land Rovers. 'God, they all look exactly the same – caps pulled down, rain streaming off their Barbours, and miserable. Couldn't Sheikh Matab cancel the fourth drive? I wish he would. It might get better after lunch.'

'You're right, sir. The beaters hate it in this weather and the birds don't fly well,' Old replied. 'I asked Sheikh Matab to cancel the drive, but he refused. He's very keen on big bags, you know, sir.'

'Not quite like the old days, Colin.'

'Not quite, sir.'

Angus found that his peg for the Home Drive was out on a stubble field twenty yards from the wood. The peg on his right, number one, was only fifteen yards away and empty, but he assumed that Jim was walking down with the beaters and would come on to his stick after the drive had started.

Colin's whistle blew, and Angus heard the beaters starting to move through the wood. He looked quickly to see where the gun on his left was standing and picked out the cap and uniform brown waterproof coat just inside the wood. It must be Graham Blackie – he remembered that Blackie had been standing next to him at the second drive. Angus watched as the gun efficiently killed the first two pheasants flying towards him. Obviously, he knew how to shoot.

Then Angus heard a beater shout 'On the left', three

pheasants broke out of the wood, and he swung and missed the first bird with both barrels. He shook his head in mock despair. Out of the corner of his eye, he saw the gun on his right turn away from the wood and move to his peg.

His heart sank. He knew that this was the moment when he had to decide to shoot Jim. He would never have a better chance.

He felt the rain trickling down his neck and was trying to button up the collar of his Barbour when the gun on his left shouted 'Partridges'. He looked across the field and saw that a small covey of twenty redlegs had got up at the edge of the wood in front of the beaters. More wary than pheasants, they were flying low at the gap between the first two pegs. Angus calculated instinctively that he had time for one shot in front of him. He raised his gun but the butt slipped on his wet shoulder. Steadying himself, he pulled hard on the trigger as the birds crossed the line between the gun on his right and himself. Both barrels went off, it seemed simultaneously, and a partridge in the middle of the covey fell to the ground.

And so did the next gun.

'Oh my God!' Angus dropped his gun on the ground and ran to the peg. He saw a face streaming with blood, pouring out of the broken flesh by the eyes. It was Graham Blackie.

Angus Fyffe went over the numbers for the twentieth time in his mind as he waited to be interviewed by the Inspector. He had been number four at the first drive; Jim Bishop, he knew, was number one. At the next, going up, he had been number six and Jim, going down, had been seven. Blackie was five on his other side. Then they had lost sight of each other but, it was obvious to him now, Blackie would be number one, on his right, at the fourth drive and Bishop would have been number one a drive later. He had got confused, and everyone looked exactly the same in their Barbours and tweed caps, with their heads down and rain running off them.

Sheikh Matab had said nothing to him while they waited

for the police to arrive but at Jim's request had cancelled the shoot for the rest of the day. Angus would never forget the look of horror in Colin Old's face as they had carried Blackie off the field. He hated letting Colin down.

The door opened and a police constable asked him to follow him to the Inspector's office. The room was featureless and dark, with a collection of beer mats stacked incongruously on a plastic table. There Angus spent the next two hours. The local Inspector was joined by a Superintendent from Sussex police headquarters and the questioning seemed interminable. He was asked about his guns, his eyesight, his shooting skill, his acquaintance with Blackie. He told them at great length about the rain, the wooden butt slipping on his shoulder, the partridges flying too low, the over-sensitive trigger mechanism on the second Boss gun, the Belgian cartridges that could be faulty. It was cold in the Inspector's little room but Angus could feel the sweat trickling down his chest, and his stomach contracted with a sick sense of worry.

'I gather you had trouble with your other Boss gun at the second drive. You knew the triggers on the Boss guns needed adjusting?' the Superintendent asked.

'I tried them out the other day; they seemed to be working perfectly.'

'But I see from our records that there are two William Evans on your gun licence. They're old guns, too, but not as old as the Boss. Why weren't you shooting with them?'

'It's a bit hard to explain,' Angus said slowly. 'I shoot a great deal. I like to try out my different guns – I suppose it's like trying different golf clubs. I don't shoot exactly the same with all of them. It makes the day . . .' he shrugged his shoulders '. . . more interesting.'

The Inspector coughed and intervened. 'You said you shoot a great deal and your keeper has confirmed that to me. But swinging through the line, I think that's the right expression, is surely, Lord Fyffe, the first thing you're taught not to do. Any boy being taken out shooting is told that.'

Angus had his answer prepared. 'You're right, Inspector. That was inexcusable, a terrible mistake on my part. I can only blame it on the rain, the gun slipping on my shoulder and my instinctive pressure on a very light trigger as I steadied myself. But that doesn't excuse it. I shall never, never forgive myself.'

The Inspector looked back at the Superintendent who, in turn, stared at the piece of paper on the desk in front of him, then said, 'Lord Fyffe, I imagine you know the Chancellor, Mr Blackie, quite well.'

'Yes, well enough, although you could say he's only risen to fame since I left the House.'

'You're ultimately responsible to him for the advice you give on the lottery?'

'Yes. Of course, I would always talk to the Board first.'

'Of course.' The Superintendent sounded hesitant. 'Have you had any great row with the Chancellor about the lottery?'

For the first time Angus started to feel confident. 'You mean, that would give me a motive for killing him?' he asked with a half-laugh. 'Good Lord, what an extraordinary thought. The lottery is going very well – tonight we're going to have a record jackpot. The Chancellor has every reason to be pleased with the suggestions I've made on the way it's run. We've had no recent disputes.' He leant back in the steel-framed chair. 'You can ask the Prime Minister about that, Superintendent. I'm sure he'll confirm what I say.'

The Inspector picked up the ball again. 'These new cartridges, the ones you fired at the partridges – Mr Old confirms you borrowed them from him. Have you ever used this make of cartridge before?' He passed the box over the table.

Angus peered at the label, then shook his head and passed the box back. 'I don't think so. I always buy my cartridges directly from William Evans. I'd just run out before that last drive.'

The questioning finally petered out. The Superintendent

looked at his watch, spoke quietly to the Inspector about talking to the Chief Constable and left the room. While he was away, the Inspector offered Angus a cigarette. He had known him for several years and had called at Strudwells after some Georgian silver jugs had gone missing the year before.

'Terrible accident, sir,' he said. 'Terrible for you and for the Prime Minister. I'm afraid it'll be all over the press tomorrow. We're expecting the journalists here any minute.' There was a certain tone of satisfaction in his voice.

Angus winced. 'I suppose that's inevitable.'

'Absolutely.' The Inspector drew on his cigarette, then tapped some non-existent ash into a large ashtray. 'We're having a press conference at six. I don't yet know who'll take it. I expect it'll either be me or the Chief. It depends.' He gave Angus a look that was intended to be full of meaning.

At that moment, the Superintendent came back into the room. 'I've got some encouraging news, Lord Fyffe. Mr Blackie is out of the operating theatre, and he's out of danger. Unfortunately there is still some concern about his eyes – the surgeon has said he won't know for a day or two yet whether he can save his sight.

'Anyway, the Chief Constable is quite content for you to go home. We'll keep the gun and the cartridges for further testing – we'll be making more enquiries about the reliability of those cartridges – but at the moment we don't expect to lay any charges.' He smiled at Angus. 'The Chief Constable authorised me to say that. That'll be a relief to you, Lord Fyffe, and to all your friends at Strudwells.' He made as if to shake Angus' hand but then thought the gesture out of place and withdrew his arm.

Angus got to his feet. 'Thank you both for your courteous handling of the investigation. As you can imagine, the whole thing has been an awful shock to me. I'll never forget it. I only pray that Graham Blackie will get his sight back.'

Angus managed to maintain his composure as he shook the policemen's hands, walked out of the station and got into his

car, but once he'd started the journey back to the cottage on
the Strudwells estate where he was staying, he found his right
hand was shaking uncontrollably. He pulled into a lay-by and
shut his eyes. Immediately he could see the covey of
partridges flying between Blackie and himself. He pulled on
the trigger and there was Blackie on the ground, with blood
gushing out of the wounds to his face, looking as if an animal
had taken a bite out of his cheek. He knew that he would
never be able to shoot again.

Sheikh Matab had put the panelled sitting room at Bishop's
disposal. The Prime Minister made a series of phone calls and
finally agreed on a statement with his Press Office, deeply
regretting the tragic accident to the Chancellor but expressing
relief that his life was no longer in danger. An announcement
would be made after the Commons debate on Monday about
possible changes in the Treasury team. Until then, as First
Lord of the Treasury, he would take personal charge of
Exchequer matters.

This done, Bishop took the key that had been brought
down by special courier from Whitehall and unlocked the
personal red box that Blackie had brought to Strudwells. He
felt exhausted and sickened by the tragedy but he knew he
must be totally in command of any further developments in
the foreign exchange markets.

The file on top had a blank cover. Bishop opened it and his
eye fell immediately on the draft fax to journalists now headed
From A Confidential Whitehall Source. It was dated and timed
for that evening. He read on and discovered that he was to
announce on Monday that he would personally require
Britain to join the Euro at the rate of one–ten to the pound.
'Good God!' he exclaimed. 'This'll cause chaos!'

He looked at the note pinned to the front of the fax: 'Ring
me before six on Saturday, if we're to get this into the Sunday
papers.' It was signed WW. He looked at his watch and saw
that it was just after five. Seconds later, he was on the

telephone to the private exchange at Number 10 and, within minutes, they had located David Armitage and he was in his car on the way to Strudwells.

'I bought twenty tickets this time,' Phil Darby said to Agnes as they settled down, plates laden with sausage, egg, fried tomato, chips and ketchup, to watch the lottery draw.

'You didn't! That's extravagant, Phil, that's what it is. You shouldn't 'ave.'

Phil smiled with smug satisfaction. He did not think it necessary to mention that it was actually Bobbins' money that had paid for these tickets. He had guessed right. Neither Bobbins nor the clerk checking his returns had noticed that he had pocketed this batch of twenty from the current week, substituting his twenty from the previous week with identical combinations of numbers. Christ, there would be a fuss if he won, but he reckoned he could get away before anyone caught up with him. He had checked on flights to Peru – that was somewhere he had always wanted to go to. He had decided not to take Agnes. On the whole, he thought he would get on better in his new life without her.

'Ten to eight. I mean it's time to switch over to BBC 1,' he said.

'Lovely sausage,' said Agnes, tackling her plate with gusto. 'Where did you get them, Phil?'

'Up north somewhere; they're called Cumberland sausage. Now shut up and listen.'

Stars shot across the screen, then turned into dots and dashes in all the colours of the rainbow, which resolved into the message 'TONIGHT'S KINGPOT £50 MILLION!!!'

'Christ! What a lot of dosh!' said Phil.

'These chips aren't as good as the ones we had last week, Phil.' Agnes picked up a chip off her plate and looked at it with disgust. 'It's all soggy. Can you pass me the relish?'

'Shut up, you stupid cow! Can't you get it into your head that I want to watch the draw?'

Streppie Pepper was already on the stage in a startling red silk gown with frills round the neck and more frills round the bottom of the three-quarter-length skirt.

Agnes condescended to stop shaking the relish bottle on to her chips. 'She looks stupid, like a Christmas cracker,' she said disapprovingly.

'I think she's lovely,' said Phil. 'Smashing, a real doll.'

'You're disgusting! You'd go off with anything in a skirt.' Agnes jabbed at her plate with her fork, and egg yolk squirted over her skirt and onto the settee. 'Get me a cloth, will you, Phil?' she asked, squinting down. 'I've egg all over meself.'

'Get it yourself.' Phil turned up the volume on the television until he was sure he could not hear Agnes' voice.

Streppie introduced a pale, bearded man in a baggy light grey suit to the audience as the musician of the year, the star of this year's World Music Festival. Considering they had never heard of the musician or the Festival, the applause was rapturous. Everyone was in an excited mood. Lottery sales that day, Streppie announced, had beaten all previous records. The jackpot, after two roll-overs, was now the kingpot and, at an expected £50 million, it was the biggest prize ever, ever in Britain's history.

'Fifty million.' Phil rolled the words round his tongue. His hands were shaking so much that he put his unfinished plate down on the floor.

'What's all the fuss about?' Agnes enquired. 'You've got as much chance of winning as I 'ave of being a super model.'

'You just don't understand. I'm on the inside track – I mean I've got information.'

'What! Why didn't you say so before?' Agnes wiped a large piece of white bread round her plate, collecting the remains of egg, grease from the chips and relish, and popped it into her mouth, then turned back to the little screen with a grunt of satisfaction.

The musician pressed the starting button and the great cylinder started to turn. The carefully stacked pile of pink, green, white, yellow and blue balls disintegrated as the balls jostled with each other and then broke away like single sheep leaving a flock, one following another down the shute and into the public eye, fame and the record book.

'Thirty-nine,' Streppie announced. And then, 'Thirty-six!'

'Fantastic!' Phil exclaimed. 'I've got 'em. Same first two numbers as last week.'

'Thirty-five.'

'I've got it! I've got it!' Phil was beside himself. He rolled over on the settee, clutching his tickets, and for the first time in months gave Agnes a huge hug. 'I'm going to win, I'm going to be a millionaire.' He broke into song: 'Who wants to be a millionaire? I do,' suddenly seeing himself with the riches and fame of Frank Sinatra.

'Eighteen,' carolled Streppie. 'Eighteen and never been kissed.'

'Got it. Got it!' Phil searched frantically among his twenty tickets and pulled one out. 'Here we are.' He read out the numbers. '18, 35, 36, 39, 45, 46.' He gave a loud whoop of triumph.

Agnes, despite herself, was impressed. 'Cor, Phil, you might make it. We could go on holiday to the Canaries. Lanzarote looks nice.' She collected travel brochures from all the travel shops in the neighbourhood and read them avidly, gazing at pictures of never-never lands that she did not expect to visit.

But that was the end of Phil's success.

The last three numbers rolled out one by one and each was presented to the studio audience by Streppie as a huge personal success. Thirteen. Nineteen. And, finally, twenty as the bonus. The audience cheered and shouted and laughed as Phil's heart sank.

Agnes was philosophical. 'Never mind, love. I don't think we'd really like Lanzarote – it's right out in the sea. With four numbers right, you'll have won something, though,' she

219

added hopefully. 'We could go to Blackpool or to Harrogate. Harrogate looks very posh.'

Phil was inconsolable. 'Just a hundred pounds,' he muttered, his vision of a new life with a young, dark Latin American beauty shattered, 'perhaps two hundred if I'm lucky and there aren't too many winners.' He pulled out his plate from under the settee and found it licked clean.

'That bloody Scottie!' He turned accusingly to Agnes. 'It's all your fault. That bloody dog of yours has finished off my supper.'

Margaret looked at her watch again. She could not help herself. It was insufferable having to sit in the Strudwells drawing room, making formal conversation with Matab's dinner guests. An air of gloom hung over the party. Everyone arriving at the house expressed their regrets at Graham Blackie's terrible accident and then waited, half hopefully, for further details. It was not the evening of laughter and keen political gossip the guests had expected.

Jim, sitting on the other side of the room, had noticed Margaret's regular glances towards her wrist. Now he caught her eye and shook his head. It was not a suitable time to ask Matab if he could arrange for the television to be turned on so they could watch the lottery result; indeed, it might cause great offence to some of the guests.

Margaret gritted her teeth. She would have to sit through two hours, perhaps three, of a boring dinner, talking to people she did not know and did not like, without hearing the result of the lottery. It was intolerable. Trust Jim not to understand. She was wondering whether she might make a special appeal to Matab – he would appreciate the reason for her impatience – when the butler, white-coated with black tie, came into the room and loudly announced that dinner was served.

Matab immediately walked over to her side, linked his arm through hers and started to lead the guests towards the dining room. As they passed through the open doors, he turned to her and, calmly, as if he were discussing tomorrow's weather, mentioned that Harry Plank would ring him as soon as he knew whether they had won the big prize. 'Don't give anything away,' he added.

Margaret, seated on Matab's right, found herself staring at a plate filled with a dozen oysters. She put her fork into one of them, and pale grey-brown juice oozed out into the shell. She turned away, a sense of nausea welling up in her stomach.

'Don't you like oysters tonight?' Matab asked with his usual quietness. 'I chose them especially for you. You told me they were your favourite food.'

Margaret smiled at him, a reluctant, hesitating smile. 'I just can't stand the suspense,' she said, finding it difficult to match his quiet tone. 'There's so much hanging on this lottery win for me. It's a crossroads.'

At that moment, the butler re-entered the room, stood behind Matab's chair and murmured, with his apologies, that His Excellency was urgently required on the telephone.

Matab was out of the room for ten minutes. Margaret's neighbour on her right wanted to know what effect the Chancellor's accident would have on the debate on Monday. He supposed there would be a sympathy vote for Blackie, and Margaret tried to formulate some sort of answer while her mind was on Matab. She kept on looking towards the door, wondering desperately why it was taking so long for him to be given a simple piece of information.

The oysters had disappeared and roast pheasant, with a chestnut, cream and brandy sauce that was the chef's special invention, served before Matab came back into the room. He turned to Margaret with profuse apologies for his absence and explained, in a distant, formal voice, that his brother, the Emir of Medevan, had insisted on a talk about some state problems.

Matab's usual, studied nonchalance seemed to have failed him. 'Is there anything wrong?' Margaret asked.

'We have some difficulties,' he replied. 'I cannot talk about them now.' He started to cut the pheasant on his plate, then looked up again at Margaret. 'I'm sorry, I've had to give instructions that I cannot take any more telephone calls during dinner. It would be too rude to my other guests.'

Margaret sighed with impatience. 'Oh, Matab, you can't . . .' she began, but he had turned to talk to the guest on his left.

Ten minutes later, Margaret was toying with the macaroon biscuit on top of her zabaglione when the butler came back into the room and whispered confidentially in Matab's ear that there had been another call for him. The caller had not given his name but had asked him to write down an urgent message for the ambassador. He put a card in front of Matab, which he read and then passed to Margaret. It said simply THE MAGIC FLUTE HAS SOUNDED THE RIGHT NOTE.

'So we've won the jackpot?' Margaret had slipped away from the other guests as soon as dinner was over and hurried to her bedroom to telephone Angus at his cottage on the Strudwells estate.

'Definitely. No doubt about that – 13, 18, 19, 35, 36, 39 and bonus 20.' Angus sang the numbers down the line and the enthusiasm bubbled out in his voice. 'We've made it, my darling Margaret, we've made it. Harry Plank rang me twenty minutes ago. I'd been on tenterhooks. Bet you had, too.'

'That's fantastic!' Margaret said. 'You know, I had to sit right through a ghastly dinner, talking about the debate on Monday and Graham's accident, when all I wanted was to hear about the lottery result. Oh, Angus, I feel like dancing round the moon!'

'Margaret,' Angus' voice went cautious, 'any news about Graham? What were they saying?'

'Nothing special, don't worry. Everyone accepts, of course, that it was an awful accident and they feel very sorry for you . . . They don't know yet about Graham's eyes, poor chap.'

Margaret paused for what she felt was a decent interval, then she said, 'Have we any idea yet how much we've won?'

'No. No one has said how many jackpot winners there are.' Angus put on his best lottery adviser's voice. 'Total sales were around a hundred million, so, on our one in fifty million chance, we hope there'll only be us and two others, but even if there were seven – that's the mathematically correct figure – with a jackpot of around fifty million, we would make close to a hundred and fifty thousand each, with another fifty thousand from the smaller prizes.' Angus did not mention his special commission of six per cent.

'In fact,' he went on, 'Harry's very bullish about the smaller prizes. The winning combination has got one sequence in it – eighteen, nineteen, twenty as the bonus – and another broken sequence – thirty-five, thirty-six, thirty-nine. Punters very rarely back on sequences of more than two numbers, and that's why this is in our list of one in fifty million chances. Harry thinks there'll be very few winners other than us of the match five plus bonus number.'

Margaret sat silently as Angus' excited calculations poured over her. It was impossible to believe that her gambling dream was coming true. She couldn't take it in. 'Are you still there?' Angus asked.

'Yes, but I'm dazzled. I don't know what to think. I don't know whether to laugh or cry.'

'Laugh, certainly. It's got to be the best news ever for us. But one thing, Margaret – don't tell Jim anything about our win. Tell him nothing at all. Harry's most emphatic about that, and I think he's right. There's just a possibility that Jim might insist that a syndicate that included his wife shouldn't win the jackpot.' Angus gave a nervous, forced laugh.

'He couldn't do that,' Margaret said. 'We just couldn't give it all up.'

'Well, you never know. Listen, Margaret, I'm sitting here celebrating all by myself. I've got rid of the journalists, thank God. Why don't we meet on Monday? By that time Harry will have cashed the winning tickets and got the cheques. So the money'll be in our hands.' Margaret agreed immediately.

After Angus had rung off, she continued sitting in her chair. They had made it – they had gambled and they really had made it. She got up and smiled at herself in the mirror. Everyone had been against her but she had stood up for herself and won. She gave a nod of approval to her reflection. Angus was right about Jim, of course. In his high-minded way, Jim certainly might try and make her at least give up her share. Well, she wouldn't do it. She deserved better than that.

By the time Jim came to bed, Margaret was fast asleep. For once, a little smile twitched the corner of her mouth. She must be dreaming, Jim thought, and he looked lovingly at her, his heart lightening, as he undressed.

CHAPTER NINETEEN

Sheikh Matab woke at six, as usual. He needed no alarm clock to rouse him.

He got dressed and spent some time in the room he used as an office, then slipped quietly out of the house and walked through the park towards the Home Wood.

He loved this time of day. It was quiet, the air was fresh and clean and, this cold November morning, the branches of the shrubs were laced with hoarfrost, the twigs curling upwards, minutely decorated with ice.

Matab walked fast with the long, relaxed stride of someone used to covering great distances. He opened the oak gate which led to the path through the Home Wood where the guns had stood the previous day. The gate swung noisily on its half-broken hinge and a dozen pheasants, already pecking at the ground, bustled back towards the release pen.

He stopped momentarily at his own peg, number six, and looked to his right. The path, cut through the trees in order to give the guns space to see the birds, curved away round the end of the pen. He could not pick out the peg where Jim Bishop had been standing, nor the pegs in the field beyond.

A few minutes later, he stood at the peg where Fyffe had shot Graham Blackie. The empty cartridge cases had been removed by the police but they had insisted that the pegs stay in place. Matab half-closed his eyes and imagined the covey of partridges flying between the two guns. Of course, it was possible that Fyffe had made a mistake. Blackie and Bishop had both been wearing tweed caps and identical brown shooting coats; the pegs were too close to each other – he himself had insisted on that to Colin Old. But Fyffe was surely too experienced a shot to swing through the line unless he intended to.

He wondered, just as he had been wondering ever since he first heard Angus Fyffe's agonised shout. Fyffe was, of course, one of Bishop's oldest friends, and Blackie was challenging Bishop for the leadership of his party. Fyffe could have had a political motive for getting the Chancellor out of the way, and of course he didn't know, when he shot Blackie, that he was going to win the lottery.

Matab watched as a small line of partridges walked quietly towards him across the stubble field, their heads up. He thought they were more interesting birds than pheasants, and much less predictable. They had a will of their own – sometimes they went the way you expected, sometimes quite the opposite. Shooting them helped him to swing better on to pheasants. They seemed to fly faster, although that wasn't the case.

The partridge were about twenty yards in front of him when, sensing him upwind, they took off and flew in a tight group to his right. Matab raised an imaginary gun to his shoulder and swung with the birds as they passed, shoulder high, between him and the next peg. This must, he thought, have been just their line yesterday.

As he walked away, Matab knew he had established nothing of importance. The simple fact was that Jim Bishop was not dead. He had promised his brother that the matter of Bishop would be attended to and that had not happened. That had been the sole point of his brother's telephone call the previous evening. He heard someone moving through the wood, whistling – Colin Old. He decided to go and have a word with him.

As he walked, he thought back to that telephone conversation. In all the years he had lived, talked and worked with his brother, he had never known him so furious.

Sheikh Abdulla had seen the news of Blackie's accident on

WorldWide television. He had accused Matab of shameful incompetence, and, at one angry moment, he had shouted down the line that, if the truth came out that Matab had had the British Chancellor shot by mistake for the Prime Minister, Medevan would be the laughing stock of the Arab world. He, Matab, would be refused permission to return to his country, and Abdulla would disown him. In the meantime, the value of Medevan's sterling reserves continued to fall sharply . . . The situation of his country was becoming dangerous.

Matab crossed over the stile into the wood and saw Zeppelin running in front of him with a cock pheasant in his mouth.

His last words to his brother were like cold stones packed round his heart. He had assured him that matters would be put right as far as the Prime Minister was concerned, that was his promise, but the deed could not be done while Bishop was a guest in his house. Two accidents in one weekend would be impossible.

Abdulla had not accepted his word. He had repeated the rude old proverb that tomorrow there might be apricots, and then he had put down the telephone without a word of friendship or farewell. That was the final insult.

Matab walked through the bare trees to find Colin putting a pheasant into the game bag round his neck while Zeppelin sat a yard away, his black tail swinging backwards and forwards over the ground.

'Morning, sir,' Colin said. 'I've been to see if there were any more runners. I didn't have any time yesterday afternoon, what with all those interviews with the police. Zeppelin's picked up three already, and a dead woodcock about twenty yards behind your peg.'

Old was another friend of Fyffe's and Bishop's. Matab looked at him assessingly, but all he saw was an open, weatherbeaten face with wrinkled lines below the tweed cap and blue eyes that gazed straight at him.

'Thank you, Old,' he said. 'I remember that woodcock. I hardly saw it; it slid through the trees on my right.'

'It must have been a lovely shot.' Old hesitated, then went on: 'A dreadful accident, sir, to Mr Blackie. It must be terrible for you and Lord Fyffe.'

'Have you ever known anything like this happen before at Strudwells?' Matab asked.

'Oh, no, sir,' Old replied quickly. 'I've been keeper here for thirty-one years. I've often loaded for Lord Fyffe and he's one of the most careful guns I know. He must be very distressed.'

Matab did not reply and, after a respectful pause, Old said, 'Do you think the next shoot will be as planned in two weeks' time, sir? It seems . . .' he searched for the right word '. . . pushing to ask, but I've to book the beaters and the pickers-up, and they're all very busy at this time of the year.'

Matab saw the worry in Old's face and felt a rare surge of sympathy for him. The shoot was, after all, his job; his wage depended on it. 'I don't know, Old. We'll have to decide in the next few days, but you couldn't have done better. Thank you very much.' He reached into his inside pocket for his wallet but found that, dressing quickly that morning, he had left it behind.

'Thank you, sir, it's very good of you to say so. When you see Mr Blackie, would you give him good wishes from all of us at Strudwells? You see, sir . . .' Embarrassed, he turned and started to pull Zeppelin's ears gently. 'You see, on the estate, we're very proud to have people like you and the Prime Minister and the Chancellor coming here to shoot. We'd hate the shoot to lose its reputation.'

Matab thanked Old again.

He took another way back to the house and walked round the ornamental lake. He noticed the mallard swimming in busy circles in the middle with two elegant little teal keeping a respectful distance. The sun was now well above the trees, but a faint haze hung over the water which seeped gently and regularly out of cracks in the broken stone surround.

Matab stopped and looked at the softly curving landscape around him. It was all very typically English, and very unlike his own home. At least, he thought, if Bishop was removed, there would be no question of the lottery result being challenged. Fyffe would be able to spend money on restoring Strudwells and Margaret Bishop would be rich. Perhaps one day she would join him in some other country.

The butler was waiting inside the hall for him. 'While you were out, sir,' he said, managing to make it sound as if walking in the park before breakfast was a faintly indecent activity, 'a gentleman rang. I think it was the same caller as last night – he has a bit of an American accent. He did not leave his name but said to tell you that he had just heard that there was only one winner last night.' He paused, hoping for some enlightenment from his employer, but none came. He added, 'He sounded very happy. Very happy indeed. I hope it's good news for you, too, sir.'

Matab did not reply immediately. He moved towards the dining room, where he could hear sounds of breakfast, then he turned round to face the butler. 'Thank you, Horton. We'll be returning to London this afternoon.'

The one o'clock news picked up the story. The National Lottery Board had confirmed during the morning that the jackpot in last night's draw was £49,700,087 and there was only one winner who, so far, had not claimed the prize. The media were in full cry in pursuit of the new multimillionaire.

The lottery's press release pointed out that, as a result of the very unusual winning combination of numbers, there were few winners of the other prizes, but they had all won exceptionally large sums. The prize for Match 5 plus bonus number was £850,000 instead of an average figure of £200,000, and even Match 4 won £257 rather than the £105 the previous week. Listening to the news, Phil Darby stood a round of drinks at his local while Agnes, chuckling with pleasure, booked herself a Eurostar round-trip to Paris.

But to Jim Bishop, listening to the radio in his ministerial car going back to London, the press release sounded defensive. He soon learnt why. It was followed immediately by an interview with a talkative bishop, a frequent speaker in the House of Lords, who denounced the jackpot as obscene. The lottery management had, in his judgement, lost all sense of reality and decency. The monies available should all be spent on education and health and the necessary repair of Britain's dilapidated churches, and he personally intended to raise the matter with the Prime Minister at the earliest opportunity.

The radio commentator added tartly that they had sought an interview with Lord Fyffe, the special adviser to the Lottery Board who had been involved in the Chancellor's serious shooting accident on Saturday, but he was unavailable for comment.

Jim shook his head sadly and turned to Margaret, sitting beside him, to discuss the lottery result, only to find that her eyes were firmly closed. She appeared to be fast asleep. Reluctant to disturb her, he asked his driver to turn off the radio, and went back to the heavy file of papers on which he and David Armitage had started working the evening before.

The Hussars had intended a great eve-of-battle rally in Trafalgar Square but, with Graham Blackie in hospital, public celebration had been vetoed by Spencer Gray in favour of a final session at Saint George's tavern.

'Rather like playing Hamlet without the Prince,' Doug Mesurier remarked to Spencer as they walked into the large meeting room at the back.

'If you remember your Shakespeare,' Gray said in a tone of tart rebuke, 'Hamlet was killed by Laertes with a poisoned rapier. Even by the wildest stretch of the imagination, I don't think old Angus Fyffe is into the poisoned rapier game. Brainpower-wise, he and Laertes are not in the same league.'

Mesurier started to laugh, then decided this was inappropriate to the occasion. He wore a suitably serious expression as he sat down next to Spencer at the top table.

The Hussars had once again turned out in full force. Every chair was occupied and there was a noisy, excited crowd standing between the tables and the doors into the saloon bar. Everyone was dressed as they thought appropriate for patriotic Britons. Some wore tweed coats, corduroy trousers and striped Brigade of Guards ties, others T-shirts with 'THE BRITISH ALLIANCE' emblazoned on the front and a picture of a lion roaring on the back. One of the few girls, slim-waisted and pretty, in tight blue jeans and Doc Martens, walked round the room distributing copies of the advertisement that would appear in all tomorrow's tabloids, headed LAST CHANCE FOR BRITAIN.

Spencer Gray opened the meeting with a bulletin on Graham Blackie. He was certain to be in hospital for another week or two and the Hussars voted unanimously to send him a message of support and encouragement. In his absence, Spencer himself, Wally Wallace and Doug Mesurier would all take part in the debate the next day. There was bound to be massive support from various members of both front benches, and all their forecasts showed they would win the vote with a large majority. Conviction rang through Spencer's voice as he said this, and he was cheered to the echo. Next Sunday, he promised, would be their Victory Celebration. He was sure Graham would send them a triumphant message, even if he could not be with them himself.

Pint glasses banged enthusiastically on the wooden tables and someone shouted, 'Blackie for Prime Minister!' The cry was taken up until Spencer held up his hand.

'My friends,' he said in ringing tones, 'there is one more day of fighting to be done before the victory parties start.' He looked at Mesurier. 'Doug, would you like to report on the progress of our British Alliance?'

'We haven't got quite the million we're looking for; we're a

231

bit behind that target,' Mesurier confessed. 'It's been a filthy wet week and there was a lot of rain yesterday when I know a lot of you would have liked to have been out canvassing for us.'

'What about the ten-thousand-pound prize for the one who collected most signatures?' a voice shouted from the back.

'I'm coming to that.' Mesurier paused and his normally confident voice sounded troubled. 'So far, the person to produce most signed forms,' he pointed at several fat bundles lying on the table in front of him, 'is none other than our vice-chairman. By intensive use of his constituency computer, he has managed to get three thousand and seventy-two signatures. Can anyone here tonight beat that?'

There was total silence in the room, broken only by a noisy belch followed by laughter.

'Then I am proud to announce that the winner is our own, the one and only, the terror of the Europeans . . . Wally Wallace.'

Spencer Gray put all the enthusiasm he could muster into his announcement, but it was greeted with a cynical groan that swelled as it passed round the room and took a long time to die away. Soon afterwards, the Hussars started to drift out of the room, some to go home, some to drink with friends at the public bar.

'That announcement went down like a lead balloon,' Spencer commented to Wallace as the two men walked down Whitehall towards Millbank.

Wallace did not reply. He seemed abstracted.

They walked on in silence, then, as they went past the pugnacious statue of Winston Churchill in Parliament Square, Spencer spoke again. 'I never saw anything about the Euro leak in today's papers.'

'That's what I'm worrying about,' said Wally. 'I never got a reply from Graham to my message with the draft faxes. Without his permission, I couldn't send them out.'

CHAPTER TWENTY

The bullion lorries turned sharp left in front of the Mansion House and passed under the massive fortress-high west wall of the Bank of England. Then they swung to the right, into Princes Street, and then right again, as the double metal doors cautiously opened, into the bullion yard of the Bank.

There were fifty of them.

As they came to a halt, their tailgate doors were unlocked from inside and security guards, in black uniforms, jumped to the ground, pistol-holsters bouncing against their thighs. A queue of trolleys, each one holding four pallets of gold ingots, led back from the yard into the cavernous passage that sloped down to the gold vaults.

The first trolleys were quickly pulled into place and distributed alongside the vans, then a grey-coated official stepped forward, stood in the middle of the yard and looked up at the figure standing at the window above. Sir Geoffrey Williams gave a vigorous nod of the head. The twin prongs of the forklifts on the trucks edged under the front pallets and, straining at the weight, started to lift them up to the back of the armour-plated vans.

Sir Geoffrey looked at his watch. It was two thirty-one in the afternoon. Everything was, as he would expect, precisely on schedule. Sir Geoffrey did not tolerate sloppiness in the running of the Bank, least of all in the handling of the gold reserves.

At two thirty-five, a black Rolls-Royce, sporting the number-plate MED 1 and flying the pennant of the State of Medevan, was waved into New Palace Yard by the two policemen at the gate. Sheikh Matab was one of the few ambassadors who had not switched his allegiance to Mercedes, and his Rolls-Royce made a stately circle of the cobbled yard before stopping at the entrance to Westminster Hall.

The chairman of the International Parliamentary Union was waiting for him. As soon as the car halted, he stepped forward, opened the door and with obsequious eagerness shook Sheikh Matab's hand. A personal message had reached him from the Foreign Secretary during the morning, saying that Matab was currently not best pleased with Britain and asking him to do his utmost to placate the ambassador.

With a wave of the chairman's hand towards the waiting policemen, they bypassed the security gates, went through the crowd in the Central Lobby and started up the steps that led to the Diplomatic Gallery. As they walked, the chairman uttered his fulsome regrets at Blackie's unfortunate accident on Saturday and then talked of the historic importance of the debate that would start in an hour's time. It would change the future of Britain. He thought the result was very much in the balance, although he personally would of course be supporting the Prime Minister.

Matab said nothing in reply. As he walked, he could feel the holstered 9mm Browning pistol bouncing gently against his thigh in the deep pocket of his white *thob*, under the folds of his black *bisht*. He had come early in order to make certain he had a central seat in the row reserved for the Diplomatic Corps. It was essential that he have a clear line of vision to his target.

At much the same time, Marie Claude walked into Graham Blackie's room at Saint Luke's hospital. The head lying on the double white pillows seemed almost mummified, with bandages covering the eyes and the nose and upper cheeks. She started to cry as she ran up to the bedside.

'My darling, *mon chou*, what have they done to you, *ces*

salopards? You look terrible, I can't bear it.' She reached out and took hold of Graham's hand and kissed it. She felt his fingers tighten round hers and hold on with an agonised grip.

They sat like this for a minute in silence, his fingers interlocked with hers. His thumb started to stroke the inside of her palm, gently and confidingly. Then a nurse bustled into the room.

'He had to be kept very quiet, so you're the first visitor that's been allowed to see him, Miss . . .'

'Moisan. Marie Claude Moisan.'

'Miss Moisan. Would you like a cup of tea?'

'I would adore one.'

After the nurse had left the room, the silence continued. Marie Claude bent forward and kissed Graham on his cheek, just below the line of the bandage.

At last he spoke, murmuring into her ear, 'The doctors say I'll get my sight back. The eyes are scarred but not destroyed. If necessary, they'll do a transplant.'

Marie Claude slid a hand behind his neck and pressed her cheek softly against his face. '*Je t'aime tant, mon jules, je t'aimerai toujours,*' she whispered. 'I nearly died when I heard the news. I wanted to come and see you immediately.'

She heard the door handle turning and sat upright as the nurse came in again. 'I've brought you your tea.'

Blackie's voice spoke with a sudden urgency from the bed. 'Could you please switch on the television?' he asked.

'Of course, you want to listen to the big debate in the Commons, don't you?' The nurse spoke with the tone of someone used to humouring the difficult. 'It starts in just a few minutes. I'm sure Miss, er . . . Miss Moisse . . .' she raised her eyebrows as she tried to pronounce Marie Claude's name and then abandoned the attempt, 'you'll want to hear it too, dear, and you can tell him just who's speaking and all.' Without waiting for any further answer, she moved over to the set in the corner and switched it on.

★

Matab stared down into the Chamber from the front row of the Gallery. As he had planned, he was placed in the centre and had a clear view of the Speaker, the dispatch boxes and the Ministers sitting in front of them. The green leather benches were jammed from end to end, there was already a crowd standing behind the Speaker's chair and some latecomers sat on the floor between the benches. A constant hum rose, making it impossible for the back-benchers to be heard as they asked questions, but this seemed to Matab to make no difference to the ministerial replies.

A buzz of approval greeted the arrival of Roger Beacon, the Leader of the Opposition, and a louder noise, mixing cheers with some heavy groans, welcomed Jim Bishop as he took his seat on the Government front bench two minutes before Question Time ended.

The Prime Minister had hardly sat down when a note from the civil servants' box was passed along the bench to David Armitage, sitting directly behind him. Armitage read it, looked amazed, then tapped the Prime Minister on the shoulder and passed it to him. Seconds later, Jim Bishop was speaking urgently to Armitage who rose from his seat and walked back to the row of civil servants, sitting apprehensively in their pen. Then questions ended and the Prime Minister was on his feet at the dispatch box.

'I have just received this astonishing note, Mr Speaker,' he said, waving the paper in the air. 'It tells me that at this very moment Britain's gold reserves are being loaded into lorries at the Bank of England, apparently to remove them from the control of this House, should we vote to join the European Central Bank.'

A collective sigh, a vast intake of breath mingled with murmurs of 'impossible, fantastic, traitors', rose from both sides of the House.

The Prime Minister gestured, seeking silence. 'All nineteen million ounces of our reserves are lined up to be taken by armoured lorry to some unknown destination. I can assure the

House that this is being done without my agreement. Apparently, it has been organised by the Governor of the Bank, acting with the approval of the Chancellor.'

Marie Claude saw Graham's hands clench as he listened, his bandaged face turned towards the television. 'I should be there, I should be there,' he muttered. He rocked his body to and fro on the bed in frustration.

'It shows the extraordinary lengths to which those opposed to the European Union will go in their blind pursuit of the nationalism that has led to so many wars in past centuries.'

'I could explain, I could explain.' The tone in Blackie's voice was more and more tortured.

'I am forbidding immediately the removal of the gold from the Bank.' Two civil servants got up from the box behind the Speaker's chair and hurried out of the little door at the back. 'This amounts to the biggest bank robbery in history and I am sure it would be the wish of the House that I suspend the Governor of the Bank from his post immediately.'

Jim Bishop paused and looked around him. It seemed to Marie Claude that every MP in the sight of the camera nodded his head and shouted 'Hear, hear!' at the top of his voice. She felt the tears starting to roll down her cheeks again as Graham sank back into his pillows, his mouth puckered.

'Oh, Christ, Christ, they don't bloody understand! And I'm not there; Geoffrey Williams isn't there to explain. It isn't a robbery, it was to keep the gold safe for Britain,' Blackie raged. He banged his fists on the bed.

Marie Claude sensed the growing confidence in Bishop's voice as he continued. The incident with the gold reserves had given him more support than he had expected. Patiently, he rehearsed the arguments for Britain joining the Euro, and he was listened to without interruption for ten minutes.

Then he said, 'I have another announcement to make that will surprise the House. Many of us have been very worried at the fall in sterling in recent weeks. A number of senior bankers and economists have told me they considered it unjustified, a view with which I agree.'

Matab felt with his right hand under the *bisht* into the pocket of his *thob* until his fingers touched the metal of the pistol and he started, gently and slowly, to ease it out of its holster. He did not know for how much longer the Prime Minister would be speaking.

'After the Chancellor's unfortunate accident at a shoot on Saturday, and I am glad to be able to tell the House that his sight is not now in serious danger,' the Prime Minister continued, 'some draft faxes were found among his papers at Strudwells, the house where he and I were both staying. In the Chancellor's absence in hospital I took personal charge of these.'

'Oh, my God!' Blackie shook his bandaged head in agony. 'I can't believe it, I just can't believe it.'

The Prime Minister paused, picked up a pile of papers from the table at his side and, leaning forward on the dispatch box, dropped his voice as if he was sharing a secret of the greatest importance with friends and colleagues.

'The House will have difficulty in believing what I am about to say. But I have checked it out with the utmost care as it concerns a Privy Councillor and a senior member of my ministerial team.

'These faxes were personally drafted by the Chancellor and were to be sent to the press on Saturday evening, anonymously but coming from a Whitehall source, leaking the rate at which we had reputedly decided to join the Euro.'

The House was spellbound, every member listening with rapt attention. 'These faxes suggested,' the Prime Minister continued, dropping his voice even further, 'that the rate would be as low as one-ten to the pound, ten points below the rate on Friday.

'This would of course have caused panic in the market and would have led to turmoil in the hours immediately before this debate. I can only assume that that was the reason for the faxes.'

'Oh, Christ, that's only part of the story.' Blackie's voice was now so low and miserable Marie Claude could hardly hear it.

'Why have you done this, my darling?' she asked.

'I thought it was right for the country.'

'There is of course no truth in what these faxes purported to announce. No truth whatsoever. I have to tell the House,' Bishop's voice had become very solemn, 'that I am now dismissing the Chancellor of the Exchequer.'

Marie Claude leant down and put her cheek against Blackie's face and her hand on his chest. She could feel his heart racing and her tears trickled gently on to his chin. 'I shall always love you,' she said.

Matab pulled forward his voluminous black cloak so that it covered the Browning as he rested the pistol on the rail in front of him. It seemed an easy target, but there were people all around him and he knew he would have very little time in which to aim. He looked at the Prime Minister's head as he would at an antlered stag, calculating angle and distance.

'The Chancellor showed devastating misjudgement,' the Prime Minister continued. 'He and the Governor convinced themselves that joining the Euro would, in simple terms, be bad for Britain and they therefore took extraordinary steps to stop this happening.

'The Leader of the Opposition and I are convinced of the opposite. Of course, there are many challenges, difficult unresolved questions to be answered. But I believe that Britain's industry and services can only prosper in this new millennium as part of a united and successful Europe. In the end, however immediately uncomfortable, that united Europe requires a single central bank and a single currency.'

The Prime Minister threw out these words as if he were throwing a gauntlet at the disbelievers. He turned sharply and looked up and down at the challengers on his own benches.

Wally Wallace stared at Spencer Gray, who stared in turn at Doug Mesurier. No one rose to deny what Jim Bishop had said.

'You'll have to start a new career.' Marie Claude put all the comfort and warmth of her love into her voice. '*Tu pourrais commencer par être un père,*' she bent down and whispered into his ear. 'Let's call her Concorde, an Anglo-French production.'

Graham was silent but he felt the smile spreading across Marie Claude's cheeks as he traced the line of her lips with the tip of a finger.

'You are amazing,' he said. 'I shall be scarred, jobless, a failed politician. Anyone else would run a mile from me.' He paused, then said, 'I like the name William. If it's a boy, we will call him William after the Conqueror. That villain must have been an ancestor of yours.'

Marie Claude knew she was winning. She climbed on to the bed and lay alongside Graham, holding his hand tightly and nestling her face in his shoulder. 'I hope the nurse does not come with another cup of tea,' she murmured in his ear. '*Je ne souhaite pas la rendre jalouse.*'

'Yesterday I consulted with the chairmen of all our clearing banks,' the Prime Minister continued, 'on the rate of exchange between sterling and the Euro that I should recommend to the House today.'

Matab remembered the cold early morning when he and his brother had stalked through the courtyards in the royal palace on their way to their father's rooms. He had followed his brother's lead then; he must do the same now. There was no turning back.

'We considered a number of alternatives, starting I may say with the rate of one-ten to the pound that the Chancellor was apparently going to recommend. This, of course, we rejected.'

Roger Beacon laughed and the nervous tension in the Chamber was broken. On both sides of the House, members settled back on to the benches and nodded and started to look around them. It was becoming like a normal debate. The noise caught Blackie's attention. He turned his bandaged face to the television and asked anxiously, 'Marie Claude, darling, tell me, just what's happening now?'

She looked up at the little screen. The Prime Minister seemed in total control of the House. Relaxed, hands on the table by the dispatch box, he was pointing this way and that as he wooed supporters and dissidents alike.

'Jim Bishop is fantastic, brilliant,' she said and Blackie groaned. 'They are, how do you say it, eating out of his palm.'

'After hours of discussion and with the full agreement of all European Union heads of government, we decided on a very generous rate, which will encourage other countries to join the Euro and which at the same time reflects the great strength of our economy.'

Matab looked at the neighbours on his right and left. They were all leaning forward intently, hands on the brass rails in front of them, memorising the Prime Minister's words for their dispatches home that evening. He dropped his robed left arm to his side, raised his right hand and placed the sight at the end of the short barrel in line with the Prime Minister's head, then he brought up his left hand again to steady his right.

One of the television cameramen, in the television room at the side of the Strangers' Gallery, noticed the glint of light on the metal and swung his camera on to Matab. Within seconds, the producer, watching a battery of six cameras, ordered the film from that camera to be used live and rushed out of the room.

'*Merde*,' whispered Marie Claude, 'someone has a gun. I think he's going to shoot Jim Bishop.'

'Oh, God, no,' Blackie groaned. 'That's just not possible. Not him as well. Stop it. For God's sake, stop it!'

'We will join the Euro.' The Prime Minister turned again sharply to address the dissidents' row immediately behind him where Wallace, Gray and Mesurier were sitting in glum disbelief at the changing mood of the House. Matab's Browning followed with precision the arc traced by his quickly moving head. 'We will join at a rate fifteen per cent higher than when this turmoil started two weeks ago. We will join at one-fifty Euros to the pound. This will be a vital help to those who have held sterling through the last difficult weeks and is fully justified . . .'

Fifteen per cent higher . . . one-fifty Euros to the pound . . . The words percolated through to Matab's brain as he again trained the bead of the Browning's barrel steadily on to the right side of Bishop's head, two inches above the right ear, and started to take the strain of the trigger smoothly on to his crooked index finger.

He must consult Sheikh Abdulla immediately. The run on Medevan's reserves was stopped; the contracts with British industry could stand.

Matab was moving to lower his pistol into his lap when an attendant, his chain of office clinking on his neck, hurled himself across the row behind and cannoned into Matab's back. Reaching out with his outstretched arm, he hit Matab's wrist with his fist, and the Browning fell to the floor.

In the same instant a Member jumped up, pointed to the Gallery and yelled, 'Up there, Mr Speaker, where they're fighting. The man in the black robe with the white shirt – he was pointing a gun at the Prime Minister!'

The whole House rose instinctively to its feet and stared as two attendants, their arms locked through Matab's, pulled him away over the feet and across the knees of a serried line of ambassadors who were between him and the gangway.

'Order, order!' shouted the Speaker from the far end of the House. 'The Gallery will be cleared immediately and the sitting suspended for thirty minutes while I have this disgraceful incident investigated.'

'The angels were on his side,' said Bertrand de Toussaint to his German colleague as they walked back to their diplomatic limousines.

'I'm not a Catholic, as you well know, Bertrand,' the German replied. 'I am a Lutheran, and I do not believe in angels, but I respect economic logic. It is logic that is on Bishop's side. Britain has to swallow structural change, to accept a constitutional revolution, in order to move forward with us into the next century. You see that, I see that, Bishop and Beacon see that. But will the majority of his colleagues?'

'We'll know in a few hours' time,' the French ambassador said.

The Mercedes and the stretched Citröen were parked side by side. The two ambassadors nodded gravely to each other and got into their separate long black cars.

'There's no point in the debate continuing any further, Jim. You'll never get a better result than now.' Roger Beacon spoke with force and passion. 'You've got three things going for you – the removal of the gold, Blackie's false faxes, and finally that ambassador waving a pistol at you. You're very lucky.'

They had retreated to the Prime Minister's room with David Armitage, who had brought them both cups of tea and now sat listening intently. Fifteen minutes had elapsed since the Speaker had suspended the sitting, and Bishop needed urgently to reach a decision.

'I've had a quick spot check done on our lot by the whips,' Beacon went on. 'They reckon we're up by at least ten votes. I'm sure the same'll be true on your side – the sympathy vote. It may be ridiculous and it has nothing to do with Europe, but grab it while it's there.'

The Prime Minister stared into his teacup as if he was trying to read the leaves, then he slowly looked up. 'Do you agree, David?'

'Yes, Prime Minister, I do. Two waverers came up to me just now, behind the Speaker's chair, and said they were horrified at the thought you might have been shot and they were certainly going to support you – they couldn't not. Another, who's never, never been a friend, was furious with Blackie. He said he had no idea Blackie could be so stupid.'

Beacon nodded his agreement. 'Seize it, Jim. There's a tide in the affairs of men and all that. Take it at the flood.'

The Prime Minister put down his teacup and smiled at them both. 'I really wanted to win on the arguments, not on sentiment. I had about an hour of my speech still to go, but of course you're both right. No more talking. I'll move the motion to join the single currency, immediately and formally, as soon as the Speaker reopens the debate.'

'And I will second it. There's no need for me to speak. My side know exactly where I stand.'

Beacon stood up and Jim Bishop got up from his chair and shook his hand. 'Thank you, Roger. I know what you've been through. I'm very, very grateful.'

He turned to Armitage. 'David, perhaps you could tell the whips on both sides of the House to expect a vote straight-away. Of course, it's a free vote. I'd like you to join personally in counting the ayes.'

The annunciator on the wall showed that there were now four minutes until the debate resumed. Armitage hurried out of the room as Beacon and Bishop moved towards the door, discussing a joint statement to the press.

'I wish to make a short statement to the House before the debate continues.' The Speaker stood in his black silk gown with its broad gold bands, his wig flowing down his neck on to his shoulders. Time seemed to have stood still as he announced that the ambassador of Medevan, on being taken from the Gallery, had pleaded diplomatic immunity. On the instructions of the Foreign Secretary, the ambassador would be required to leave the country by ten o'clock that evening. The House listened in silence.

The Speaker then called on the Prime Minister to resume the debate.

'I propose the motion on the order paper, standing in my name and that of the Leader of the Opposition,' said Bishop.

'Formally?' the Speaker asked.

'Formally,' Bishop replied.

The Speaker looked inquiringly at the Opposition front bench and Roger Beacon rose to his feet.

'I second the motion on the order paper.'

'Formally?'

'Formally.'

A collective sigh of relief rose from the members. At last, they could get down to the nitty-gritty of voting. No more words, no more argument.

'Those in favour say aye,' the Speaker demanded in the traditional words. A huge roar of voices shouted 'Aye' from all sides of the Chamber, to be followed a few seconds later by a loud volume of 'Noes'.

'Division!' shouted the Speaker. And, as custom demanded, his cry was taken up by policemen all over the Palace of Westminster. With their helmets held in their hands, they walked down the library and into the bars and tea-rooms crying, 'Division!' It was unnecessary, as every member of the House was already crammed into the Chamber.

CHAPTER TWENTY-ONE

The division was in progress. Members coming out of the corridors on either side of the Chamber, the Aye lobby and the No lobby, gave their names to the clerks and were ticked off the division list. Then they walked through the open door and turned, some walking towards the Members' lobby, others back into the Chamber. Wally Wallace stood on the outside of the doorway with a folded piece of paper in his hand, cross-checking David Armitage's counting of the Ayes. 'Two eighty-nine, two ninety,' said Armitage as two members filed past them, and Wally pencilled the last figure on his paper.

A few yards behind Wallace, Spencer Gray stood with Doug Mesurier. Each had a crumpled list in his hand which he studied from time to time. 'Adsetts,' said Spencer. 'Adsetts, what the hell are you doing with the Ayes? You promised us your vote.'

Adsetts looked down from his six-foot-six height. 'Sorry. My constituents would never forgive me,' he said, shaking his head with a gesture of mournful hopelessness and moving quickly away.

'That's at least twenty lost from our side,' Spencer said.

'Rats,' commented Mesurier, 'they've no bloody principles. Hi, Fergus, what's gone wrong?'

Fergus Aston beckoned to Spencer Gray, who followed him into a quiet corner of the Members' lobby behind the message board.

'You knew the terms,' said Aston coldly. 'The Lords and, or, a job.'

Spencer nodded.

'There's no way Blackie will deliver on those terms now. He'll be looking for a job himself.'

Spencer reacted furiously. 'I thought you had talent and you really wanted to keep Britain independent. I was wrong on both counts.'

Aston's fist tightened but Spencer wheeled round and strode back to the doors from the Aye lobby. As he arrived, he heard Armitage intoning like a plainsong chant, 'two hundred and ninety-nine, three hundred'. There was an upbeat, triumphant note on the three hundred.

'Anything over three hundred and twenty through this lobby,' Doug Mesurier said, 'and we've lost. The Speaker and his three deputies don't vote, and Graham and five others are away sick.'

'I know, I know,' Spencer interrupted. 'I've been doing the damn calculations since dawn this morning. God, there are Cynthia Ainger and John Apps. We worked hard enough on those two.'

Before he could say any more, Cynthia walked up to him. 'Very sorry, Spencer. John and I agree. We're that rare species. We listened to the arguments and changed our minds during the debate.'

'Oh, God, spare us from such sinners,' Doug muttered behind him.

Jim Bishop sat on the Government front bench, as the Chamber slowly filled up again. He felt relieved and exhausted, like a helmsman who had just taken a thirty-foot boat through a force ten storm. There was nothing more that he could do about the vote. The die was cast and in a few more minutes he would know the result.

His mind turned to Matab. He could not believe he had really been in any danger. Did Matab really want to kill him? He had regarded him as a friend. He wondered if the whole thing was a gesture of some sort, but, if so, there was no obvious purpose to it. Granted Matab had been furious the week before about the fall in sterling, but he had now put that right.

Then there was that ghastly business at Strudwells last Saturday, when Blackie had been shot. He never liked the feel of coincidences, but it was impossible to see any connection between the two events.

Poor old Blackie. That was an extraordinary story. Bishop nodded at two back-benchers walking past him and leant back against the green-cushioned bench.

It was hard on Graham Blackie that he had not had a chance of replying during the debate but, really, he had behaved astonishingly badly. And Geoffrey Williams, too. It was amazing what fools the issue of Europe made of Britons.

He looked slowly around the Chamber. If he won the debate, it would be one of the greatest victories ever in this House of Commons. It was an immodest thought, but true. Peel and reform of the Corn Laws, Chamberlain and tariff reform, Macmillan and Heath and their battles to join the Common Market: they had all been famous parliamentary fights but it seemed always to have been a case of Britain against the rest of the world. That was fine when Britain had an Empire, but she could no longer afford the luxury of grand isolation. The change should start tomorrow.

Damn Matab. He had wanted to say all this in his speech; he had sweated over it for hours. He wanted to convince first Parliament, then the country; not win on the sympathy vote. Still, as Beacon said, better win after a bad argument than lose after a good one. Beacon was a good ally. He wondered what he could do for him.

Coming out of his dreaming, with the Chamber loud with rumour and talk and gossip around him, Jim realised David Armitage was looking at him from behind the Speaker's chair and pointing urgently at a small piece of paper in his hand. The division figures. By tradition, whoever held that paper had won the vote. A huge smile split his face from ear to ear.

Others saw Armitage's gesture and leaned over from their benches and started to congratulate Bishop. He urged caution. 'Wait, we haven't heard the figures yet.'

Then David moved forward, accompanied by three whips. Turning by the dispatch box, he nodded to the Speaker, opened the paper and read out the result. He made it sound like the opening words of a victorious Te Deum. 'The Ayes three hundred and seventy, the Noes two hundred and seventy-one.'

He handed the paper to the Speaker, who repeated the words, 'The Ayes three hundred and seventy, the Noes two hundred and seventy-one, so the Ayes have it; the Ayes have it. Unlock.'

As the attendants moved forward to unlock the division lobby doors, a cheering roar broke out in the Chamber. Roger Beacon crossed over by the mace to shake Jim Bishop's hand and colleagues struggled to touch him, to congratulate him, to assure him that they had always known he would win.

Bishop walked back to Downing Street with David Armitage. As they passed the Cenotaph, still surrounded with wreaths from Remembrance Day, their walk turned into a triumphal march. For the last hour, radio and television bulletins had been broadcasting news of an attempted assassination of the Prime Minister, and already hundreds were standing in Whitehall waiting to congratulate him on his escape.

Now the news came through of the vote in the Commons and, to his huge surprise, Bishop found himself being clapped on the back, kissed and thanked.

As his security guards moved forward to protect him, a woman pressed a bunch of chrysanthemums into his hand. 'Well done, Jim!' She reached up to kiss him on the cheek. The Prime Minister told his guards to stand away. 'This is much too much fun,' he said. And he found himself laughing and joking with the crowd.

'My holidays on the Costa Brava'll be a lot cheaper, won't they?' a voice shouted.

'Yes, and you won't come back with a pocketful of useless pesetas,' Jim shouted back. He felt, suddenly, that a huge burden had been lifted from him and he could start enjoying politics – and life – again.

'I can't wait to tell Margaret,' he said to Armitage as they walked through the double gates into Downing Street. 'She had come to hate all those European meetings. There was so much anger and violence around. Now that's all finished. We've won with a clear majority – ninety-nine, far more than I ever hoped for.' David nodded his agreement. 'I think the Euro will become very popular. It will be the making of Britain.'

Bishop smiled and waved at the members of the press who were gathering on the far side of Downing Street. 'I'll be with you in a few minutes,' he shouted.

CHAPTER TWENTY-TWO

Inside Number 10, the long hall passage seemed marvellously quiet after the noise outside. The Prime Minister smiled at the eager, thrusting portrait of Ellen Terry as he passed it. The dreams and aspirations in that lovely profile had always reminded him of the hopes of their daughter, Sally. She had just got her coveted place at the Royal College of Music when she'd been killed in the car smash.

A private secretary was waiting by the door to the Cabinet room. 'You were brilliant in the House, Prime Minister, really brilliant, but thank God the Medevan ambassador didn't shoot. We were all watching on television and we just couldn't believe it. The seconds when he had the gun in his hand and you were still speaking . . .' The private secretary shook his head, for once lost for a word. 'They were quite unbearable. I shall never forget them.'

Jim Bishop smiled at him. 'I was better off than you. I knew absolutely nothing about it until it was all over. Now . . .' He gestured to David Armitage to follow him towards the curling staircase. 'The Leader of the Opposition and I are going to do a joint press conference outside in a few minutes. After that, I want to have a celebration, a party here for everyone who's helped. David, will you get on the telephone and start organising that? Of course, Margaret must be there. Is she upstairs in the flat?' he asked the private secretary.

'I don't think so. She went out around one, and I don't think she's come back yet.'

Some of the joy went out of Jim's step as he turned and ran up the staircase. He so wanted to share this moment of success with Margaret, the pleasure of it and the relief. If they could start to rebuild their partnership, that would make all the agony worthwhile. He sent up a quiet prayer that she would be back in a few minutes.

He opened the door of the flat and immediately noticed the large piece of paper tucked under the bronze head on the hall table. As he picked it up, his instinct suddenly told him it was going to give him some terrible news. He paused, shut his eyes for a moment and said out loud, 'Lord, Lord, please, please, please, let it be all right.'

The note was on 10 Downing Street headed paper. As he started to read it, he noticed, incongruously, how much Margaret's handwriting sloped backwards. It used to be quite straight and up and down. The note was quite brief.

Dear Jim,

I'm going away with Angus.

I've known for some time, and I imagine you have, too, that nothing was working out right between us. Angus and I have been part of a syndicate that has just won the lottery jackpot. The head of our syndicate, the American you met at Strudwells, collected the cheques this morning.

We've won a lot of money. My share is well over a million – a million pounds, think of that! – and it just seems to me, and Angus as well, that it's the right moment to start again, somewhere and something fresh, while there's still energy and hope in us.

Forgive me, Jim, and don't take it too hard. In a funny way, you can trust Angus to look after me. And you know me – I can't make the sun stand still but I do want to make him run.

Please don't send Scotland Yard or Interpol or anyone else to look for us. Even if they found us it wouldn't work; it certainly wouldn't make anything any better between you and me. And don't worry about Giles – I'll send him enough money to buy a house or a flat.

I hope you win in the debate this afternoon. I don't agree with you, but you deserve to win for your own sake.

Good luck. I shall always love and, pompous word, respect you.

Margaret

There was a scribble below the signature. It looked as if Margaret had started to draw a heart with an arrow through it and then stopped halfway.

Jim sat down abruptly and hid his face in his hands. It seemed as if the world had come to an end – the world, not just his own personal world. He stared into the dark under his hands. He just loved her so much; it was impossible to believe she would leave him, and leave him for ever. It was like experiencing a death: someone was with you for twenty years, thirty years, in bed with you, at supper with you, working, walking, sharing everything, loving, hating, crying, laughing, and suddenly they were gone, and there was no calling them back, no apologies for mistakes or angry words, no chance to change.

God, he wanted Margaret so much. He wanted to see her, to touch and kiss her, to repair bridges, to hold her in his arms, to plan the years ahead.

The telephone rang by his side, and his heart seemed to come up and fill his mouth. It was all a mistake – Margaret must be back and on her way up to the flat now, at this moment.

'The Leader of the Opposition has arrived, Prime Minister,' his private secretary said. 'He's waiting in the anteroom. If I may say so, sir, I think you should start the press briefing straightaway. They want, of course, to make you the lead story in the five o'clock news.'

'Of course, I'll be down in a minute.'

Jim put Margaret's note into his pocket, stood up, wearily shook his head and rocked his body backwards and forwards. He did not know which way to turn or which path to follow. Then, moving like an automaton, he opened the door and walked down the stairs.

His private secretary was waiting for him. 'I hope you don't mind, Prime Minister,' he said, 'I thought you might be tired after the debate, I've prepared a short list of bull points, points you might like to make to the press, if you need them.' He added, protectively, 'There are hundreds of them outside.'

'That's very thoughtful of you, thank you very much.' Bishop took the list and greeted Roger Beacon. Together they walked back down the same passage, past the same portrait of Ellen Terry. It seemed an age since he had smiled at her.

'You know, I hate to say this,' Beacon said, 'but I expect you've done yourself a lot of good this afternoon. You'll probably win the next election now. There's nothing like someone having a shot at you to make you popular. Think of Reagan. Margaret will be enormously proud of you.'

Jim could not find an answer to this.

The police, with their sense of occasion, and nose for popularity, had allowed the public into Downing Street, and the little street was crowded all the way past the Treasury to the gates into Whitehall. As the two men appeared through the black door of Number 10, the serried cameras in front of them flashed like sparklers at a fireworks party and a group of children wearing school blazers cheered. The hurrahs rippled infectiously through the crowd, whipping elderly tourists and homegoing office workers into sudden excitement. A party of Japanese tourists climbed on to each other's backs to get a better view and waved the little European Union blue and gold-starred flags that they had bought at Brussels airport.

A tall young man, long-haired and in ragged jeans, produced a mouth organ and started to do a jig on the pavement. The world's television cameras focused on the street party at the heart of Government.

'Christ,' said the man from Universal News to the reporter pressed against his elbow, 'perhaps the whole bloody thing is going to be popular after all.'

After a few minutes, Bishop and Beacon moved forwards to the microphones and slowly the street fell silent. 'I'm very grateful to you all for coming to celebrate this evening,' the

Prime Minister began. Roger Beacon was surprised at the painful break in his voice. 'And I'm grateful to the Leader of the Opposition for his whole-hearted support in our difficult decisions about Europe. The vote in the Commons today was for a new future for Britain . . .'

Jim dried up. He simply could not think of anything more to say. He reached into his pocket for the prompt note given him a few minutes before. By mistake, he pulled out Margaret's note instead and opened it. Tears came into his eyes as he looked at the first, short sentence. 'The show must go on,' he said, catching his breath. 'And it will go on.'

He stepped back from the microphone and gestured to Roger Beacon to take his place.

'The Prime Minister is a very brave man,' Beacon said and the crowd roared their applause and approval.

'One of Britain's great Prime Ministers.' The crowd whistled and clapped. 'He deserves our support.' They cheered.

'I've never seen anything like it.' The man from Universal News was still mystified and spoke in a tone of near indignation to his neighbour. 'Not since my dad showed me the films of VE Day. Everyone just seems so happy; it's not what we're used to.' He shook his head in wonder.

'Perhaps it will last this time,' he said. 'I hope so. I do hope so. It would be good for Britain.'

INSECURITY

Matthew Lynn

'A near-perfect thriller . . . you will never look your boss in the eye again'
Sunday Express

Jack Borrodin has a new job. He thinks he is just one step away from a seat on the board of one of the country's leading pharmaceutical companies.

Tara Ling has a new job. An expert in leprosy, she has been hired by Jack's company to work on creating a vaccine against a deadly new virus.

Outwardly a respectable conglomerate, the closer to its core Jack and Tara get, the more rotten it appears. Framed for crimes they did not commit, Jack and Tara have two weeks to strike back at the company that deceived them. Unless the company strikes them down first.

'A rattling yarn in the best traditions of the classic thriller . . . an excellent debut'
The Times

THE RAINMAKER

John Grisham

'He keeps us turning the pages until well after bedtime . . . as exciting as a car chase with a load of dynamite thrown in'
Tim Binyon, *Daily Mail*

John Grisham returns to the courtroom for the first time since *A Time to Kill* in this riveting tale of legal intrigue and corporate greed.

Rudy Baylor is a newly-qualified lawyer: he has one case, and one case alone, to save himself from his mounting debts. It is a bad faith suit against a giant insurance company which could have saved a young man's life, but instead refused to pay the claim until it is too late.

The settlement could be worth millions of dollars, but there is one problem: Rudy has never argued a case in court before, and he's up against the most expensive lawyers money can buy.

'The book stays in the hands as if super-glued . . . compelling'
Stephen Gallagher, *Sunday Express*

'A classy, gripping tale . . . a guaranteed page-turner'
Empire

'A taut and terrific page-turner'
Entertainment Weekly

THE PARTNER

John Grisham

'A narrative triumph and a stylish joy, this novel has me gasping for more of the new, satirical Grisham'
Gerald Kaufman, *Daily Telegraph*

They kidnapped him in a small town in Brazil. He had changed his name and his appearance, but they were sure they had their man. The search had cost their clients three and a half million dollars.

Four years before, he had been called Patrick S. Lanigan. He had died in a car crash in February 1992. His gravestone lay in a cemetery in Biloxi, Mississippi. He had been a partner at an up and coming law firm, had a pretty wife, a new daughter, and a bright future. Six weeks after his death, $90 million had disappeared from the law firm. It was then that his partners knew he was still alive, and the long pursuit had begun . . .

'All the ingredients of suspense, drama and meticulous attention to detail that have made Grisham's novels bestsellers . . . A terrific read'
Sally Morris, *Daily Telegraph*

'Excellent'
David Pannick, QC, *The Times*

THE RUNAWAY JURY

John Grisham

'Riveting . . . Grisham is a superb, instinctive storyteller'
Marcel Berlins, *The Times*

Every jury has a leader, and the verdict belongs to him.

In Biloxi, Mississippi, a landmark trial with hundreds of millions of dollars at stake begins routinely, then swerves mysteriously off course. The jury is behaving strangely, and at least one juror is convinced he's being watched. Soon they have to be sequestered. Then a tip from an anonymous young woman suggests she is able to predict the jurors' increasingly odd behaviour.

Is the jury somehow being manipulated, or even controlled? If so, by whom? And, more importantly, why?

'Beautifully paced and plotted and full of delightful twists. Grisham's mastery of form has never been more evident . . . a marvellous read'
David Robson, *Sunday Telegraph*

'This book is a joy. One of those books you regret having to finish'
Neil Shand, *Daily Express*

'Grisham creates a terrific level of suspense. I could not put it down'
Frances Hegarty, *Mail on Sunday*

OTHER TITLES OF INTEREST

ALL ARROW BOOKS ARE AVAILABLE THROUGH MAIL ORDER OR FROM YOUR LOCAL BOOKSHOP AND NEWSAGENT.

PLEASE SEND CHEQUE/EUROCHEQUE/POSTAL ORDER (STERLING ONLY) ACCESS, VISA, MASTERCARD, DINERS CARD, SWITCH OR AMEX.

EXPIRY DATE .... SIGNATURE...

PLEASE ALLOW 75 PENCE PER BOOK FOR POST AND PACKING U.K.

OVERSEAS CUSTOMERS PLEASE ALLOW £1.00 PER COPY FOR POST AND PACKING.

ALL ORDERS TO:

ARROW BOOKS, BOOK BY POST, TBS LIMITED, THE BOOK SERVICE, COLCHESTER ROAD, FRATING GREEN, COLCHESTER, ESSEX CO7 TDW.

NAME ....

ADDRESS...

....

Please allow 28 days for delivery. Please tick box if you do not wish to receive any additional information ☐

Prices and availability subject to change without notice.